THIN BLOOD

Vicki Tyley

ISBN 978-0-9874603-6-3

PROLOGUE

Craig Edmonds stared at hands sticky with darkening blood.

His hands.

He held them away from his body and looked down at his chest in horror. Large, dirty-red blotches marred the once pristine white shirt. Forgetting the blood on his hands, he tore at the buttons, ripping the shirt open.

Breathing in short, sharp gasps, he frantically examined his torso, looking for the wound. No cuts. No injuries. No holes where there shouldn't be any. His chest heaved in relief. He wasn't dying, after all.

But then, mid-sigh, it struck him: if it wasn't his blood, whose was it? His head whipped around, his eyes scanning the room like radar on overdrive.

Even in the half-light, he quickly saw all was not as it should be. The glass shade from one of the bedside lamps lay in shattered fragments on the floor. The curtain rail over the bedroom's bay window hung at a precarious angle. Usually a black-and-white photo of a nude, tattooed woman hung above the bed; now the frame lay in pieces in the doorway.

He focused on the queen-sized bed. His stomach clenched as he took in the twisted and disheveled bedclothes. Instinctively, he knew the dark patches on the sheets weren't shadows that would disappear once the curtains were opened.

He swallowed, the acrid morning-after taste of whisky harsh in his parched mouth.

"Kirsty?" he croaked. Clearing his throat, he called again, hesitant but louder.

In the crushing silence, time stood still.

"Kirsty!" he screamed, as he dashed into the master bedroom's compact, white-tiled en suite. He stumbled, clutching at the doorframe. He took in the bloodied handprints adorning the vanity unit and walls like some sort of macabre finger-painting. Fighting an intense wave of nausea, he looked down at the blood-smeared floor.

Trying desperately to rein in his growing panic, he raced to the main bathroom. His wife wasn't there either. Next room.

Out of breath, heart hammering, he reached the internal door that led to the double garage and opened it. The external roller door was down and his red Alfa Romeo and Kirsty's silver Lexus were parked next to each other.

Gripping the door handle, he sagged against the door. He took a deep breath. Fought for control of his adrenaline-charged body. He lurched into the kitchen, heading for the sink.

Hands shaking violently, he somehow managed to turn on the cold water tap. He watched, mesmerized, as the blood from his hands, diluted by water, swirled in a pink eddy in the bottom of the sink before disappearing down the plughole.

Oblivious to the water dripping from his hands, he dropped onto the pine storage-box-cum-bench beneath the window at the end of the kitchen. Elbows on knees, he dropped his forehead into his hands. If only the infernal pounding would let up, he could think straight.

His memory of the previous evening was patchy, to say the least. He had a vague recollection of arriving home stressed after a late-night meeting at the office and, bypassing the dried-out dinner Kirsty had kept warm for him, heading for the bottle of Chivas Regal. After that, it was anyone's guess as to what had happened.

A series of short clips flashed through his mind. In one, he saw himself shouting at Kirsty, her throwing up her hands and yelling back. What had they been arguing about? In another, he was picking up his car keys, and...

Damn it! Why can't I remember? he thought, glancing towards the door leading into the garage. It was then he saw the set of four smudged, rust-brown streaks low on the doorframe. He closed his eyes, praying for the nightmare to end.

Except he had a feeling the nightmare was only beginning...

1

'MISSING' shouted the large, white capital letters. Jacinta Deller studied the green and white poster pinned to the shopping centre noticeboard. Underneath, in smaller type, was the question, 'Can you unravel the mystery?' The rest of the poster was taken up with a collage of headshots of men and women missing from all over Australia.

She edged closer, setting down her heavy shopping. The white noise of voices, footsteps and cash registers, echoing in the domed confines of the multi-storey shopping centre, receded as she concentrated on the small print under each photograph.

People of all ages and ethnicities were missing; had been missing for months, years and, in some cases, decades. Had these people met with foul play, or had they disappeared of their own accord? Whatever the reason, what must have been the impact on the family and friends they had left behind?

She could understand what might drive a person to up and leave, to start life anew somewhere else, as someone else. A fresh start. That, or jump off the nearest bridge.

The look on her boss's face that day had told Jacinta the news wasn't good, but she hadn't expected to be sacked as investigative journalist for *The Acacia Tribune*. Technically, not sacked... 'retrenched' was the word used. It made no difference to her, though. The end result was the same: she was out of a job.

Stunned, she had left the building carrying only her handbag and the meager few personal possessions collected from her desk. She hadn't stopped to say goodbye to anyone; nor did anyone stop her. Perhaps they thought it might be contagious.

Her life was a mess. Even with a job she had struggled to meet her monthly mortgage payments, and more so after kicking out her slob of a flatmate. On top of that, and only five months earlier, her mother had died unexpectedly from a brain aneurysm. And to make matters worse, she and Brett Rhodes, her boyfriend of three-and-a-half years, hadn't been on speaking terms as a result of a massive row. Sparked by something trivial, no doubt. She couldn't remember what exactly.

When Brett had stormed off, all she had wanted to do was run as far away as possible. Away from all her problems. Away from her screwed-up life. How much easier it would have been than staying and facing reality. She wondered if that was what some of the people on the poster had done – she liked to think so, anyway, because the alternative was certainly far worse. With a sigh, she picked up her shopping and headed for the underground car park.

2

"That's odd."

"Hmmn?" Jacinta said, her attention not wavering from the laptop's screen.

Brett stopped munching and set his bowl of corn flakes and milk on the frosted-glass tabletop, amidst the screeds of printouts and lined pages of scribbled notes. "That," he said, stooping and pointing at an one of the many webpages she had printed. He swallowed the mouthful of half-chewed cereal and tapped the corner of the picture under the banner, 'Have you seen this person?'

She frowned, first at the bowl of cereal plonked in the middle of her research, and then at the photograph of the young fair-haired woman Brett had his finger on. "What did you say?" she snapped, making little attempt to hide her irritation at being interrupted.

"I said, that's odd," Brett repeated, picking up his bowl from the table.

He had her attention now. She leaned back in her seat and, turning her head toward him, waited for him to go on. Instead he winked at her, continuing to spoon his afternoon-breakfast, as he called it (one of his little idiosyncrasies she still hadn't quite come to terms with), into his mouth from the bowl cupped in his left hand.

She sighed. And though too many hot, sleepless nights on end had left her feeling tired and cranky and definitely not in the mood for Brett's games, she took the bait. "What's odd?"

Brett's hazel eyes widened. "What? You mean you don't remember the case?"

Remember what case? she thought, shifting in her seat so she could see him without twisting her head right off. With one hand resting on the back of a dining chair and the other balancing the cereal bowl at shoulder height, he looked like one of those bronze male nude statues bearing a light-filled orb.

She reached for the webpage printout.

"The Edmonds case. Surely you can't have forgotten, even if it must be nearly ten years. It was in the news for months on end. You couldn't turn on the TV or open a newspaper without seeing something about it."

"You're forgetting, I wasn't in the country when this happened," she said, running her finger down the listed details. Name, date of birth, last seen, age, hair, eyes, complexion, weight, height. "This woman," she checked the name, "Kirsty Olive Edmonds, disappeared four months after I went traveling overseas." She continued reading. "It says here she's been missing since the twentieth of January 1996, from her home in Camberwell, Victoria. Left wallet and personal effects... Motor vehicle still at home... There are grave concerns for her safety and welfare."

Brett spluttered. "Grave concerns? You can say that again! Doesn't it say anything about the two murder trials?"

She raised her eyebrows and scanned Brett's face, looking for confirmation he wasn't winding her up, and then back at the printout. Besides a link to another website and what she had just read out, there was no further information. "Why don't you just tell me about it?" she said, exasperation tinging her voice. She was grumpy enough without having to contend with her boyfriend's teasing.

After getting over the initial shock of sudden joblessness and not having the security of a weekly pay packet, she had decided freelance was the way to go. She had always wanted to be her own boss. All very well in theory, but theory didn't pay the bills. Sure, she'd had some success in the intervening year, with a few articles published and even others that had been commissioned, but not enough if she wanted to eat *and* keep a roof over her head.

When Brett had suggested he move in, she thought all her prayers had been answered and readily agreed but, almost at once, had had second thoughts. Financial hardship was not a good reason to move your lover in. In fact, it was a bad reason.

She loved him, he made her laugh, made her feel alive. But, they had only just made up – what woman could have resisted Brett's corny 'roses are red' apology and white-handkerchief surrender on bended knee? Despite her misgivings, she helped Brett shift all his stuff, clearing wardrobe and drawer space like the dutiful girlfriend. Had it been a mistake? Lying awake at night worrying only made her less tolerant, solving neither her love nor money woes.

"Fill me in. I'm listening," she prompted as she reached for her notepad and pen.

Brett pulled out a chair, straddling it backwards before launching into a monologue about 'The Edmonds Case', as he referred to it. It had a practiced air, as if he had been rehearsing, waiting for the right moment.

His take on the case had stockbroker Craig Edmonds slaughtering his wife, Kirsty, bundling her up in a blanket, dumping her in the boot of her car and then driving who knows where to dispose of the bloodied corpse.

Her husband reported her missing a couple of days after this. What had started as a typical missing person's case soon evolved into a full-blown homicide investigation when blood traces and dark-blonde hairs were discovered in the boot of Kirsty Edmonds' Lexus, parked in the garage of their home.

Forensic investigators found further evidence pointing to foul play inside the house, particularly in the master bedroom and the adjoining en suite. The house had been thoroughly cleaned, but although the bloodstains weren't visible to the naked eye, they were still there.

Further suspicions were raised when the police delved into the affairs of the Edmonds. The couple had taken out term life insurance policies of $1,000,000 on each other's lives, less than six months prior to Kirsty's disappearance. Kirsty was worth more dead than alive.

Everything pointed to her husband. If he'd had the word 'guilty' tattooed on his forehead, it couldn't have been more conspicuous. One small problem, though: there was no body, and the evidence was all circumstantial.

Nevertheless, that didn't stop the authorities from charging Craig Edmonds with the murder of his wife. The fact that he had changed his story did not help his credibility. First, he denied he was in the house the night his wife went missing; then he claimed he had passed out on their bed from too much drink in the late evening, not waking until the next morning.

Brett paused in his recitation long enough to take a breath, then continued. "An innocent man wouldn't have attempted to conceal evidence, would he? Why didn't he report Kirsty missing immediately, instead of waiting two whole days? His answer: he panicked. What sort of defense is that?"

Even if Brett had Craig Edmonds convicted of murder, two trials, both resulting in hung juries, failed to do the same. Much to Brett's disgust, the man — guilty or innocent — had walked free.

All talked out, Brett took a deep breath, crossed his arms across the back of the chair and waited patiently for Jacinta to finish her scribblings.

If everything he had told her was correct, it was indeed an odd case. Were the authorities just keeping their options open by listing Kirsty Edmonds as a missing person, over whose safety and welfare they held 'grave concerns', at the same time as they had charged her husband with her murder? Twice.

And twice the jury had failed to convict him. Not surprising, really. She knew that gaining a murder conviction without a body was difficult, although not impossible.

Jacinta stopped writing, setting the pad and pen on the table beside her laptop, and turned back to Brett. "Thanks for that. How do you know so much about it, anyway?"

Brett rolled his eyes. "Everyone who was around at the time knew about it. As I told you, the media coverage was intense. I suppose there couldn't have been anything more newsworthy happening at the time." He paused. "That, and the missing woman's sister, Narelle Croswell, is our credit officer."

The 'our' he was referring to was Woodridge Research, the market research company where he worked as IT Systems Analyst.

For a moment he held her gaze as if trying to decide if he should continue. "I may live to regret telling you this, but what the hell, you'd find out one way or another, anyway. Our dear Narelle married Craig Edmonds last October. Kept her maiden name, though." He watched her face, waiting for the information to sink in, the corner of his mouth lifting in a smirk.

Her jaw dropped. "You can't be serious? Are you telling me Narelle married her sister's accused killer?"

"And oh yes, Narelle and Craig were having an affair at the time Kirsty disappeared."

"Jesus, Brett! You can be a pain in the arse sometimes." She hated the way he drip-fed information to her. Was he deliberately trying to antagonize her? "So, is that it? Have you told me everything?" She glared at him, her lips pressed together in a thin line.

3

Brett held his hands up, palms out. "No way!" Shaking his head vigorously, he backed away. "Absolutely not!"

From his reaction, you would have thought she had asked him to assassinate the Prime Minister. Instead all she had asked him to do was introduce her to Narelle Croswell, the missing woman's sister.

"You must have some staff function or after-work drinks you could invite me along to. Then I could introduce myself to her. You wouldn't have to be involved."

Brett's face paled. Behind his nervous eyes she could almost see the frenetic acceleration of his brainwaves, looking for a way out of the predicament in which he had landed himself.

"Look, she doesn't even have to know I'm a journalist." She paused. "Not immediately, anyway."

"But... but," he stammered, "I thought the article you were working on was a general overview on missing persons, not specific cases." He glanced past her, and then back at her face. "And anyway, I doubt the public would be interested in a rehash of that old case. Everyone had had more than enough by the time it was all over. Why would you want to dredge it all up again?"

He was right. She had been working on an article about the 30,000 people reported missing in Australia each year. And if Brett hadn't said anything, she would still be looking at that broader picture. She wagered that right about now, he was kicking himself.

As for dredging up an old case, he had a lot to learn about human nature. Mankind's morbid fascination with murder and intrigue verged on the voyeuristic. The more gruesome the better.

Softly, softly might be the better approach. "You're probably right. I'll just keep working with what I have," she said, waving a hand over the paper-littered table. What she had was more than enough to get started. Brett could live for another day.

His face softened, visibly relaxing.

After convincing him that deserting her for his mates at the pub wasn't a bad thing, she turned her attention back to the laptop. Although a night out was tempting, her future success as a reputable investigative journalist was more important. And Brett had unwittingly provided her with what could be just the boost she needed.

First things first: she needed to check the information he had given her. Typing "Craig Edmonds" into Google's search engine resulted in 618 hits. She quickly scanned various news articles, all of which more or less covered what Brett had told her.

One thing he hadn't touched on was the question mark over the part Narelle had played in her sister's disappearance. With speculation rife, many media reports painted her as the scarlet woman, a woman capable of stealing her own sister's husband, a woman without conscience. But a small band of supporters had jumped to her defense, claiming she was no more than an innocent victim drawn into a web of deceit and betrayal.

A clap of thunder overhead startled Jacinta. The room darkened as the gathering heavy clouds blocked out the sun. The air, still and humid, felt claggy on her skin. *The calm before the storm*, she thought, standing and crossing the wooden floorboards to the open, double-hung window at the end of the room.

Leaning against the windowsill, she breathed in the heady perfume of her herb garden, the scent intensified by heat and rain. A simple pleasure in a complicated life.

She sighed and headed back to her laptop, realizing her problems were nothing compared to those of the Croswell sisters. One was missing, presumed dead, while the other had married the man accused of her sister's murder.

A fine film of sweat developed on her face as she trawled through website after website. Then she found it: the original court transcript for the first trial, Regina v Edmonds. Elated, she raced to download it as if it might vanish before her eyes.

Her jaw dropped. The document consisted of 283 pages of what appeared at first glance to be mainly verbose, longwinded legal prattle. She blinked, her eyes already gritty with fatigue.

Pulling her long, corn-blonde hair away from her face and neck, she pinned it in a loose knot on top of her head and then, gathering up the laptop and her notepad from the table, made herself comfortable on the daybed near the window. She had a long night ahead of her.

4

Smiling to himself, Craig Edmonds closed his briefcase, turned off his desk lamp and stood up. If anyone had told him that after everything he had been through in the last decade he would ever find happiness again, he would have laughed in his or her face.

He had been to hell and back. Months in remand, accused of murdering his wife, had taken its toll on him, both mentally and physically. But the one constant through it all had been Narelle — his sweet, loyal Narelle. His own family had disowned him, but her belief in his innocence had been unwavering. He admired and loved her for that, but there were times when even he didn't believe in himself. How could he, when no matter what he did, he couldn't remember what really happened that night.

Was he capable of murder? Could he have mutilated his wife like they said he had? No, not under normal circumstances. He was sure of that. But why couldn't he remember?

5

Jacinta heard the front door close and touched her lips. Had Brett said goodbye? She had been so preoccupied with the Edmonds case that she couldn't remember talking to him. What sort of mood had he been in?

She shook her head. Another black mark against her name. Much to Brett's chagrin, she had spent the whole weekend reading, rereading and trying to absorb 283 pages of murder trial transcript.

Even without a body, the prosecution's case had been incriminating, to say the least. Forensic testing had matched the blood and hairs found in the house and car boot to the missing woman. Craig Edmonds' attempt to clean up the blood, his delay in reporting his wife missing, the life insurance policies and the gaping holes in his statement would have roused the suspicions of the most trusting of people.

However, the evidence from Kirsty Edmonds' best friend, Grace Kevron, had been especially damning. According to her, Kirsty had phoned her during the week before she 'went missing,' saying she wanted to talk. They had met the next day in a café not far from the Royal Melbourne Hospital, where Kirsty worked as a nurse.

Jacinta flicked back through the pages marked with bright purple Post-it flags until she found the record of Grace Kevron's evidence.

It seemed Kirsty had told Grace that she and Craig were having problems but, other than saying she was scared of him and didn't know what she should do, didn't confide exactly what those problems were. Grace had also noticed what appeared to be relatively recent bruising on Kirsty's lower forearm. When Grace had questioned her about it, Kirsty had jerked her arm back, reflexively covering it with her other hand and dropping it out of sight under the table. The conversation had ended shortly after that. And even though Grace had tried phoning Kirsty, she had neither seen nor heard from her friend since.

Nevertheless, even with the prosecution's weighty arguments, Craig Edmonds' lawyer had managed to instill enough doubt in the mind of at least one of the jurors to ensure his client wasn't convicted. The evidence that wasn't circumstantial was hearsay, and therefore could not be substantiated.

Yawning, Jacinta stood and stretched her body, stiff from sitting in one position for too long. Collecting the coffee pot from the table, she headed to the kitchen to replenish it.

While she waited for the kettle to boil, she paced back and forth across the kitchen's slate-tiled floor with her arms crossed, mulling over facts and suppositions.

On the surface, it certainly seemed Craig Edmonds was guilty of, if not murder, hiding some terrible secret. But the question was, did he realize it? Had he been genuine in his claim that he had blacked out that night, waking the next morning without any memory of the preceding night? Or was it just a con to convince the jury of his innocence?

And if Craig Edmonds hadn't killed and disposed of his wife, who had? No question, the blood splattered through the house and car boot had belonged to Kirsty Edmonds.

Jacinta shook her head, dropping her arms as she turned to the kettle. Only two people really knew what had happened that night: Kirsty and her killer.

6

"Please, Grace," Jacinta called through the closed door. "Just ten minutes. That's all I'm asking for. Don't you think you owe Kirsty at least that?" If straight pleading wouldn't work, playing the conscience card might. "You were Kirsty's best friend. She trusted you." She was overplaying it, but if it succeeded in getting Grace to open the door, that was all that mattered.

Jacinta had studied the transcript of Grace Kevron's evidence in depth, but it was all too clean-cut. It didn't really tell her what sort of person Kirsty had been. How deeply had her husband's infidelity affected her? How devastating had the impact been on her marriage? What had been the state of the Edmonds' marriage before then? Had Craig caused the bruising on Kirsty's arm? Was there any other evidence he had harmed her in the past, physically or emotionally? Jacinta was brimming with questions to which only someone who knew the Edmonds intimately might be able to provide answers, or at least clues.

Grace Kevron, Kirsty's purported best friend, was the obvious choice. She had moved house since the trial, but thankfully her phone number and address were listed in the White Pages. Almost too easy.

"Please, Grace," she implored again, her voice tightening in frustration. "If you were Kirsty, wouldn't you want your best friend to speak up for you? She can't."

The door remained shut. Sighing, she stepped back and turned to face the street.

From behind her, she heard the faint click of the door being unlocked. She spun around. A tall, angular woman stood in the narrow door opening, one hand against the doorframe, the other clutching the edge of the door. Her chin-length, straight, jet-black hair accentuated the paleness of her skin.

"What can I add to what I said all those years ago? There is nothing more," said Grace, in a flat, resigned tone. "Nothing I could say will bring Kirsty back. Please just go."

"No, wait!" Jacinta leapt forward as Grace moved to close the door, planting her palm against the polished timber. "I know how hard this must be for you, but if you can just give me a few minutes of your time…" Her voice trailed off, her eyebrows drawing together as she held Grace's gaze.

Grace's shoulders sagged as she dropped her hand, releasing the door, and without a word gestured Jacinta inside. Grace, dressed in a loose, white, gauzy dress, seemed to float from the small entrance foyer into the next room on the left, making Jacinta wonder if she was just some ghostly apparition. She didn't even dent the carpet. In comparison, Jacinta felt like she was wearing concrete boots as she plodded in her wake.

As if suddenly remembering her manners, but probably more to forestall, Grace offered Jacinta a cup of tea or coffee. While Grace busied herself in the kitchen, Jacinta waited in the white, bare-walled, sparsely furnished formal sitting room, seating herself in one of the contemporary, but austere, white leather armchairs just inside the door. She gathered her thoughts, hoping that the cold, almost clinical room wasn't a reflection of its resident.

*

Brett Rhodes sat near the back of the conference room, his legs outstretched with his ankles crossed under the seat in front of him. A PowerPoint presentation of the latest product release of computer peripherals flashed in a blur of meaningless color across the large screen at the front of the room. Even the booming voice of the presenter failed to grab his attention.

In fact, his mind really wasn't on the job at all; hadn't been all day. What had possessed him to open his big mouth and tell Jacinta about the Edmonds murder case? Worse still, that he worked with Narelle Croswell? Perhaps it was to get her attention. Well, it had worked, even if only momentarily, but at what cost?

Jacinta had backed off when he refused point-blank to introduce her to Narelle, but he knew it would only be a short reprieve. He knew her too well to think she wouldn't pursue the story with the same dogged determination she applied to everything else in her life. That same trait that had drawn him to her in the first place.

Funnily enough, it was at a new product release, similar to the one he was at now, that he had met Jacinta Deller. She had been seated in the front row, her brow furrowed in intense concentration, when he first spotted her. But it wasn't until the session was well underway that he really became interested.

Initially it was because she was asking questions that he considered extremely basic, like 'what is the function of a hub?', leaving him curious as to why an obvious amateur would be attending a presentation aimed at IT professionals. But when she stood her ground, undeterred by the barely disguised sniggers and the occasional guffaw from those around her, he wanted to know more.

At the mid-morning break, he had searched for her amongst the people milling around the tables set out with row upon row of white cups and saucers, plates of cakes and bite-size savories. The panicky fluttering in the pit of his stomach when he couldn't immediately see her passed as soon as he glimpsed her collecting brochures and specification sheets from the table just inside the double doors.

Taking a deep breath, he picked up his cup of coffee and, trying to appear as nonchalant as possible, wandered her way. He was taken aback when she continued looking through the papers on the table, completely ignoring him. Of course, now he knew from experience that she hadn't done it intentionally.

If the theory that men could only focus on one thing at a time while women were capable of multitasking held, then either Jacinta was a man, or she just didn't fit the stereotype. And with her long blonde hair, her petite but curvy figure, her button nose and deep-blue eyes that sucked you right in, he vouched she wasn't a man. More like a shortened, freckle-faced Barbie doll with attitude. Not that he would ever tell her so.

After much throat-clearing and cup-tapping, he eventually attracted her attention. She looked around at him, starting in surprise to find that she wasn't alone. Then she smiled, her whole face lighting up.

He could smell her perfume, a light floral scent. The fluttering sensation in his stomach returned, worse than before. He remembered standing there like a paralyzed idiot, unable to speak or breathe for what seemed like an eternity.

Just then the presenter called everyone back to their seats, rescuing him, or rather her, from an awkward situation.

He spent the next hour and a half fidgeting, unable to concentrate on anything more than the back of the blonde head in the front row, mentally rehearsing what he was going to say to her — if he could stop acting like some fumbling, lovelorn schoolboy.

The session ended at noon, providing him with what he thought would be the perfect opportunity to ask her to lunch. But she seemed to be in too much of a hurry to bother with him, scarcely pausing as she turned him down flat, glanced at her watch and strode off.

Dejected and feeling like he'd been kicked in the stomach, he had walked head down through the hall to the exit.

About a week later, he had received a call. It was her. It was Jacinta. Caught by surprise, he regressed to gibbering nonsense. They hadn't been introduced, so how had she known who he was, or where to find him?

She laughed and reminded him that even though she didn't know much about computers, she could read. It took him a moment to comprehend what she was talking about. He felt his face reddening, glad that she couldn't see him, as he recalled the large plastic-encased tags detailing name and company with which each attendee had been issued on registration. How blind was he?

Somehow, he had managed to pull himself together enough to agree to meet Jacinta after work that day, at some bar he had never heard of in the city centre.

Over drinks, he learned that the only reason she had been at that IT product release was to cover for *The Acacia Tribune*'s AWOL regular technology columnist.

That had been over three years ago, and yet he still hadn't fathomed her completely. She was as unpredictable as ever. And that was his predicament. Should he pre-empt Jacinta and get to Narelle first, forewarning her as well as apologizing? Or should he do nothing except stand back and prepare himself for the inevitable fallout?

*

Waiting for Grace to answer, Jacinta leaned forward, setting her empty cup on the narrow, bleached-pine coffee table.

Grace stopped twisting the fine gold band on the little finger of her left hand and looked up. "I don't even know for sure that Kirsty knew about the affair. I knew something was bothering her, but that's all." She dropped her gaze, adding in a half-mutter, "I only found out about it myself at the trial."

Even after all these years, Grace's disappointment that her best friend had been unable to confide in her was still evident. Had Kirsty known about the affair between her husband and sister? Reading between the lines, Jacinta felt sure that at least Grace thought she had. How could she not have?

So far, Grace had not revealed much more than what Jacinta had read in the trial transcript. Not surprisingly, she remained guarded, only divulging information already on public record. What had Jacinta expected? She was a complete stranger to Grace and, what was more, a journalist.

A different approach was called for.

"Grace..." She paused, waiting for Grace to lift her head, only continuing when she held her gaze. "Were you aware that Craig Edmonds and Narelle Croswell had married?"

For a few long seconds, Grace sat there frozen. Then, as if a switch had been flicked, her dark eyes suddenly widened, her jaw dropping as her mouth gaped in a giant 'O'. She tried to hide her shock behind visibly trembling hands.

Jacinta had expected some sort of reaction, but nothing as dramatic as this. *So, the wedding really has been kept hush-hush after all*, she thought. She had searched the Internet for any mention of the wedding, but had not come up with one hit. Considering the hype surrounding the original case, that in itself was odd. But she would still have expected someone like Kirsty's best friend to know about it.

With a horrible mixture of guilt and glee at provoking such a response, Jacinta took a deep breath, her mind racing as she tried to untangle her thoughts. One part of her wanted to reach out as a friend to Grace, but the journalist in her was spurring her on to strike while Grace's defenses were down.

Why not both? she thought, leaping to her feet and making her way around the coffee table. She couldn't let the opportunity slip by.

She crouched beside Grace's chair, still unsure of what she should say. Before she could open her mouth, Grace had dropped her hands and, with a fire in her eyes that hadn't been there before, turned to Jacinta.

"That bitch! How could she do it? How could she do it to her own sister?" She shook her head, her dark hair grazing her pale cheeks. "Tell me, what sort of person could do that?" She stared down at Jacinta as if she should have all the answers.

Jacinta had no answers, only questions. What was she supposed to say? That only a cold, calculating person with no morals could do that? Was that what Grace wanted to hear?

In the end, what Jacinta thought didn't matter. Grace had risen from her seat and was pacing backwards and forwards across the room, wringing her hands and talking to no one in particular.

Feeling like an eavesdropper, Jacinta remained crouched beside the vacated chair, listening and trying to make some sense of Grace's incoherent ramblings. The news had clearly disturbed her, and most of what she was raving about centered on murderers and evil adulterers. What had Jacinta unleashed?

It soon became obvious that Grace held the same view as Brett in that Craig Edmonds, although not convicted of his wife's murder, was guilty all the same. Nor did she consider Narelle an innocent party. Was it possible that the pair had been in it together, as Grace was implying?

Jacinta felt the beginnings of cramp nipping at her calf muscle. Flexing and bending her leg, she used the arm of the chair to ease herself up. She continued to watch as Grace, seemingly oblivious to

Jacinta's presence, swept from the room. Jacinta moved to follow her, almost colliding with Grace when she stopped abruptly and turned.

Grace stared straight through her and for a moment, Jacinta thought she had become invisible. Then she blinked, her eyes slowly focusing on Jacinta's face.

"I can't help you." Grace's voice quavered. "I need to be alone."

Jacinta nodded.

She collected her satchel from the floor beside the chair, opened the zippered side pocket, drew out one of her business cards and handed it to Grace. "I'm sorry. I didn't mean to upset you; I assumed you would already have known about Craig and Narelle."

At the mention of their names, Grace's eyes narrowed. She looked on the verge of tears, her lips trembling as she opened the front door.

Jacinta was about to say something about the futility of burying the truth, but then thought better of it, and quit while she was still ahead.

"Please, Grace, think about what I said. You can call me any time of the day or night." She stepped through the doorway, turned and added, "About anything, anything at all."

"You're talking to the wrong person." The door swinging closed, Grace's ashen face disappeared from view.

7

"You're unbelievable, do you know that?"

Jacinta held the phone at arm's length and could still hear every word Brett was saying. Not that she could entirely blame him.

Grace's words rang in her ears: *You're talking to the wrong person.* What had she been alluding to? What wasn't she saying? Perhaps it had just been a passing comment, intended only to send Jacinta scurrying off in a different direction.

She had spent more than an hour sitting cross-legged on the daybed, staring out the window at nothing, carefully weighing up her options before finally coming to a decision. Why couldn't Brett understand that it wasn't personal? It was business, nothing more. *Anyway, his reputation is still intact and if he would just stop kicking up such a fuss, he'll soon realize that I would never deliberately undermine him*, she thought as, shifting position, she pulled her legs up under her.

What was wrong with inviting a few people to dinner? They had been talking about it for long enough. She would do her utmost to play the perfect hostess, making sure it would be an enjoyable evening of good food, wine and conversation. She was already planning the menu in her head. Something simple and elegant, she decided. It would have to be; her cooking skills didn't stretch much further than simple.

Brett still wasn't convinced. "Don't do this to me, Jacinta." He sighed and dropped his voice. "Don't do this to us… please…"

"Brett, I really don't know what you're so concerned about," she said, knowing full well what was on his mind. "I invited," she added, trying to allay his fears, "Patrick and Shauna as well."

Patrick Malcolm, an old school friend of Brett's, had recently become engaged to his partner of eight years, Shauna Boise. The start-up of a new florist's business on top of wedding arrangements had kept the couple busy. Consequently, Brett hadn't seen much of his friends of late. Jacinta hoped that inviting them to dinner might offset, partially at least, her ulterior motive for inviting Craig Edmonds and his new wife, Narelle Croswell.

Brett paused in his tirade. Perhaps he was coming around to her way of thinking. Perhaps that was just wishful thinking on her part. More than likely, on the other end of the phone, he was shaking his head and trying to work out what her ploy was.

Jacinta seized the opportunity. "I swear I won't mention anything at all about the case. You have my word." And she always kept her word.

"So, what's your agenda? Why have you invited a couple of people that you've never even met to dinner?" He sounded tired. "And besides, I'm really surprised that Narelle accepted your invitation. From what I know, they don't socialize much. What else haven't you told me?"

It had taken a lot of talking and coaxing to sway Narelle into accepting the dinner invitation. Jacinta had implied, if not actually stated, that it had been Brett's suggestion and that he would be offended if they didn't accept. Her tactics had been a little underhand, to say the least, but they had worked. And, true to her word, she had no intention of discussing the disappearance of the first Mrs Edmonds or the ensuing murder trial. Initially, all she wanted was to get an impression of what sort of people they were. Nothing more.

Even after she told Brett all that, he still sounded skeptical. She hung up, vowing to prove him wrong. After all, journalism and integrity didn't have to be mutually exclusive terms. *Quite the contrary*, she thought as, unfurling her legs, she moved to the edge of the daybed and stood up.

With the phone still in her hand, she wandered over to the dining table she had commandeered and looked down at the paper and documents laid out in piles around her laptop. It was only a slight exaggeration to say the stack of overdue bills was almost as high as the trial transcript next to it.

Brett had wanted to pay them for her. However, they were bills she had incurred, and she didn't think it right that he should bail her out. Although she disliked being indebted to anyone, even her lover, she could make exceptions for banks, credit card providers and utility companies. But they wouldn't wait forever.

Dropping the phone on the table, she reached across and picked up a yellow-covered, spiral-bound notebook. She had filled it with research notes, her thoughts, and any other snippet she thought might be pertinent to the story. Somewhere amongst all the scribblings were the threads of an exclusive. Her big break, if only she could tie them all together. And hopefully without snapping too many along the way.

8

After kicking off her high heels, Narelle Croswell padded in bare feet across the kitchen's cool, tiled floor to the refrigerator. Feeling oddly buoyant, she hummed as she grabbed an open bottle of Hunter Valley Chardonnay from the fridge door.

With the wine bottle tucked under her arm and her fingers wrapped around the stem of a wine glass, she made her way to the sliding glass doors that led out to the swimming pool, collecting the phone from its cradle on the way. She had yet to tell Craig what she had done.

Stepping out onto the sandstone paving, she paused, savoring the light breeze as it caressed her flushed skin. The hint of dampness in the air reassured her that the promised cool change was on its way. Early evening sunlight, dappled by the branches of eucalypts, bounced across the tiny ripples on the saltwater pool's surface. A scene set for entertaining.

Narelle couldn't remember the last time she had socialized, let alone entertained. *But maybe that drought is about to break*, she thought. A small smile tweaked at the corners of her mouth as she deposited her load onto the polished aluminum table, poured herself a glass of wine, and settled down in the nearest sling chair. Maybe they could start living like normal people again. Maybe they could stop hiding from the world.

Her first reaction had been to turn down the invitation, but Brett Rhodes' girlfriend, Jacinta, had been especially persuasive. What did she have to worry about? Brett and she had worked for the same company for nearly three years with no problems. A private dinner party wouldn't leave them feeling exposed and vulnerable the same way a public restaurant would. It could be fun.

Now all she had to do was sell the idea to Craig. She set her wine glass on the table, picked up the phone and pressed the quick-dial button that would connect her to Craig's direct line. Although he was due to leave the office shortly, Narelle hoped that by phoning him while he was distracted by his work, he wouldn't say no outright. He would want to talk about it at home. And that's exactly what she wanted. Then the drive home would give him time to mull over the proposition. Or at least that was the theory.

He answered on the fifth ring. Keeping her voice light and cheery, she asked how his day had been, making small talk before adding, almost as an afterthought, that they had been invited out to dinner. She tried to make it sound like it was no big deal, that dinner invitations were commonplace for them.

She heard a sharp intake of breath and knew she had failed.

Silence.

"Craig?"

He responded with a sharpness of tone that she hadn't heard before. "We'll talk about this when I get home."

Click. He had hung up.

Stunned, Narelle set down the phone and picked up the wine bottle to refill her glass. She had predicted that he would want to discuss it at home, but nothing had prepared her for how he had said it. It was a side of her husband she had never experienced before. But she had heard something else in his voice. Could fear be behind his uncharacteristic behavior?

She picked up her wine glass from the table and skolled its contents in two gulps. Craig would be home soon.

9

Domesticity wasn't Jacinta's greatest virtue. The kitchen looked like a hurricane had just passed through it. Dirty pots, bowls and utensils littered the bench. A thick, garlicky pasta sauce bubbled like a hot mud pool on the stove, splattering cooked tomato in all directions. Salad greens sweated inside plastic bags, sharing the sink with empty tomato cans and onion skins.

Wiping her hands on a tea towel, she glanced at the clock, feeling a flutter of panic. Salads still had to be made, lemons squeezed for the dressing, the pasta sauce finished, parmesan cheese grated, the antipasto platter organized...

The list seemed endless, not to mention that she still had to shower and change. If she wasn't careful, their guests would arrive and she would still be standing there, looking like a victim of the same hurricane that had hit the kitchen.

Fortunately, Brett had volunteered — or rather, had been recruited — to look after drinks and the music, as well as set the table. Mentally crossing those chores off her list, she went in search of the glass dessert bowls she knew she had; she just wasn't sure where they were stashed. She was quickly remembering why they didn't entertain often. Brett couldn't understand what all the fuss was about, but he wasn't the one running himself ragged.

Somehow she managed to finish the food preparation, clean the kitchen, and check that Brett hadn't set the table with the forks on the right and the knives on the left.

The doorbell rang just as she was putting the final touches to her makeup. She paused, relaxing on hearing voices she recognized. Patrick and Shauna were punctual, as always. That should make it a little less stiff when Craig and Narelle arrived. If they arrived. Narelle had confirmed with Brett on Thursday, but who was to say they hadn't changed their minds since then.

The doorbell rang again, filling Jacinta with trepidation this time. Whose bright idea was it to invite a man accused of his wife's murder and his new wife to dinner? What if they saw straight through her? What if she unintentionally stared at them? Or worse, avoided eye contact? What if she had one too many glasses of wine and blurted out something she shouldn't? The more she thought about it, the more perilous it seemed.

After checking herself one last time in the mirror, she fixed what she hoped was a welcoming smile to her face and went to meet her guests. As she shut the bedroom door behind her, she heard laughter and the clink of glasses coming from the other end of the house. A good start.

She found everyone congregated in the brick-paved courtyard off the living room, drinks in hand, being entertained by one of Patrick's infamous tall tales. Jacinta smiled to herself. As long as he was the centre of attention, he was happy. He could be guaranteed to liven up any party. So far, so good.

Long-legged Shauna stood beside her sturdier red-haired fiancé, rattling the ice cubes in her glass and giving a good impression that she had heard it all before. And more than once, too.

Brett and their other two visitors had their backs to her, but all turned in unison when Patrick, without missing a beat in his performance, blew her a theatrical kiss. Now she was the centre of attention.

Smiling sweetly, she waited for Brett to make the introductions. Narelle Croswell, with her mass of brunette curls and model looks, was a marked contrast to her relatively plain, fair-haired sister. The only photos of Kirsty Edmonds that Jacinta had seen were cropped images posted on various websites. Still, the sisters looked so different that it was hard to imagine they shared the same genes.

Next to her, scuffing his feet on the ground, Craig Edmonds looked much less at ease than his wife. He had aged considerably since the photos plastered all over the Internet had been taken. His face had thinned and his dark hair was flecked liberally with grey. The moustache was gone and he wore rimless glasses. Despite the ageing, he was still an attractive man, and Narelle and he made a striking couple. They certainly didn't look evil.

But what did evil look like? If Grace Kevron was to be believed, she had just shaken the hands of two cold-blooded murderers.

Brett kept casting her sidelong glances and she kept pretending she didn't see them. They had talked in depth about what subjects were off limits and what weren't, but from the looks he was giving her, he wasn't taking anything for granted. Pouring a glass of Evans & Tate's Sparkling Pinot Noir Chardonnay, he moved to stand directly in front of her, only releasing the champagne flute to her fingers when he held her gaze. It was the telepathic equivalent of a stern reminder.

After a few minutes of idle chitchat, she headed inside to the kitchen. She had originally intended to make the dinner a formal, sit-down affair in the dining room, but since the evening was so balmy and everyone seemed to be comfortable outside, she decided to take the meal to them. First course, anyway.

As she passed through the lounge room, Kate Ceberano's soulful voice reflected her thoughts: *"Will you still love me tomorrow? Tonight with words unspoken..."* If she kept to her promise not to start asking questions of Craig and Narelle, there would be no reason for Brett not to love her tomorrow. She knew she had nothing to worry about, as long as she stuck to her role of the perfect Stepford wife.

Hoping she was better at acting than cooking, she started removing the lids from the plastic containers of olives, semi-dried tomatoes and marinated eggplant she had bought that morning. Although she had bravely attempted to grill the eggplant slices, they had come out looking like charred bits of dish sponge. What was more, they tasted worse than they looked.

While Jacinta was in the middle of arranging curled, wafer-thin slices of prosciutto and coppa on the platter, Shauna turned up with the wine bottle, offering both a refill and assistance. Or, in Jacinta's case, salvation.

"Narelle and Craig seem like a nice couple. How do you know them?" Shauna popped a black chili olive into her mouth.

Jacinta hesitated. "Ummm… Brett works with Narelle at Woodridge." She quickly changed the subject, delegating Shauna the task of setting the outside table.

By the time she had carried the antipasto platter, a floury ciabatta loaf and a bread knife out to the courtyard, Katie Melua's bluesy jazz voice was flowing from the stereo speakers. The light, lemony scent of the citronella lamps wafted through the air.

With the aid of a couple of bottles of an excellent King Valley Riesling, the party had soon devoured the first course, leaving little more than crumbs and olive pits. Any tensions that might have been there dissolved as the couples laughed and talked. Even Jacinta had started to relax. So, when Craig suddenly asked her what she did for a living, she was thrown off balance for a second.

Brett quickly stepped in, filling the void. "Jacinta is, as they say, between jobs right now. Unfortunately," he dropped his lower lip in an exaggerated pout, "my idea that perhaps she could devote all her new-found free time to being my slave didn't work out."

The original question was soon lost in the ensuing laughter. Breathing a silent sigh of relief, Jacinta collected the dirty plates, excused herself and headed back inside.

No sooner had she started stacking the plates in the dishwasher than she heard the click-clack of high heels on the slate behind her. She turned, expecting to see Shauna again, and almost dropped the plate in her hand when she saw Narelle standing there instead, a couple of empty glasses in her hands.

"I'm sorry, I didn't mean to startle you."

Jacinta smiled at her. "No problem. I just didn't see you, that's all." She reached for the glasses, adding a "thanks" as she placed them in the dishwasher.

Like Shauna had earlier, Narelle then offered to help. Had they arranged to take turns, or had it just turned out that way? Jacinta's first thought was to politely decline and send Narelle straight back to the party, but then a little voice in her head piped up. When else would she get the chance to talk one on one with Narelle? Even though she couldn't ask the hard-hitting questions she would dearly have liked to, there was no reason she couldn't get to know her better.

"Thanks," she said, gesturing toward the stove. "What are your sauce-stirring skills like?"

Initially, the conversation between the two women was a little stilted, but Jacinta soon found herself warming to Narelle. She came across as such a genuine and likeable person that Jacinta had difficultly imagining how she could possibly have been involved in something criminal or sordid. But did first impressions really count?

While she waited for the pot of salted water to come to the boil for the ravioli, she put the finishing touches to the salad, adding a few leaves of fresh basil from her herb garden. Everything was running like clockwork. She couldn't have planned it better if she'd tried.

She was starting to feel quite smug, but then Narelle caught her off-guard and asked her what sort of work she did when she wasn't being a domestic goddess.

Jacinta felt like a kangaroo caught in the glare of headlights, rooted to the spot and not knowing in what direction to flee. She blushed, a rapid surge of heat radiating up her face. There was no hiding it.

"I'm sorry, I didn't mean to embarrass you," Narelle said, running the words together in her rush to apologize.

Unable to look Narelle in the eye, Jacinta stared down at her feet, frantically trying to come up with some response that wasn't going to push her even further into the corner.

She forced a laugh. "You name it, I've done it." She wasn't lying. Backpacking around the world in her early twenties meant finding work wherever she could. "Everything from waitressing to fruit-picking to working in a bank." She didn't mention her stint as a deckhand on a fishing trawler off Iceland, or her time spent as a holiday rep in Rhodes. From experience, she knew that would only invite more questions.

Thankfully, Narelle, perceptive enough to sense Jacinta's reticence, didn't press the issue. Or perhaps it was because they both had something to hide.

10

The pounding in her head grew louder. Without opening her eyes, Narelle rolled onto her back and flung her arm out to the side. The bed beside her, though warm, was empty.

The peal of the doorbell ricocheted through the house, embedding what felt like sharp darts behind her eyes. She groaned, lying as still as possible, waiting for the pain to subside. It didn't make any sense. Had she really had that much to drink?

Then it all started coming back to her. The champagne, the wine, the liqueurs... She had been so wired in, she hadn't realized how much she'd had to drink. Why hadn't Craig tried to stop her? She groaned again, remembering. He had, but she'd brushed him off as a party pooper. Now she was paying for it.

Oh, God, she suddenly thought, *did I make a complete fool of myself? Way to go, Narelle.* She felt embarrassed and peeved with herself all at the same time. *What must they think of me?*

The doorbell rang again, and before the chime had petered out, it was pushed again and again in rapid succession. She pulled the bedclothes up over her head, her face contorting against the resulting off-key heavy metal jangle.

Cotton sheets proved a poor sound barrier. Hearing a woman's strident tones, she yanked the sheets off her head. She couldn't quite make out the words, but there was no mistaking the voice. Her chest felt like it was clamped in a giant vice, the air in her lungs being squeezed out.

She scrambled out of bed, her brain like liquid sloshing from side to side in her skull as she stumbled from the bedroom.

Craig, motionless and mute, stood about two meters back from the front door, his fists tightly clenched by his sides. He didn't turn as she approached, but she didn't need to see his face to know how he must be feeling.

He flinched as she reached out and touched his naked back with her fingertips. She paused, opening and closing her hand before dropping it back to her side.

"Craig," she whispered. Focused solely on the door, he either hadn't heard or chose not to hear her.

"You depraved, sick bastard! You killed your wife and then you married her sister." Grace Kevron's voice rose to a screech. "You should both be rotting in hell for what you did to Kirsty. If it's the last thing I do, I'll make sure you pay."

Narelle grabbed Craig's forearm, trying to draw him away. He shook her off and moved toward the door.

"We have nothing to say to you. If you don't leave, I'm going to call the police." His voice sounded remarkably calm, but both fists twitched as if each hand was kneading a stress ball.

"And what will they do? Lock me up? You know I'm not the criminal here, don't you?" Mocking laughter followed.

Narelle tried again to pull Craig away from the door. She looped her arm through his, feeling the tremor in his body.

"Restraining order!" Craig shouted at the door as if the idea had suddenly occurred to him. "I'm going to take out a restraining order against you if you don't leave my property this instant."

Grace laughed again, before dropping her voice to a hate-filled snarl. "Perhaps if Kirsty had taken out a restraining order against you two, she would still be alive. You haven't heard the last of me. Believe me, you will pay for what you did."

11

Jacinta tossed the morning newspaper onto the daybed and headed to the kitchen to make coffee. She passed the dining table, strewn with paperwork and once again reclaimed as her work desk.

She still couldn't quite believe how well Saturday night's dinner party had gone. Even cynical Brett had grudgingly admitted to enjoying himself. But what had she achieved, besides proving to herself that you didn't have to be a gourmet chef to produce a tasty meal for six?

In her mind, she had achieved a lot. At the beginning of the night, Narelle had been as reserved as her husband, but a few glasses of wine had soon unleashed a bubbly, outgoing woman who possessed a wicked sense of humor. She'd had Jacinta in stitches, laughing so much that tears ran down her face.

Although she still wasn't quite sure about Craig, she had begun to think that she and Narelle could be good friends. Craig Edmonds and Narelle Croswell were no longer just impersonal names in print; they were real people. People with feelings. People with emotions. And yes, perhaps, people with secrets. But what right did she have to meddle in someone else's life?

After that night, she had given a great deal of thought to her career direction. When she looked inside herself, she didn't see the ruthlessness and hunger needed to make it in the cut-and-thrust world of investigative journalism. Nor was she prepared to ride roughshod over people's lives, regardless of what they had or hadn't been accused of.

The clincher, though, was her bank balance. Or lack thereof. She had been forced to transfer money from her credit card to her check account just to pay her living expenses. What she needed was a job with a regular pay packet, and fast.

As hard a decision as it was, she knew Brett, for one, would be ecstatic when she told him. Starting from today, she was no longer an investigative journalist ready to expose the truth and wow the world, but a job searcher prepared to compromise for almost any job — except selling her body — she could get. She truly believed she had made the right decision. So why did she feel so flat and uninspired?

She had finished making coffee and was carrying it through to the dining room to make a start on the employment pages when the phone rang. Maybe it was news that a previously unheard of great-aunt she didn't know she'd had died and left her a fortune.

Instead it was good news of a different kind; the kind where some effort would be required on her part. Anthea Sutton, her old boss and the editor of *The Acacia Tribune*, was calling to let her know that one of the newspaper's regular advertisers, Alvico Media, was looking for a copywriter. Anthea had recommended Jacinta.

A regular job with regular money. Jacinta didn't know whether to laugh or cry. Although she would still have to apply for the position, Anthea's recommendation would certainly go a long way.

With nothing more to do until Anthea emailed through all the details, she decided to read the newspaper. She set the cooling mug of coffee on the windowsill, hooking one leg under the other as she sat down and spread the newspaper out flat on the daybed in front of her.

As usual, the front page was full of doom and gloom. Interest rates were set to rise. 'Health costs us an arm and a leg' proclaimed another headline, which certainly wasn't news to Jacinta. A teenage boy behind the wheel of a stolen car had managed to evade police, only to later wrap the car around a power pole, killing himself and all three of his young passengers. Even the photo of convicted terrorist Abu Bakar Bashir flashing a toothy smile from centre page was nothing to feel good about.

Sipping her coffee, she turned the page.

ACCUSED WIFE-KILLER WEDS VICTIM'S SISTER.

For a split second, time stood still, her mug frozen mid-air. She blinked, hoping her eyes had deceived her. Then she read the headline again.

ACCUSED WIFE-KILLER WEDS VICTIM'S SISTER.

The day that had started out so promisingly came crashing down around her. In slow motion she reached out to the side and placed her coffee back on the windowsill. Transfixed by the words, she sat staring at the article. How was this possible? A pure coincidence?

Problem was, she didn't believe in coincidences.

Leaning forward, she gripped the sides of the newspaper in both hands and lifted it up to her face, as if somehow that would make the words easier to comprehend.

She took a deep breath and started reading the smaller type under the heading, feeling sicker by the second. The writer, although careful to skirt any outright libelous statements, implied that the justice system had failed in its duty to bring Craig Edmonds and Narelle Croswell to account for their part in the murder of Kirsty Olive Edmonds. Craig and Narelle's nuptials had been cleverly used to throw even more suspicion their way. The article's only redeeming feature — from the Edmonds' point of view, anyway — was that it wasn't accompanied by a picture.

How was she going to explain it to Brett? How was she going to make him believe that she wasn't responsible? He wasn't one for coincidences either. The fact that it hadn't been published under her byline wouldn't be proof enough for him. After all, she had published under pseudonyms before.

Someone somewhere had to have leaked that information about the wedding to the newspaper. Why else, months after the event, would the news suddenly have come to light?

Then the image of Grace Kevron's shocked face popped into her head. Had Grace, looking for some sort of vengeance, alerted the press?

With a heavy, sinking feeling, Jacinta realized that she was responsible, indirectly if not directly, for thrusting the Edmonds case back into the limelight. But wasn't that what she had wanted? Wasn't that the aim of all the research? If she were honest with herself, she would have to say yes. In the beginning, anyway.

Since then she had come to her senses, understanding that no good could come from playing with other people's lives and stirring up old emotions. Her conscience had stopped her, but had it already been too late by then? She had unwittingly opened a Pandora's box. The question was, could she close it again, or was the damage already done?

Shoving aside the newspaper, she leapt from the daybed, making straight for the phone. Halfway across the room, she stopped. She hadn't thought it through. What was she going to say to Narelle? Shouldn't her first step be to confront Grace and confirm her assumptions? Or maybe she should talk to Brett first. Standing there with her face buried in her palms, she wished she could turn back the clock.

Her hands were shaking by the time she picked up the phone. Her first call had to be to Narelle. It would be better coming from someone she knew, even if not that well, than reading about it in the newspaper. The old saying about 'shutting the gate after the horse has bolted' came to mind as she waited for the call to connect.

A snooty-sounding woman on the switchboard answered, informing her that Narelle was on sick leave. And no, she didn't know when she was expected back. Could someone else help?

I very much doubt it, thought Jacinta as she hung up the phone.

12

Jacinta hung her head. How many ways were there to say 'I told you so'? Brett was up to number ten, each louder and more agitated than the last.

"Okay, okay, okay! I get the message. I should've listened to you. But I swear I did not write that article. You have to believe me."

"Believe you?" Brett's nostrils flared. "Oh, yes, I always believe you. Believe you when you tell me that it's all just one big coincidence. Believe you when you tell me this wasn't meant to happen. Believe you when you tell me you love me. Believe you when…" His voice trailed off. "Jacinta, I don't know what to believe any more."

"Believe what you want, then," she spat, regretting the words the instant they left her mouth.

Brett sighed, not just his shoulders but his whole demeanor sagging as he turned and walked away from her. She watched his retreating back, feeling like a stranger in her own body. Desperate to undo any wrongs, real or imagined, she wanted to stop him and tell him how sorry she was. Instead all she could do was sit numbly by.

The pillow on the daybed where Brett had slept last night still held the indentation of his head. She gathered up the quilt, hugging it to her chest as she closed her eyes and inhaled Brett's musky scent. Tears brimmed in her eyes, spilling down her cheeks unchecked as she rocked back and forth on the end of the daybed.

The sound of drawers and cupboards being opened and slammed shut from the far end of the house quickly brought her back to her senses. Now was no time to be feeling sorry for herself.

She entered the bedroom just in time to see Brett throw the contents of his sock basket into his suitcase.

"What are you doing?"

"What does it look like I'm doing?" Brett said, tossing a bundle of shirts on the haphazardly heaped mountain of clothes on the bed.

"You can't leave. Not like this."

"Why not? You do as you damned well please, so why can't I? No one dares get in the way of the world-wise Jacinta Deller lest they get trampled, do they?"

Ouch!

Biting her tongue, she swallowed hard, trying to rein in the welter of conflicting emotions. Couldn't he understand that she had only been trying to do her job as a journalist? Besides, it was the information he had given her that had started it all. Then it clicked. He wasn't only angry with her, he was angry with himself for telling her about the Edmonds case in the first place.

Still smarting from his outburst, but now at least with a modicum of understanding as to why, she tried reasoning with him. However, he wasn't in the mood to be reasonable and her very presence seemed to be more than enough to antagonize him.

Momentarily defeated and with no energy left to continue the pointless battling, she left Brett jamming clothes into the open suitcase on the bed.

A short time later, she heard the front door close, followed soon after by the deep-throated V8 rumble of Brett's 1966 Chevrolet Impala as he backed out of the driveway.

The house felt strangely empty, as if all the life had been sucked out of it, leaving her sitting in a vacuum. In the heat of the moment they had both said things they hadn't meant but that, nevertheless, had cut deeply. Could they ever go back to what they had before all this happened?

Jacinta shook her head. Her world had come to an end, and the only person she could blame was herself. She had been taking risks all her life but none had backfired as spectacularly as this one. But life, she reassured herself, was full of gambles. Where would she be if she had always played it safe?

The picture-perfect scene of a husband and brood of kids standing in front of a weatherboard cottage, complete with white picket fence, flashed through her mind. She shuddered, the mere thought incomprehensible.

Later, perhaps; but for now, she was in charge of her own life and regardless of the mistakes she made along the way, she had to live it as she saw fit. Logic was all very well, but logic couldn't override her feelings for Brett. It had taken him walking out on her to make her see what her single-mindedness had cost her.

She felt so alone, and so very tired. Craving the respite sleep would bring, she lay down, resting her head in the same hollow where Brett's had once been, and pulled the quilt up over her body.

For what seemed like hours, she lay motionless with eyes closed, sleep evading her. Brett's words played over and over in her mind. Did she always put herself first, regardless of the impact on others? She had always thought of herself as ambitious, but was it possible she had crossed the threshold into mercenariness without realizing it?

Opening her eyes, she threw the quilt off and sat upright.

No, damn it! Brett was wrong. Hadn't she made the decision to drop the story for the sake of everyone involved? If only he had let her explain, instead of constantly talking over the top of her.

She conceded she was no angel, but everyone made mistakes, even him. At least she had made an effort to understand when he confessed to having a one-night stand while in Sydney, attending an IT conference. In her eyes, infidelity was a far greater wrongdoing than passing on information that was on public record anyway. Of course, that didn't excuse her own behavior.

Intent on taking control rather than playing the poor, misjudged victim, she abandoned the refuge of the daybed and headed for the bedroom to get changed. The oversized men's blue-and-white striped pajama top she wore had to go.

She was standing in the walk-in-robe, contemplating what to wear, when she heard her mobile ringing. For a moment, she considered ignoring it and letting it divert to voicemail. However, curiosity and the possibility that it might be Brett had her sprinting for the dining room.

Without time to check the caller display, she snatched the still-ringing phone from the table, answering it with a breathless "hello".

"I'm not interrupting anything, am I?"

The voice was familiar, yet unfamiliar. She clamped the phone to her ear, her breathing slowly returning to normal. "Grace, is that you?"

"At your service," cackled Grace. "Had to thank you for that snippet of news..." She laughed again. "Talking about news, read the newspaper today?"

Forget ghost; think witch. "Grace, do you really think that was the wisest thing to do?"

"They deserve everything that's coming their way, and more," Grace retorted, her voice hardening. "You might like to know I also called on the newly-weds."

Jacinta held her breath, hoping she really hadn't heard what she thought she had.

"For some reason, they weren't pleased to see me. Craig, the bastard, even threatened to call the police. What a fucking hypocrite. Can you believe that?"

Yes, she could believe that. The venom in Grace's voice had Jacinta more than grateful that the demented woman wasn't there in person.

There were mistakes, and then there were mistakes. If contacting Grace Kevron hadn't been bad enough, telling her about the wedding had been disastrous. Surely, if she had been astute enough, she would have realized that Grace still hadn't come to terms with losing her best friend. Maybe Brett was right after all. Maybe her zealousness was her undoing.

Her suggestion to Grace that perhaps she should leave the Edmonds to the law was met with more derision and contempt. Grace then started screaming about blood, bodies, vengeance and the devil, scaring the hell out of Jacinta.

Could grief do that to a person? The woman clearly needed psychiatric help of some kind. Jacinta was way out of her depth and could do nothing except wait and hope that the tirade would eventually stop.

At least Grace didn't know where she lived…

13

Narelle stared blankly at the phone. Although she remembered writing down Jacinta Deller's phone number, she couldn't remember where. Closing her eyes, she tried to picture the sequence of events: answering the phone, scribbling the details of the dinner invitation on the corner of her deskpad, hanging up, reaching into her…

Snapping her fingers, she opened her eyes and went in search of her black handbag. Somewhere in the depths of it was her seldom-used pocket diary, with all the information from the deskpad neatly transcribed into it.

She had been remiss in not thanking Jacinta and Brett for Saturday night sooner, but her good intentions had been lost in the week's dramas. Grace Kevron's Sunday morning visit had left both Craig and Narelle shell-shocked. What had suddenly awakened the beast, as Narelle liked to think of Grace, after so many years?

The Edmonds hadn't recovered from that attack when another bomb exploded in their faces. Somehow, the press had found out about their marriage, raking up what Narelle thought was old and buried and mixing it with the new. She couldn't understand what anybody had to gain from the seemingly unprovoked attack. None of it made any sense. How much longer would they have to live with the malicious insinuations?

Wasn't it enough that she had lost her only sister? Wasn't it enough that her parents had disowned her because of her involvement with her sister's husband? Wasn't it enough that she would always carry the guilt of the affair? Wasn't it enough that she had been implicated in her sister's disappearance and murder?

Apparently not.

Narelle believed in Craig. She couldn't have married him if she hadn't. She had no answers to what had happened that fateful night. All she was certain of was that Craig could not have killed Kirsty. Drunk and passed out on the bed, a full-scale riot could have been happening in the house and he wouldn't have known anything about it. Anything could have happened.

She was sick of living life as a social hermit, sick of looking over her shoulder. *Sick of being sick*, she thought suddenly, as a new bout of nausea had her running for the bathroom. Since Sunday, she had been battling an upset stomach, spending more time with her head hung over the toilet bowl than not. Craig hadn't been sick and it didn't feel like food poisoning, so she blamed it on stress.

Some time later, feeling drained and exhausted, she resurfaced from the bathroom. Like a little girl lost, she stood in the doorway, looking left, then right. Was stress playing havoc with her memory as well? What had she been doing? What day was it?

She wandered around the house, careful to avoid the windows. Most of the reporters and photographers who had camped out on the front verge earlier in the week had given up, but a few determined stragglers remained. She had no idea what they expected to achieve, and didn't much care.

Gazing at the phone, she had a sudden sense of déjà vu, finally recalling that she had been in the middle of looking for Jacinta's phone number when her stomach had had other ideas. With a quiet sigh, she picked up the phone and headed to the bedroom.

Despite overindulging, she had really enjoyed the dinner party. Both the food and the company. Jacinta and she had clicked immediately, nattering away like old girlfriends. Narelle would've relished the chance to get to know her better. As it was, Jacinta must have thought it extremely rude of her not to have contacted her already. Sure, she had a good excuse, but how was Jacinta to know that?

Narelle dug out her pocket diary from the bottom of her handbag, sat on the edge of the bed and flicked through blank page after blank page until she came to last Saturday's date. Her round handwriting, detailing time, address and phone numbers, spilled over into Sunday.

Mentally rehearsing what she was going to say, she dialed Jacinta and Brett's home phone number. She forced a smile, hoping to portray a lightness she didn't feel. It felt strained and unnatural. The phone rang seven times, then she heard a click, followed by Jacinta's cheery tones asking her to leave a message. Narelle hesitated, reluctant to talk to a machine.

"Umm… Jacinta, it's Narelle Cros—"

"Hold on a sec." After a series of clicks and squeals, all went quiet. "Sorry about that. I wasn't fast enough getting to the phone."

Narelle stammered out a few disjointed words, her carefully rehearsed little speech of thanks in tatters.

"Narelle." Jacinta paused. "Is everything okay?"

If the concern in Jacinta's voice wasn't enough, asking her that question was like turning on a tap.

Narelle opened her mouth to speak, but what came out sounded something like a cross between a loud hiccup and a thwarted cough. Uncontrollable, choking sobs followed.

As mortified as she was, there was nothing she could do to stop it. Struggling to regain her composure, she dropped the phone onto the bed next to her, and picked up her pillow. Like some never-ending battle, each time she thought she'd won and was back in control, she would start bawling again. What was wrong with her?

Over the years she'd become an expert at keeping her emotions in check, so what had changed?

After what seemed like an eternity, her sobs weakened to a low snivel. The pillow she had used to smother her blubbering was sodden. Releasing it into her lap, she took a deep breath, holding it for a count of ten before slowly exhaling.

The sight of the neglected phone face-down on the quilt almost set her off again. She swallowed and picked up the phone, praying that all she would hear was a disconnected tone. Before it reached her ear, she heard Jacinta's anxious voice, frantically calling her name.

Narelle bit down on her lip, tasting blood. Somehow she managed to speak, blurting out a garbled apology. Jacinta brushed aside the apology, clearly at that moment more concerned with Narelle's welfare than anything else. Before she knew it, Narelle was giving Jacinta her address.

Knowing that Jacinta would be there shortly at least gave Narelle the impetus she needed to pull herself together. Breaking down over the phone had been bad enough. In person, it could only be more humiliating.

She allowed herself a few minutes for some yoga stretching and deep breathing, feeling the benefits almost immediately. Cold water splashed on her face further revived both body and soul.

Running her fingers through her hair, she pushed and poked wayward curls into position. A touch of lip-gloss added some color to her otherwise washed-out face. She tried smiling at the sad face in the mirror, but it didn't reciprocate. She tried again. The corners of the lips lifted slightly but the eyes remained impassive.

Even though she had been expecting it, she jumped when the doorbell rang. With more purposefulness than she felt, she turned and strode to the front door. Remembering at the last moment to smile, she flung the door open.

Her face crumpled. She had seen enough of police detectives over the years to recognize them when she saw them. The first officer, standing about a meter back from the doorstep, was a tall woman in her mid to late thirties, her fair hair pulled back in a ponytail. Just to her left and slightly back stood her partner, a clean-shaven, solidly built man in his twenties. Both wore suits, the male detective looking distinctly uncomfortable in his.

She would have slammed the door in their faces if the woman hadn't already put her foot in the doorway.

"Police," said the woman, holding up her identification badge. Introducing herself as Detective Sergeant Renee White and her partner as Detective Constable Mark Fratta, she then asked to come in.

Even though Narelle knew she had every right to refuse them entry, she didn't have the energy to fight. She hadn't considered why the police might be there. In her experience, police equated to endless accusations and questioning.

Feeling outnumbered and vulnerable, she stepped back from the door, wondering if she should be calling a lawyer. At any other time, she would have wanted Craig by her side, but his state of mind was already fragile enough.

Sunday's visit from Grace had been the trigger, but Tuesday's newspaper article compounded it. She desperately wanted to help him but every time she tried, he just withdrew further. He had become remote, to the extent of sleeping in the guest room. Or not sleeping.

At night, alone in their bed, she would lie awake, listening to her husband prowl around the house. She would hear the clink of glass against glass and know that he was seeking solace in the bottom of a bottle. It frightened her.

Being confronted by police officers, whatever their reason for being there, would bring it all back, perhaps pushing him over the edge. She couldn't risk that. She could, and would, deal with it on her own.

As she turned to close the door, she heard raised voices. She kept her body shielded by the door and peered out. Standing on the footpath, dwarfed by a posse of reporters, was Jacinta, slapping her hands at the air like she was trying to shoo off a couple of pesky flies.

But the reporters, like flies, weren't about to be deterred. It wouldn't matter what Jacinta did, they weren't leaving. Quite the contrary.

The visit by the police and then Jacinta seemed to have revved up their interest somewhat. Undaunted by Jacinta's accusations of trespassing, the cameras followed her every movement, microphones poised to catch every sound.

It wasn't until Jacinta's foot left the top step that Narelle managed to catch her attention. Jacinta's eyes widened, but she said nothing as Narelle reached out, hooked her arm and pulled her through the narrow opening of the door.

14

Jacinta rubbed her arm, surprised at the intensity of Narelle's grip. Narelle stood barefoot in front of her, her skin as pale and translucent as the white, loose-woven shirt she wore. Almost as if the vivid scarlet and yellow hues of the close to mural-sized abstract painting on the wall behind her had sucked all the color from her. She looked ill.

The muffled sound of a male voice coming from somewhere in the depths of the house startled Jacinta. From the phone call, she had expected Narelle to be home alone. Was Craig at home, too? If so, why wasn't he comforting his wife?

Narelle answered Jacinta's unspoken questions with a barely audible whisper: "Police."

Jacinta's mind went into overdrive. What would the police be doing calling on Narelle? Her first thought was that they were delivering bad news. Had someone been seriously injured — or worse, died? Was it Craig? Was it something to do with Grace Kevron? Had it anything to do with the old murder case?

Her thoughts were cut short when Narelle headed up the hall, signaling for Jacinta to follow. As they passed the airy kitchen and meals area, drawing closer to the northern end of the house, a softer feminine voice joined the male's.

The open cathedral-ceiling space Jacinta stepped down into took her breath away. Her whole home could have fitted into the room without a squeeze. The polished timber floors, the plush rugs, the buff leather couches and armchairs all exuded wealth and taste. An eclectic mix of artworks, undoubtedly originals, adorned the walls. Bright sunlight streamed in through the expanse of glass overlooking the swimming pool.

Awestruck, she wondered if this was Narelle's or Craig's influence at work. But then it suddenly occurred to her that she was standing in a crime scene, albeit an old one.

Jolted back to reality, she shook her head and blinked. On the far side of the room she saw, rather than heard, Narelle offering a seat to a tall, fair-haired woman and a younger, stocky man, who Jacinta presumed were police detectives. As curious as she was, she hung back, not wanting to intrude.

The detectives shifted in their seats, looking as uncomfortable as Narelle, who was perched awkwardly on the couch opposite with her knees together and ankles splayed. Her eyes darted left and right, anywhere but directly at the officers. Then her gaze caught Jacinta's. Narelle's eyes widened, her hand flying to her mouth as if Jacinta had suddenly materialized from out of nowhere.

Eventually, recognition dawned in Narelle's eyes. She beckoned, frantically patting the seat beside her. Jacinta hesitated, unsure of what she should be doing. It felt like she had walked onto a film set in the middle of a take and forgotten her lines. What was her role supposed to be?

Taking a deep breath, she moved across the room to join Narelle. A long, narrow, blue gum coffee table acted as a barrier between the police and Narelle. As Jacinta sank down onto the couch next to her, she glanced across at the detectives' faces. Their expressions portrayed nothing, not even the slightest impatience at being kept waiting.

Narelle didn't introduce Jacinta to the officers, nor did they seem particularly interested in her presence, their focus firmly centered on Narelle.

The female detective spoke first, her voice low. "Ms Croswell," she said, sitting forward in her seat and pulling a plastic bag from her jacket pocket, "do you recognize this at all?" She slid the bag across the coffee table toward Narelle.

For a few moments Narelle just stared at the bag, seemingly unable to bring herself to pick it up. "What is it?" she asked in a hoarse whisper. She began to mangle the ball of scrunched-up tissues in her hands.

Even though the question was directed at the female, it was the male officer who spoke. "When your sister, Kirsty…" He paused for a fraction of a second, as if weighing his words, before continuing, "…disappeared, you gave us a description of a gold cross that she always wore."

Narelle had visibly stiffened at the mention of her sister, but still made no move to examine the bag.

The detective continued, "Would you mind looking at this," he picked up the bag from the table and tried to hand it to her, "and telling us if this is like the one Kirsty owned."

Narelle's hand trembled when she finally reached out and took the bag from his fingers. Her breathing labored, she maneuvered the cross into the corner of the sealed evidence bag. Laying it flat on her palm, she stared at the small, tarnished gold cross, a deep-blue sapphire set in its centre. She stopped breathing.

All eyes were on Narelle. The heightening tension hung like a pall over them. No one moved.

Sandwiching the bag between her palms, Narelle closed her eyes tight, bringing her hands up under her chin in a silent prayer. No one else moved.

The male detective cleared his throat, breaking the spell.

Narelle's eyes popped open, giving her the wide-eyed, vacant look of a child's doll. And then, without warning, she lurched from the couch. The plastic bag containing the cross tumbled to the floor. With one hand covering her mouth and the other clutching her stomach, she fled the room.

The detectives looked sideways at each other before turning their attention to Jacinta. If they were looking for an explanation, they were definitely looking in the wrong place. Jacinta was as much in the dark as they were. Regardless, she didn't need to be Einstein to work out that Narelle was ill.

Jacinta stood up, intending to go after Narelle, but stopped when she heard the young male detective muttering under his breath. His partner shot him a reproving glance, but by then it was too late. It had taken less than a second for his words to register.

Outraged, Jacinta turned on him, lashing out at him for his snide remark. 'Murderer's whore' or 'murderous whore', she wasn't sure which; it didn't matter. And even though she knew the words weren't intended for her ears, they were uncalled for and totally unprofessional coming from a police officer.

She had jumped to Narelle's defense, not because she believed in her innocence, but because she felt strongly that everyone deserved a fair go. Any personal prejudices the detective had should have been left at home. After all, Narelle was the victim's sister, and not, as far as Jacinta knew, a suspect.

Out of the corner of her eye, she glimpsed the senior detective. The female officer's mouth was moving, but if she had spoken, Jacinta hadn't heard her. Too angry by this time to bother with niceties, Jacinta reached down and grabbed the evidence bag from the floor, thrusting it into the startled woman's hands before storming off to tend to Narelle.

It wasn't until she reached the kitchen that it occurred to her she was in a strange house, with no idea where Narelle might be. Except for the strident whispers of the police in the living room, the house was silent.

She sighed, consoling herself with the flippant thought that at least she knew her way to the front door. If all else failed, she could make a run for it.

A toilet flushed.

Jacinta started walking in the general direction of the noise, feeling like a prowler casing the house as she checked each room she passed. She was zeroing in on a closed door at the end of the hall when it opened. Narelle emerged from the doorway, wiping her mouth with the back of her hand and looking paler than she had before, if that was possible. Her hairline was damp, a couple of wet curls clinging to her cheek.

Narelle smiled weakly at Jacinta. "Just a stomach bug," she said, patting her flat stomach. Then, lowering her voice to a whisper, she asked, "Are they still here?"

Jacinta nodded. "Do you want me to tell them you're too sick to see them?"

Narelle shook her head wearily. "No, if it's not today, it'll be another time. Might as well get it over with."

"Would you prefer me to leave?"

Perhaps Narelle's reluctance to speak to the police came from having an outsider present.

"No." The word echoed in the hall. Narelle leaned closer to Jacinta, dropping her voice. "I mean, please don't go; I could do with a friend about now." Pausing briefly, she added, "That's only if you want to, of course."

It's the very least I can do for you, thought Jacinta. She felt like a fraud. If only Narelle knew the truth about her newfound friend, she wouldn't be standing there, pleading with her eyes for Jacinta to stay. It didn't matter that Jacinta had renounced her journalistic ambitions: the damage was done. Thanks to her, old wounds had been opened. The media, along with Grace Kevron, were baying for blood.

Not trusting herself to speak, Jacinta simply nodded and followed Narelle down the hall.

The two detectives had given up waiting in the living area and were loitering near the kitchen. The female officer held a mobile phone to her ear with one hand and was busy writing notes with the other. The male officer stood head down, hands in pockets, scuffing his feet on the tiled floor. He looked up briefly without acknowledging them, and then returned to acting like an insolent schoolboy.

When the female officer finished on the phone, Narelle switched into hostess mode, introducing Jacinta to the detectives but leaving it to them to introduce themselves when she stumbled on their ranks and names. Detective Sergeant Renee White extended a hand, which Jacinta happily accepted. Detective Constable Mark Fratta, on the other hand, kept his hands firmly planted in his pockets, a thinly veiled scowl on his face. The feeling was mutual.

Narelle was acting as if it were a social occasion, fluffing around in the kitchen, filling the kettle, opening cupboards. Her offers of coffee, tea, juice, water or perhaps something stronger were all turned down. She opened drawers, closing them again before moving on to the next, as if searching for something. That, or playing for time. One look at Narelle's wringing hands told Jacinta it was the latter.

Looking to Narelle for confirmation, DS Renee White suggested they all take a seat at the round glass table in the meals area next to the kitchen.

DC Mark Fratta made the first move, taking the seat closest to him. The DS opted for the chair next to him. Narelle was dallying at the end of the kitchen bench, seemingly waiting for all her visitors to be seated before joining them.

Jacinta glanced at the two remaining chairs, settling for the chair opposite Mark Fratta rather than the one beside him. She sat down, immediately wishing she had chosen the other seat. If she kept her eyes down, she looked straight through the glass tabletop at the fabric bunched around the DC's groin, and if she looked up, she was staring him in the face.

Thankfully, Narelle joining them provided them all with a temporary distraction. She didn't know about anyone else, but Jacinta found the whole situation disconcerting and rather farcical. All it would have taken was for them to join hands and they could have had a séance. Maybe then they could find out what had really happened all those years ago.

This time the sergeant did all the talking, starting by apologizing for calling unannounced. In a soft, unthreatening voice, she went on to explain that the gold and sapphire cross had recently come into their possession. Since it matched the description that Narelle had given in her statement of a cross belonging to her sister, they were seeking her assistance in identifying it.

For a few long seconds, no one spoke.

Then, in a small voice, Narelle asked, "Where was it found?" Her head remained bowed, her hair falling forward and obscuring her features.

"In the Toolangi State Forest, north-east of Melbourne, on an old logging road."

"What made you look at my statement?" Narelle lifted her head, meeting Renee White's gaze. "It must be years since anyone's looked at that file," she continued, her words stronger now.

The slightest of smirks appeared on Mark Fratta's face, vanishing the instant he caught his sergeant's look.

The DS deftly deflected the question, telling Narelle that like many of the old cases, it was reviewed regularly. Before Narelle could say anything else, the DS had the plastic evidence bag containing the cross out of her pocket, dumping it on the table directly in front of Narelle. "Narelle," she said, dispensing with the formalities, "is this, or isn't this, Kirsty's cross?" No more softly, softly.

Narelle's jaw jutted defiantly, her answer just as blunt and to the point. "No, it's not." She pushed herself away from the table, the chair scraping on the floor. "I'm sure you can find your own way out."

"Skeletal remains were also found." The DS paused for effect. "They are believed to be female."

The sharp intake of breath Jacinta heard was her own. The soft thump she heard was Narelle sliding from her chair to the floor.

15

Jacinta shivered, her thin top offering no protection against the evening chill. She could see the outline of objects around the swimming pool, but no detail. Hugging herself, she trod carefully around the pool to the far side.

While the police had long gone, the doctor had just left, assuring Jacinta that Narelle would sleep for at least eight hours. Sedative or no sedative, Jacinta wasn't taking any chances.

Nearing the boundary fence, she wondered what she would do if Brett didn't answer his phone. Craig hadn't come home yet and she needed Brett's help in finding him. She would stay the whole night, if need be, but Jacinta felt sure that Narelle would expect to see her husband's face when she woke, not that of a woman she had only just met.

At the edge of the paving, she turned and raised her mobile phone in front of her face. Even with the mobile's keypad backlit, she still had to squint to read the digital display as she scrolled through the address book.

The steady flow of distant traffic droned in the background as she waited for the call to connect. Just when she thought it was going to divert to his voicemail, he answered.

"Make it quick, Jacinta," he said, making no attempt to hide his annoyance.

Watching the house for any sign of movement, she cupped her hands around her mouth and the phone. "Brett, I'm at Narelle's. I—"

"Excuse me, did you say you're at the Edmonds' home?" Giving her no chance to reply, he ploughed on. "How could you, Jacinta? You promised me you would stay away from them. Just once couldn't you have left well enough alone? Was that too much to ask?"

Her throat tightened. "Stop! Just let me explain." She heard him sigh, the underlying message obvious: *It had better be good.*

In a hushed voice, she quickly filled him in on the events of the day, starting with Narelle's distraught phone call that morning. She told him about the police visit, the gold cross, and then the news that had tipped Narelle over the edge. The police hadn't confirmed they suspected the skeletal remains found in the Toolangi State Forest were those of Kirsty Edmonds, but they weren't denying it, either.

"Oh dear God, Jacinta, what have you started?"

Something snapped inside her. "What have I started?" she hissed, managing to keep her voice to a low roar. "I'm not the one responsible here. I'm not the one who found the body, and I'm certainly not guilty of murder." She took a breath. "Although that could be arranged."

"Okay, I get the point. When will they know for sure if the remains that were found are Narelle's sister's?"

Breathing a little easier now that Brett was no longer haranguing her, she recounted what DS Renee White had explained to her about the degradation of nuclear DNA over time.

"Does that mean they won't be able to positively identify the bones?" Brett sounded concerned.

"Not a hundred percent. However, there is something called mi-to-chon-dri-al," she sounded the word out, hoping she had recalled it correctly, "DNA that is inherited solely from the mother."

"So, what does that mean?"

"That means if the mitochondrial DNA matches Narelle's, then the remains belong to someone in the family with the same maternal lineage. And I assume that unless there are other members of the family missing, that would mean Kirsty. They should know within a week to ten days."

She could almost hear his mind ticking over, his only response a low whistle. She waited, allowing time for the possible ramifications if the remains were positively identified as Kirsty Edmonds to sink in. If his thinking was anything like hers had been, there would be a slew of conflicting scenarios playing out in his head.

On first hearing about the discovery of the skeletal remains, Jacinta's immediate thought had been that it would bring closure. At long last, Narelle and Craig would be able to grieve properly; she for a sister and he for a wife. It would mean that they could escape the shackles of the past and get on with living.

Who am I kidding?

The likelihood of that happening and everyone living happily ever after had to be almost zilch. As soon as the news got out that unidentified human remains had been found, media speculation and rumor would be rife. How soon would it be before some switched-on reporter put the police visit to the Edmonds' house together with the discovery of the skeleton?

What could a collection of old bones reveal? Did the dead woman have a tale to tell? Jacinta knew forensic science had advanced, but not to what extent. Perhaps evidence would be found clearing Craig Edmonds of the murder of his wife. But then again, what if the evidence, rather than exonerating, further implicated him? Or even more unthinkable — Narelle?

Of course, all that would be immaterial if the remains proved not to be those of Kirsty Edmonds. Narelle had been adamant that the gold and sapphire cross found near the body hadn't belonged to her sister. Time would tell.

"Brett, I have to go." She had seen a light go on in the kitchen.

"Don't—"

She hung up, cutting short whatever it was he was about to tell her not to do. Promising herself that she'd call him back as soon as she left the Edmonds' place, she retraced her steps to the house.

Opening the glass sliding door, she slipped inside. The kitchen was lit up but there was no sign of anyone. She noticed, on the bench next to the sink, a glass that she was sure hadn't been there before. Had Craig come home, or had Narelle, in her somnambulistic state, wandered out for a glass of water?

Thinking she ought to first check on Narelle, she crept down the hall toward the master bedroom. With no light to guide her, she strained to see more than an arm's length in front of her.

Her nose wrinkled. A faint, vinegary odor that somehow seemed familiar hung in the air. Stale wine. She recognized it in the same instant she touched something soft and warm. She screamed.

Light flooded the hall, blinding her. Instinctively, she ducked, her arms out in front of her, shielding her face. She heard him before she saw him.

"What the hell?"

Her sentiments exactly.

She blinked, her pupils contracting with the sudden influx of light. "I can explain," she blurted, wishing she could be anywhere else but there. "Narelle called me."

Taking a step back, he lowered the bottle he had been holding like a baton over his head and frowned at her. In the confines of the hall, he seemed a much larger man than she remembered. His clothes looked like he had slept in them. His face was unshaven, sporting a dark stubble that definitely wasn't designer.

She stared back, trying desperately to formulate something better than, *Your wife was sick, I came, the police were here, your new wife collapsed, the police went, the doctor came... And, oh, by the way, skeletal remains that might be your dead wife's have been found.*

16

Bloody interfering woman. Craig Edmonds banged his glass down hard on the table. Neat whisky sloshed over the side, spilling onto his hand.

Ever since that Jacinta Deller woman had infiltrated their lives, nothing had been the same. He had tried to tell Narelle that no good could come of accepting that dinner invitation. If only he had tried harder.

Instead, he had given in to her pleading and gone along with her wishes. He wanted her to be happy, but even he couldn't have foreseen the events of the week. Would they have happened regardless? He couldn't answer that. But although he had no evidence to back his hunch, he was certain that Jacinta Deller had been the catalyst.

Throwing his head back, he downed what was left in the glass, feeling the fiery liquid coursing through his throat into his stomach. He then refilled it with the last of the Chivas Regal. With the glass gripped in one hand, he stumbled to his feet and staggered toward the master bedroom.

Stopping in the bedroom doorway, he sagged, the doorframe supporting his weight. The light from the hall, whilst not shining directly on the bed, was enough for him to see that his darling wife was sleeping soundly. Narelle, her breathing slow and steady, lay on her back with the sheets tucked up under her chin.

The alcohol was making him maudlin. His eyes brimmed with tears, his emotions threatening to overwhelm him. He had never loved another woman with the intense passion he felt for Narelle. It was an intensity that sometimes frightened him. He couldn't imagine a life without her in it. She was his world. As far as he was concerned, they didn't need anybody else; they had each other. Two halves of one whole...

Sniffing, he wiped his eyes on his shirtsleeve. A couple of deep breaths helped him regain some composure. He gazed at Narelle's sleeping form, wondering what had possessed him to push her away? At a time when he needed her most, he had erected barriers. He loved her yet he had found himself unable to reach out, unable to share his innermost feelings. As much as he wanted to, he hadn't been able to put them into words.

He moved into the room. Placing the empty glass on the bedside table, he knelt on the carpet beside the bed and caressed her brow. He smiled.

She needed him now.

17

The hot, northerly wind whipped at Jacinta's hair as she stepped from the air-conditioned comfort of the Alvico Media offices on to the footpath. Surveying the street, she saw only the usual motley collection of shoppers, tourists, business people and truant students going about their day, none of whom seemed to be paying her any attention. Nothing looked out of the ordinary.

She shuddered, still unable to shake the prickly sensation she was being watched. It wasn't the first time. She had been feeling it, on and off, for a few days. Was it paranoia or was it actually possible that someone was following her? Rummaging in her satchel for her sunglasses, she made a mental list of everyone she knew, crossing out names as she went.

Since that first demented phone call from Grace Kevron, when she'd ranted on about blood and vengeance, Jacinta had received numerous calls from her. Most had ended up as messages on her voicemail — some strangely polite, some abusive, all scary. Notifying the police would have entailed explanations.

Jacinta blamed herself. In hindsight, contacting Grace about the Edmonds case had been asking for trouble. However, phone calls were one thing; following someone was something else altogether. Grace didn't know where she lived.

Last week's encounter with an inebriated Craig Edmonds had certainly left her reeling, but as far as she knew, he hadn't left his wife's side. She had phoned the Edmonds every day in the hope that

Narelle would answer. Instead, each time it had been like confronting a fire-breathing dragon guarding his treasure. Craig refused to enter into a discussion of any kind, let alone tell her how Narelle was faring. She tried leaving messages but somehow doubted they ever reached her. At least, Jacinta hoped, Narelle had her husband to look after her.

The ludicrous idea that Brett could be stalking her stayed with her for less than a second. They might not be living together anymore but, if nothing else, they were still talking to each other. He had phoned that morning to wish her luck for the job interview, sounding more like the old relaxed and carefree Brett. Maybe they had a future after all.

With her sunglasses not only shielding her eyes from the sun's glare but also giving her a sense of anonymity that she knew was false, she hurried down the footpath, breaking into a trot as the cross lights flashed green. As her foot touched the curb on the other side of the street, she stopped and turned. A quick sidestep prevented her from being trampled by the stampede of pedestrians.

She scanned the throng, failing to recognize any of the faces. Her breathing steadied as, feeling relieved but more than a little foolish, she continued on her way.

Outside the open-fronted Café Face, she wavered, the tantalizing aroma of coffee so intense she could taste it. Like a magnetic force, it drew her in.

Within seconds, she was ensconced behind one of the small, square tables dotted in front of the padded bench seat that ran the entire length of one wall. Out of habit she picked up the acrylic menu holder from the centre of the table, scanning both sides before putting it back. She had no appetite.

A pimply-faced waiter, dressed from head to toe in black, took her order. Waiting for her macchiato to arrive, she turned on her mobile and checked for messages. No one had called during the hour or so she had been pitching her skills as a copywriter to the directors of Alvico Media. She tried calling Brett, but he wasn't answering. She then phoned Narelle, hanging up the instant she heard Craig's voice on the answering machine. All the while, her gaze flitted back and forth, checking the faces of the people coming and going.

Her coffee arrived. She downed the demitasse of milk-stained espresso in two swallows, and immediately ordered another.

The second cup went down almost as quickly as the first. She had hoped the caffeine would keep her alert, but it just made her more anxious. When her heart started flip-flopping, she wasn't sure if it was simply an after-effect of the coffee or weeks of accumulated stress catching up with her. Clasping her hands together to stop them shaking, she waited, hoping the sensation would pass.

After a minute or two, her heart no longer felt like it was trying to escape her chest. Although keen to get home, she still didn't trust her legs. She ordered a bottle of mineral water, buying herself time and giving her a legitimate excuse to stay seated at the table. Sipping the ice-cold water helped to cool body and nerves. She finished her drink and readied herself to leave, sliding across the bench seat to the gap between her table and the next.

Then she saw him, reflected in the mirror behind the counter. Or at least it looked like him. The last time she had seen Daniel Lassiter she'd been a frightened fifteen-year-old schoolgirl.

Pulse soaring, she glanced at the backs of the customers who stood waiting to pay at the counter, and then back at the mirror. Her stepbrother's face had vanished.

She leapt to her feet, her eyes frantically searching the café and beyond, to the street. Had he been there at all? Could she have been mistaken? Had the face in the mirror belonged to a complete stranger? She wanted so much to believe that, but the square jaw and dark, deep-set eyes haunted her. No passing of time would ever change that.

Illusion or not, seeing him after all those years brought it all flooding back. It had started as a fairytale, her mother falling in love with a man who wanted to marry her and take care of her and her daughter. Life until then hadn't been easy for mother and daughter. Jacinta's father, a married man, had abandoned his lover as soon as he found out she was pregnant. It had taken years before her mother allowed herself to trust another man. Unfortunately, that man had been a charmer by the name of Tony Lassiter.

Jacinta could still remember her excitement on learning they were going to be part of a real family. A family with a father and a brother. Her mother was happy; she was happy; everyone was happy.

All that changed the day Tony Lassiter slipped the gold band onto her mother's finger. In the ensuing weeks and months, her stepfather subjected her mother to a torrent of emotional and physical abuse. He cut her off from her friends, further isolating her. He wanted to control her every move.

The night Jacinta woke screaming, her stepbrother's clammy hands groping her breasts, had been the night that her mother finally took a stand. She packed an overnight bag with the barest of essentials and promised Jacinta everything would be all right. They didn't leave straight away, biding their time until the right moment.

Two days later, in the dead of night and dressed in only her pajamas, she had fled with her mother to a women's refuge. Somehow, Tony tracked them down. When the staff at the refuge refused to let him see his wife, he became violent, brandishing a knife and threatening to kill them.

Jacinta and her mother made a break for it, carrying only the one overnight bag they had brought with them. Asking no questions, an old friend loaned them the money for the tickets to Melbourne. With all Tony's contacts, it was a testament to her mother's strength of character that they made it out of the state alive.

Years later, they learned that a few months after they escaped, Tony Lassiter had put a gun in his mouth and blown his head off. Jacinta had felt no sorrow, only relief for her mother.

Seeing the likeness of her stepbrother in the mirror had exposed memories she would much rather have kept buried. She had told no one about that time in her life, not even Brett. Pretending it never happened had been easier.

Had her eyes deceived her? *God, I hope so*, she thought, as she sidled between the tables.

A light touch on her shoulder, just as she was about to step out onto the footpath, almost sent her into orbit. She skipped sideways, dislodging the hand and spinning to face her assailant.

"Excuse me," said the pimply-faced waiter. "Haven't you forgotten something?"

Frowning, she stared at his extended hand. In her panic to get home and away from prying eyes, real or imagined, she had forgotten to pay her bill. Feeling her face redden, she apologized profusely, fumbling in her satchel for her wallet. She shoved a twenty-dollar note into his hand and took off, too embarrassed to wait for the change.

All the way to the tram stop, she kept checking over her shoulder. Even though the tram wasn't crowded, she remained standing, her back to the door. At one stage, she got off the tram using the front door and reboarded through the back door. Her behavior was bordering on irrational, but she didn't care. If nothing else, life had taught her it was better to be safe than sorry.

Two stops from home, she jumped off the tram, holding her breath as she waited to see if anyone else disembarked. With a huge sigh of relief, she watched the tram pull away, leaving her standing alone on the street corner in the midday sun.

By the time she had walked the couple of blocks to her street, her face was flushed and beaded with perspiration. Her shoes, not designed for walking, were pinching her feet. All she wanted to do was get home, have a shower and put her feet up.

She had begun to think that perhaps she had imagined it after all. Convinced that her mind was playing tricks on her, she made a conscious decision to try to forget what she thought she had seen. Her life was complicated enough — why add to it? Daniel Lassiter, and her memories of him and his father, belonged to another lifetime.

With the sun beating down on her, she trudged on, her only thought that of the refreshing shower awaiting her at home.

She reached her front gate, never happier to hear its annoying squeak as it swung inwards.

Then, before she could close it, she sensed someone behind her.

Without thinking, she rammed her elbow backwards as hard as she could, her self-defense training coming into play. She heard a sharp gasp as it connected with something solid. In one fluid movement, she dropped her satchel to the ground, brought both fists up in front of her chest and spun to face her target. With her knee up and her foot flexed, she was poised to strike.

Jacinta froze. Doubled over and clutching her stomach, Grace Kevron stared up at her. Her face contorted with hurt or confusion or rage. Or perhaps all of those things.

Bringing her knee down, Jacinta took half a step forward, her arms outstretched. Still bent over, Grace shied away, the look on her face now one of fear.

"Stay away from me!" she screamed.

Jacinta stopped, her hands held up in front of her, palms forward. Either she didn't know her own strength, or the element of surprise had been more effective than she would ever have expected. "Jesus, Grace! What the hell were you doing, sneaking up on me like that?"

"I wasn't sneaking up on you." Grace's eyes screwed up, her teeth clenching. She managed, "I did call out… but… you…" before the words trailed off into a moan.

Even though it was against her better judgment, Jacinta couldn't bring herself to abandon Grace on the street. With her arm around the woman's hunched shoulders, she guided her through the front gate and up the short path to the front door. Grace offered no resistance.

Once inside, Jacinta settled Grace on the smaller of the two low-backed suede sofas in the living room. A little of the color had returned to Grace's pale face, but the tension around her eyes and mouth remained. She hugged one of the sofa's scatter cushions to her stomach.

Jacinta stayed standing, her arms crossed over her chest, praying that she hadn't made a terrible mistake in bringing Grace Kevron into her home. But what alternative had she had? She wasn't even sure how to approach the situation. All care and concern? Sure, she felt bad about hurting Grace, but what had she been doing there in the first place?

"Look, Grace…" Sighing, she dropped her voice and continued, "I'm really sorry about jabbing you in the stomach like that, but what the hell are you doing here?"

Grace glanced up. "Remind me never to get behind you again," she said with a feeble smile. When Jacinta didn't respond, she added, "I came to offer my help."

Jacinta frowned, wondering where Grace was taking it. "Go on."

"Actually, I think we can help each other. We both want the same thing, don't we?" Grace shoved the scatter cushion aside and sat forward, evidently no longer in agony. "You came to me, remember?"

"Get to the point, Grace. What do you want?"

"Truth and justice. I want the world to know the truth about what happened in that house." The pitch of Grace's voice rose slightly, her calm exterior starting to crack. "I want the bastard and his floozy to pay. Kirsty didn't deserve what they did to her."

Pinching the bridge of her nose between her thumb and forefinger, Jacinta closed her eyes and sighed. "Grace, how many times do I have to tell you I'm not interested? Yes, I was researching the story, but I'm not any longer. I've given up my career in journalism." Grace looked skeptical. "In fact, I had a job interview today," Jacinta said, wondering why she felt compelled to justify herself. "I am truly sorry that my visit brought back painful memories for you. I never intended to do that. If I could, I would take it all back."

Grace leaned back in her seat, retrieving the cushion and clutching it to her chest. "There's something you ought to know."

Despite herself, Jacinta felt a flicker of interest. She weighed up her options. One, she could send Grace on her way and never know what deep, dark secret she was harboring, if any. Two, she could hear her out, have her curiosity satisfied and then send her on her way.

She heard herself offering Grace a cup of tea.

"Something stronger, if you have it."

Jacinta thought quickly. What did she have in the house she could offer her guest? The couple of cans of beer that Brett had left in the fridge? A half-bottle of Shiraz that was probably more vinegar than wine? Then she remembered the cognac left over from the dinner party.

Leaving Grace on her own, Jacinta went in search of the cognac, returning shortly with the bottle and two heavy-base tumblers. She poured two good measures and handed one of the glasses to Grace.

"By the way, how did you get my address?" Jacinta wasn't listed in the White Pages, her business card didn't include her home address, and she certainly hadn't given it to Grace.

Grace tapped the side of her nose. "I have my contacts."

Jacinta didn't press the point. She knew that privacy was just a delusion harbored by those who didn't know better. Finding someone's address was merely a matter of knowing where to look.

Even before Jacinta had touched her drink, Grace had downed hers and was helping herself to another. While she seemed relatively calm and in control at that moment, Jacinta had seen how rapidly she could flip. She could only hope that the alcohol wasn't going to exacerbate the situation.

For a few awkward moments, neither woman spoke.

Grace took a swig of cognac and cleared her throat. "Kirsty and I were a lot more than friends. We were lovers."

Jacinta choked on her drink. All sorts of possibilities had crossed her mind but that hadn't been one of them. Open-mouthed, she could do nothing but stare at Grace.

"You're shocked."

"No, I mean, yes, I mean… God, I don't know what I mean. Did Craig know? What about the police? Did you tell them?"

Grace spoke in a low monotone, her eyes glassy. "I think Kirsty told him she was leaving him for me, they argued and in a violent rage he killed her. Couldn't stand the fact she loved someone more than him."

"But…" stammered Jacinta, "but you told me Craig and Narelle were having an affair. If that was the case, and he was serious about Narelle, wouldn't that have worked out well for all involved?"

"He wanted both sisters."

Bewildered, Jacinta didn't know what to believe. Was the woman simply delusional, living in a fantasy world of her own making, or had the two women been lovers, as she suggested? Even if what she was saying had any element of truth to it, why was she confiding in Jacinta and not the police? "Grace, don't get me wrong here, but I can't see how I could possibly help. Surely this is a matter for the police?"

"You don't believe me, do you? I knew it would be a waste of time."

Grace was up and halfway across the room before Jacinta had time to blink. Silently berating herself, she clambered to her feet. She heard her mother's voice in her head: *The first rule when you're in a hole is to stop digging.* Unless you were Jacinta, of course.

"Grace, stop! Let's talk about it. We could go to the police together."

Grace didn't break her stride. "Forget it!" she shouted over her shoulder. "Mark my words, they'll pay. And I don't need anyone's help, least of all yours."

Jacinta stopped in her tracks, overwhelmed by a sudden sense of helplessness. She had inadvertently uncaged a monster over which she had no control. When the front door slammed, she exhaled loudly, wishfully hoping she had seen the last of Grace Kevron.

With her head pounding from heat, stress and drinking on an empty stomach, she flopped down onto the daybed and closed her eyes, her promise to herself to shower shelved. The glare of the sun shining through the window above her penetrated her eyelids, sending tiny darts of pain into her brain. Groaning, she covered her eyes with her arm and rolled onto her side.

She found that if she lay still, it didn't hurt as much. Gradually, her headache eased to a dull throb and to her surprise, she felt herself drifting into the welcome oblivion of sleep. Unfortunately, her peace was short-lived.

18

Impatient for the traffic lights to change, Craig Edmonds glanced at the folded newspaper lying on the passenger seat beside him. His grip tightened on the steering wheel. He knew Jacinta Deller had been trouble from the instant he set eyes on her. Now he had proof.

The newspaper article linking the discovery of skeletal remains in the Toolangi State Forest to the disappearance of his first wife could only have come from one person. Besides Narelle and himself, no one else except Jacinta had been privy to the reason behind the visit from the police. Unless the police had leaked the news themselves — which he doubted, since the DNA tests were still to be completed — that only left Jacinta.

Knowing he needed to back up his suspicions, he had set out to find out as much as he could about the woman. Narelle had been in bed asleep when he logged on to the Internet and entered 'Jacinta Deller' in the search engine. While shocked to discover they had been duped by a reporter, he wasn't surprised. It all made complete sense to him now.

Loud tooting broke through his consciousness. The lights had changed to green and he was holding up the traffic. Planting his foot on the accelerator, he peeled away just as the lights turned to amber, leaving a queue of irate motorists in his wake.

He had no concern for them. He was so consumed by Jacinta Deller and the destruction she was wreaking on his and Narelle's lives, nothing else mattered.

19

Groaning, Jacinta jammed the pillow over her head. If she ignored the incessant knocking for long enough, then whoever was pounding on her front door might just go away. She didn't care who it was; she wasn't in the mood to face anyone else that day.

Eventually, the knocking let up. She breathed a sigh of relief and tossed the pillow aside. Had she been asleep for minutes or hours? She opened a bleary eye. The sun was no longer shining directly into the room. Late afternoon, she guessed.

Reluctant to stir, she closed her eye again. Somewhere in the house, her mobile phone rang. Cursing but at the same time hoping it would be Brett calling, she swung her legs over the side of the daybed and stood up. Still groggy from sleep, she stumbled toward the living room, homing in on the ringing satchel.

Midway across the room, she glanced toward the French doors leading out to the courtyard. She gasped, horrified to see Craig Edmonds' cupped face framed in one of the panes. In that same instant, Craig spotted her. For a few seconds, she stood stock-still, unable to do anything except watch the obviously agitated man as he hopped from foot to foot, madly waving what appeared to be a folded newspaper. He looked like a deranged puppet, his mouth opening and closing in rapid succession only adding to the parody. She didn't need to hear the words to know he wasn't commenting on the weather.

Her mobile was still ringing as she lunged for her satchel.

"Brett! Brett, oh, thank God, it's you." Shaking violently, she gripped the phone with both hands. "Come quickly. Oh God, he's trying to smash the door down."

With each thump of Craig's fist on the door, she expected to see glass shattering. He tried the door handle repeatedly, jerking it up and down with such force that she thought it could only be a matter of time before he broke through. "Hurry!"

Distracted by the newspaper that Craig was now pressing up against the glass, she didn't hear Brett's reply. Edging forward, she squinted at the hazy newsprint, trying to focus. Although Craig appeared to have run out of steam, she was reluctant to move much closer.

Concentrating hard, she was just able to make out two of the words in the headline: 'murder' and 'skeleton'. She blinked and stepped back, knowing then exactly what had happened. Some savvy reporter had put two and two together — or rather, the police visit to the Edmonds house with the discovery of the unidentified skeletal remains. Craig clearly thought the blame lay squarely with Jacinta.

She started to shake her head but thought better of it, guessing any denial from her at that stage would only antagonize him further. Gnawing her lip, she glanced back and forth between the newspaper article and Craig's stony face. *Beam me up, Scotty,* she thought, suddenly wishing she could be anywhere else but there. Another planet, perhaps.

Craig continued to glare at her, mouthing what could only be obscenities. *Damn it,* she thought, *I am not going to be intimidated in my own home.* Thrusting her shoulders back, she marched up to the French doors. A thin pane of glass was all that separated them. She could see the spidery veins in his bloodshot eyes.

Then, with more bravado than she actually felt, she shouted through the closed doors, informing him in no uncertain terms that she had nothing to do with the newspaper article. She was in the throes of threatening to call the police when Brett rounded the corner of the courtyard, surprising both of them.

"Look, mate, I don't know what your problem is, but you're not welcome here. If you're not gone in ten seconds, I'm calling the police."

After the initial shock, Craig looked almost relieved to see Brett. "Finally, someone who can give me some straight answers." He thrust the newspaper at Brett. "Have you seen this? Your reporter…" his lip curled as he said the word, "…girlfriend is responsible for this."

Brett looked at Jacinta, one eyebrow lifting slightly. She couldn't believe it. Her word evidently counted for nothing.

Outraged, she had unlocked the door, preparing to face off against her critics.

"I repeat; I am not in any way responsible for that article."

"And why should I believe the word of a liar?" Craig asked with more than a hint of smugness.

Jacinta frowned.

"That's right, your secret's out. You're nothing but a fucking nosey reporter, happy to screw up other people's lives for the sake of a story."

"It's not like that. Please let me explain." She glanced sideways, hoping Brett would come to her aid. "But not out here." The neighbors had heard more than enough.

For the second time that day, she was inviting an unknown quantity into her home. At least this time she had Brett on her side.

Ironically, Craig chose the same seat that Grace had vacated only hours earlier. Declining Brett's offer of a drink, he sat forward on the seat, arms crossed defensively over his chest.

Brett had taken up position on one of the barstools, reminding Jacinta of a tennis umpire. She would have much preferred to have him sitting beside her, offering moral support and giving them at least some illusion of unity. Hiding her disappointment, she sat back in her seat, making a conscious effort to keep her body language as relaxed and open as possible.

A sidelong glance from Brett warned her to be careful. Not that she needed warning. As far as Craig was concerned, Jacinta was the devil incarnate, out to destroy everything he held dear. She wasn't completely without empathy. She could see how he might think that and she was the first to admit she wasn't entirely guiltless.

Her first mistake had been not listening to Brett when he pleaded with her to leave the story alone, but her biggest mistake — and the one she regretted the most — was entangling herself with Grace Kevron. The woman was plainly unbalanced. How else could her erratic and vindictive behavior be explained?

Jacinta glanced at the man opposite. Although his body remained rigid, his dark eyes betrayed him. In them, she saw a deep sadness. She found herself unexpectedly softening towards him, knowing then that underneath all the bluster existed a real man desperately trying to mask his true emotions. A real man trying to protect what was left of his life.

"Craig, you're right, I should have been straight with you and Narelle from the start. I used to be a reporter for a small regional newspaper called *The Acacia Tribune*, but I was retrenched last December." She looked to Brett to back her up. He nodded. "I've done some freelancing since, but nothing major." She paused, acutely aware that she could cause more harm than good by revealing too much. After all, there were different degrees of straight. "Um…"

"Jacinta doesn't freelance these days, though," interjected Brett, on cue. "In fact, she had an interview today for a copywriter position."

Confusion clouded Craig's face for a moment, the lines around his eyes deepening. "So what do you call this, then?" He tapped the newspaper article with his forefinger. "Just a figment of my imagination? I don't care what you say — all I know is that from the day we met you, we've had nothing but trouble. I'm warning you, stay away from Narelle."

"Isn't that up to Narelle to decide?" she snapped, his threat like a red rag. Out of the corner of her eye, she saw Brett's eyes widen. Ignoring the little voice in her head telling her to quit while she was ahead, she added, "She has a will of her own, you know!"

Craig jumped to his feet, his voice hard and steely as he loomed over Jacinta. "What do you think she would say if she knew her new buddy had been deceiving her all along? Save yourself the hassle and leave her alone."

20

"Don't you see? That's what my stepfather did to my mother. Controlled her every move. Cut her off from her friends." She grabbed at his hands and squeezed. "Craig's doing the same thing to Narelle. You can't honestly expect me to *butt out*, as you put it. What sort of friend would that make me?"

Brett's mind raced, working overtime to make sense of what Jacinta was saying. If she had a stepfather, this was the first he was hearing of it. And when had she and Narelle become such close friends that she was prepared to stand up to Craig Edmonds, a man who had been accused of murdering his wife? Certainly, life was never boring with Jacinta around. That much hadn't changed.

She stopped jabbering, her bottom lip quivering. Tears welled in her eyes as she released his hands and started to turn away. He caught her, pulling her in tight against his torso. She clung to him, silent sobs racking her body.

He held her fast, feeling the warmth of her body, smelling her perfume. How wrong could he have been? It was madness to think he could ever stop loving Jacinta. Whatever her foibles, they were part of what made her the woman he loved. His mouth sought hers, the faint, sour taste of alcohol surprising him.

Neither of them spoke, but somehow they ended up in the bedroom, the incident with Craig all but forgotten. Tearing at each other's clothes, they fell onto the bed, a tangle of limbs. In seconds, both were naked.

Digging her fingernails into his back, she locked her legs around his hips. Her aroused body moved with his, not staying still for a moment. He couldn't get enough of her. Nor, it seemed, she of him.

Later, he lay on his back and stared up at the ceiling, Jacinta's head resting in the crook of his arm. Even though her breathing had slowed and her eyes were closed, he wondered if she might be feigning sleep. Had the sex, too, been a way of putting off answering the inevitable questions? *No*, he decided, *that was my doing.* He smiled to himself, remembering. Although he had only intended to console her, not race her off to bed, she had been no passive participant.

Great sex aside, he had been rather taken aback by the mention of a stepfather. What stepfather? In the whole time they'd been together, Jacinta had not said one word about the man. He doubted it was something that could easily slip your mind, but on the other hand, whenever he asked about her past, she tended to be extremely evasive. All he knew was that Jacinta had never known her father, and that when she was fifteen, she and her mother had moved from Perth to Melbourne. Now that she had let that much slip, would she open up to him?

Brett's last thought before drifting into an endorphin-induced sleep was at least he understood what had prompted her antagonistic attitude toward Craig. He reminded her of her stepfather.

21

Tuesday dawned overcast, the dark heavy clouds reflecting Jacinta's mood. Monday had started badly with, first, her apparent sighting of her stepbrother, followed by Grace Kevron's bizarre visit, and finally the confrontation with Craig Edmonds. But surely, Brett's decision to move back in should have overridden all that. After all, wasn't it what she wanted?

She shoved aside the bedclothes, rolled on to her side and sat up, her legs dangling over the edge of the bed. No question, her feelings for Brett were as strong as they had ever been. However, she wasn't certain of his feelings. The last thing she wanted was for him to stay with her out of pity or some sense of duty. Telling her he loved her in the afterglow of sex didn't count.

Yawning, she stood up and padded to the bathroom. A long, hot shower, followed by a breakfast of tea and toast, left her feeling almost human again.

She was sipping her second cup of tea, thinking about the mess her life was in and indulging in a little self-pity, when the phone rang. Brett's cheery 'good morning' lifted her spirits no end, allaying her fears that he had snuck away from the house that morning harboring regrets. Dropping his voice to a low, sexy growl, he told her how much he wanted her. She laughed. Love or lust: right at that moment it didn't matter. Still smiling, she hung up.

The doorbell rang and she skipped to answer it, half-expecting to see a grinning Brett, phone in hand. Who else would be calling at such an early hour? With a smile at the ready, she flung the door open. Her face dropped.

Narelle stood forlornly on the doorstep, a tartan suitcase in one hand and a blue boxy toilet bag in the other. Her eyes, red and swollen shut, were no more than slits in her tear-stained face. Her brunette curls, tied back off her face, only accentuated her pallor. Without a word, Jacinta relieved Narelle of her suitcase and ushered her inside.

"I'm so sorry," blubbered Narelle. "I didn't know where else to go."

"Don't be silly," said Jacinta, lugging the heavy suitcase into the hall. "I'm glad to help." And she was genuinely pleased to see Narelle, but she could just imagine what Brett would say if he knew. Not to mention Craig. Did she have a death wish? Perhaps, but she couldn't in all good conscience turn Narelle away. Part of it, she realized, was also fuelled, rightly or wrongly, by guilt. In her pursuit of a story, she hadn't stopped to think of the possible consequences.

Narelle was dressed unseasonably in jeans, black boots and a thick, woolly red jumper. It was a muggy day, the heavy cloud cover pushing up the humidity, yet Narelle, instead of sweating, was shivering.

Jacinta collected a blanket from the linen cupboard in the hall, and took Narelle through to the living room, leaving the bags sitting on the hall floor. After settling Narelle on the sofa and swaddling her in the blanket, Jacinta excused herself.

Minutes later, she returned carrying two mugs of steaming hot tea, the one she placed in front of Narelle loaded with sugar.

Narelle's teeth had stopped chattering, but the tremor in her hands was still evident. She paused for a moment, cradling the mug in both hands before slowly lifting it to her mouth. As she sipped the hot, sweet liquid, her eyes stayed downcast.

Drinking her own tea, Jacinta bided her time, resisting the urge to ask what had happened. *Don't pressure her*, she told herself. *She'll tell you in her own time.* Peering over the rim of her cup, she studied Narelle. She had been crying. That much was obvious. From the little skin that was visible, there was no evidence of bruising. No black eyes. No split lip. Craig hadn't beaten her up, then. Or at least not so it would show.

Narelle lifted her eyes, a small, apologetic, almost sheepish smile forming on her lips as she met Jacinta's watchful gaze. She set the mug of tea down. Her hands retreated under the blanket, leaving only her head exposed.

"Are we alone?"

Bemused by the odd question, Jacinta merely nodded.

"I mean, Brett's not asleep in the other room or anything like that, is he? I mean… Oh God, I shouldn't be bothering you like this." Narelle's pale hands emerged from the blanket as she started to rise from the sofa.

Jacinta patted the air. "Don't go. Please stay. Honestly, it's no bother at all. Brett's at work. We have the house to ourselves." She didn't add that until the previous night, she had been alone in the house for the last week.

Narelle hesitated slightly before sinking back down onto the sofa. The blanket that had slipped from her shoulders bunched behind her. She gulped air, evidently on the verge of tears. Her long fingernails tore at the backs of her hands, turning them into angry red welts.

"These last few days," she blurted, "I've felt like a prisoner in my own home. I don't know what's got into Craig. He's become so paranoid. He's convinced everyone is out to get him." Pausing only long enough to take a breath, she continued her rapid-fire of words. "Jacinta, I so enjoyed the dinner party. I'd forgotten what it was like to socialize. But Craig… I don't know, Craig thinks we should keep to ourselves. After everything that's happened, he doesn't trust anyone. I understand that, I really do, but we have to get on with the rest of our lives. Let go of the ghosts of the past…" Her voice petered out, her gaze dropping to her restless hands.

Jacinta uncrossed her legs and leaned forward in her seat. Her problems had suddenly paled into insignificance. She couldn't imagine living Narelle's life: a reclusive and unsocial life devoid of any human relationships except that of her husband. Could love for a man make a woman blind?

Narelle added in a soft whisper, "Craig insinuated that you had an ulterior motive for inviting us to dinner."

Jacinta swallowed hard, a hot flush enveloping her face.

Narelle's gaze remained fixed downwards. "It's all right; I know you're a reporter. Brett probably doesn't remember, but ages ago, I asked him what you did for a living. When you invited us to dinner, I didn't think it mattered. We all have a job to do."

Jacinta's pulse quickened, her mind racing. Narelle had known she was a journalist, yet she had chosen to accept the dinner invitation. Brave, or just desperately lonely?

"That doesn't mean to say that I came to dinner unprepared. Over the years, I've learned the hard way how to circumvent the probing questions. I was pleasantly surprised when you didn't pry. I left here so full of hope that the past was finally behind us." She took a deep breath. "That is until things started happening. Then I didn't know what to think."

Jacinta opened her mouth, hoping that by magic the right words would spring forth.

Narelle continued, her voice remarkably calm. "All these years I've lived in hiding, too scared to face the world. I can't live like this anymore. I *don't* want to live like this anymore." She touched her stomach with her fingertips. "I've given it a great deal of thought, and I've decided it's time that my side of the story was told."

Both stunned and intrigued, Jacinta shuffled forward on her seat.

"Craig and I are guilty of adultery, not murder. No one knows what happened to Kirsty, but I can't believe that Craig is in any way responsible. In all the time I've known him, I have never seen him raise a finger to anyone, man or woman, in anger." She closed her eyes, her hands pressed together in her lap. "You know, Jacinta, I really pray that the skeleton they found in the forest is Kirsty's. Maybe then we'll have some answers." She shrugged her shoulders and opened her eyes. "And if not, at least we'll be able to lay her to rest."

Jacinta cleared her throat. "But weren't you adamant that the gold cross they found didn't belong to Kirsty?"

Narelle shrugged again. "It looked similar to hers, but I've only got my memory to go on and it's been so long. At the time, denial seemed my best bet."

"And now?" prompted Jacinta.

"Now, I want it all to be over with. I'm sick of living like a leper. I want a real life."

"Narelle, I hope you're telling me this as a friend and not a reporter. I want you to know that whatever you tell me stays in this room."

The tiny lines around Narelle's eyes deepened. "You mean off the record?"

"No, as a friend. I'm not a reporter anymore. In fact," Jacinta said, puffing out her chest and trying to add a little levity to the situation, "I hope you're looking at Alvico Media's next copywriter."

Narelle's face brightened, her body visibly relaxing. "Really?"

Not quite knowing which part Narelle was referring to, Jacinta nodded. Was she happy about the friend part, the not-being-a-reporter part, or the possibility that Jacinta had a new job?

"You don't know how relieved I am to hear that," exclaimed Narelle, crossing her hands over her chest. "You have been so nice to me and I'd wondered if it was only because you were looking for a story."

For a fleeting moment, Jacinta debated whether to be brutally honest and confess that perhaps her original motivation had been journalistic, or just let it slide. Common sense told her it wouldn't be in either of their interests to reveal what no longer mattered.

"It's times like this I wish I still smoked," Narelle said, wringing her hands. "Oh God, I'm blathering on like an idiot again. I should go."

Once more, she started to stand and once more, Jacinta stalled her. Narelle obviously needed to talk to someone, and Jacinta wanted to help in any way she could. It took some doing, but eventually she convinced Narelle that she wasn't being a nuisance, nor was she taking up valuable time.

Narelle exhaled, her body deflating as the air left her lungs and her shoulders sagged. With her gaze focused on her knees, she began to talk.

"It was just a fling, a stupid bloody fling. Neither of us meant it to happen. Sure, they had their ups and downs like every couple, but he loved her. God, if only we could have our time over again, it would be so different. What sort of woman falls for her own sister's husband?"

Not waiting for an answer, Narelle spoke quickly, the pitch of her voice rising and falling as she relived the emotional roller coaster of her past.

"I can't even remember how it all started. But it all came to a head after one of Kirsty's nursing conferences." Narelle sighed. "She was away a lot. Anyway, she must have got wind that all wasn't as it should be with Craig. Although at that stage she didn't suspect her own sister of being the other woman. Who would? He denied it, of course."

Jacinta listened in astonishment to the impassioned outpouring, trying to absorb the increasingly disjointed words. After years of bottling everything up, Narelle was finally letting go.

"Craig and I decided it couldn't go on. For the sake of his marriage and my sister, we had to end it. And we did – for about a month. We thought if we kept our affair secret, no one would get hurt." Tears ran unchecked down Narelle's face. "I knew what I was doing was wrong, but I couldn't stop. She was so devastated when she found out. She hated me, I hated me."

Jacinta reached around the arm of the sofa, and opened the small drawer in the side table, feeling for the box of tissues she thought was there. She found it and slid it across the coffee table. Narelle leaned forward and plucked out a handful of tissues. Her words continued uninterrupted with only a few lost in the wad of tissues mopping her face.

By the time the box was empty, Narelle's voice was no more than a raspy crackle, yet she pressed on, continuing to divest herself of years of pent-up feelings. If Jacinta had pieced all the bits together correctly, the affair between Craig and Narelle had lasted for about five or six months, ending at least a year before Kirsty disappeared. Were the two connected? Narelle was adamant that they weren't. It was Kirsty's disappearance that had thrown the two lovers back together again.

Nothing could sway Narelle's conviction that Craig was not a murderer. She had stuck by her man, her steadfast faith in his innocence carrying her through the lonely years of her estrangement from family and friends. Even when working, she had kept to herself, coming across to her co-workers as cold and aloof.

"After the court case, I suggested to Craig that he sell the house and we move to some place no one knew us. Somewhere we could start afresh. He wouldn't have a bar of it." Narelle shook her head as if still not believing it. "Said that would be like admitting he was guilty. But I just can't take it anymore. Tell me," she croaked, "what am I supposed to do? I love Craig but I'm so scared about what's happening to him."

Narelle looked to Jacinta for a response, her expression so miserable that Jacinta couldn't help herself. She jumped to her feet, skirted the coffee table, and wrapped both arms tightly around the distressed woman's shoulders.

Narelle gasped, her chest heaving as she choked on her sobs. "And I think I'm pregnant…"

22

Cradling the large, bulky bouquet of red roses in his left arm, Brett used his right to check the mailbox. He withdrew his hand, bringing with it one brown and two white envelopes. Reminder notices, no doubt. Whistling, he walked to the front door, Jacinta's financial predicament failing to dent his mood.

He had booked the restaurant for 7:30, hoping to surprise her. By his calculations, that would give her more than enough time to tart herself up without stressing. He bounced up the concrete steps, wondering if he should ring the doorbell or use the key she had returned to him that morning.

Deciding to let himself in, he clamped the mail between his teeth and fumbled in his trouser pocket for the key. He unlocked the door, gave it a gentle push and stepped inside. The doors leading to the dining room – or rather, Jacinta's makeshift office – and the bedroom were closed, leaving the hall in semi-darkness.

Puzzled, he crept up to the first door and put his ear to it. When he didn't hear anything, he opened it wide enough to poke his head through. His nose twitched; the warm, stuffy air inside was laced with an unfamiliar perfume. Light filtered through the unlined calico curtains, giving the room a hazy feel.

His gaze swept the room, taking in the dining table cluttered with various papers, newspapers and magazines; the absence of the laptop was only made evident by the small empty space it had left. Soft snoring sounds came from the daybed near the window.

He opened the door wider and crept into the room. A few steps in, he started, almost dropping the flowers and the mail. The dark-haired head on the pillow was certainly not the blonde one he had expected.

Backtracking, he left quickly, shutting the door behind him. Feeling that perhaps he had landed in some surreal video game, he took a deep breath and moved on to door number two.

From behind it, he heard light, irregular tapping. He opened the door a fraction, and saw Jacinta sitting cross-legged on the bed, typing on her laptop. Grateful that he had it right this time, he exhaled, his breath coming out in a loud huff.

Jacinta spun around, her eyes wide. "Jesus, Brett! Scare me, why don't you!" she hissed, her voice a strangled whisper.

He went to speak but she stopped him, placing her index finger to her lips and pointing at the door. He stepped into the room, nudging the door closed behind him with his foot.

"Please tell me it's not who I think it is in the other room."

She explained briefly what had happened. "What was I supposed to do? Turn her out on the street?"

"No, but..." He shook his head, knowing it was pointless to argue. Besides, what would he have done in her place?

Jacinta cocked an eyebrow, a small smile playing on her lips. With a jolt, he remembered the roses in his hands. He stepped forward, proffering the cellophane and tissue wrapped bouquet. With an impish grin, she accepted it, lifting the roses to her face and inhaling.

Dropping down onto the end of the bed, he angled his body to face her, setting the mail down next to the laptop. "I guess this means any ideas I had about a romantic evening for two are out of the question."

Jacinta pursed her lips. "Sorry, Brett," she said, laying the flowers gently on the bed beside her. "I didn't plan on..." Distracted, she picked up the top piece of mail, a white, hand-addressed envelope. She frowned and turned it over. The back was blank and it wasn't until she flipped it over again that she realized it had no postage stamp.

She ripped the envelope open, unfolded the contents and began to read. Her frown deepened, her face becoming pale and pinched as she gripped the single sheet of lined paper.

Jacinta hadn't noticed the small card that had slipped from the letter as she opened it. Brett picked it up to find he was holding a business card for Detective Inspector Daniel Lassiter. What possible reason could the police have for writing to Jacinta?

He glanced up in time to see her screw the sheet of paper into a tight ball and hurl it at the wall.

"Bastard!" she screamed, her sleeping guest in the next room evidently forgotten.

23

Jacinta buried her face in her hands, smothering another scream. Praying that their paths would never cross hadn't been enough. Daniel Lassiter was alive and well, married with two sons and another on the way. He had been living in Victoria for eight years. In a city the size of Melbourne, what were the odds of them both being in the same place at the same time?

Emerging from behind her hands, she glanced up to see Brett watching her, his eyebrows drawn together in a mix of concern and confusion. She couldn't skirt the issue any longer. At the very least, she owed him some sort of explanation.

As she opened her mouth to speak, he extended his hand, a business card pressed between his thumb and forefinger. Her eyes darted back and forth between his face and hand. She plucked the card from his fingers, read it, and then reread it. Somehow, the police mission 'to serve and to protect' did not sit well with the testosterone-fuelled adolescent she remembered.

Unable to speak, she held her hand up, palm out. Brett gave her an understanding nod, allowing her the space and time to compose herself. Uncrossing her legs, she flipped onto her stomach and stretched across the bed, her arm extended as she used her fingertips to snare the ball of scrunched-up paper from where it had landed on the floor.

Back in an upright position, she smoothed out the letter on the bed and reread it, hoping to find answers. Any answers. What galled her most about the letter was the chatty long-time-no-see tone. He apologized for not making himself known at Café Face: he had been running late and he wasn't sure it was her. As if the past had never existed, he made no mention of her mother or his father or anything that had happened all those years ago. It would have been so much simpler if he had just pretended not to see her.

Not only had the past come back to haunt her, but now she would be forced to put years of suppressed emotions into words. Voicing aloud what she and her mother had endured at the hands of her bully and tyrant of a stepfather would be like reliving the nightmare. Even his own son hadn't escaped unscathed. Nothing Daniel ever did was good enough for his father. Jacinta never saw Tony hit Daniel, but she saw the effect of the tongue-lashings. But knowing that Daniel had also been a victim didn't make it any easier. He carried his father's genes. Like father, like son?

"Are you going to tell me what the hell is going on?" Brett waited, his chin jutted forward in expectancy.

Inhaling deeply, she nodded. Brett's patience was wearing thin, and who could blame him? "It's a long story and I promise to tell you everything as soon—"

The phone on the bedside table rang. She pounced, answering it before it could ring again. The fury-filled voice on the other end had her wishing she hadn't. Listening to Craig Edmonds' slurred torrent of abuse, Jacinta understood the intent, if not the words. Finally, he screamed some incoherent threat, burst into loud sobs and slammed down the phone.

She replaced the receiver and turned to Brett. Her first instinct had been to tell him it had been a wrong number. Then she had second thoughts. If she was going to give their relationship any chance of survival, she had to start being more open with him.

"One guess who that was," she said, trying to make light of it. She nodded as he gestured in the general direction of the dining room. "Right now I don't think I'm his favorite person. But at least Narelle is safe." She slid to the side of the bed. "Perhaps I should go and check on her."

As she went to get up, Brett barred her way, standing legs apart, directly in front of her.

"Narelle is fine. Forget everyone else for the moment. We're more important." He sat on the edge of the bed, pulling her down with him. "You," he reached for her hands, "are more important. I love you, Jacinta Deller. Someday you may trust me enough to confide in me. I can wait for however long it takes." He briefly squeezed her hands before releasing them.

Intended or not, his reverse psychology worked. He hadn't pressured her — quite the opposite — yet she felt compelled to talk. She had put it off for long enough. No matter how difficult, she had to do it, if only to prove her love for him.

An uneasy silence enveloped them as they sat side by side, but not touching, on the edge of the bed. Fearing her fragile composure was on the verge of crumbling, she dared not even look at him.

She clamped her hands tightly between her knees to stop them shaking. Taking a deep breath, she filled her lungs and began.

Brett listened without interruption as she shared parts of her life she had never shared with anyone. From time to time her voice wavered, but somehow she managed to keep her emotions at bay.

Starting from her early childhood days, when life was uncomplicated, she moved into the school years. As she grew up, she had started to pine for the father she never knew. All her friends had fathers, even if they weren't living with the family. She didn't even know who her father was, and she never would. Her mother had taken the secret of his identity to her grave.

Yet Jacinta had survived and got on with making the most of what she had. That was until the Lassiters came into their lives.

Keeping her voice low and without intonation, Jacinta told Brett about what in the beginning had held so much promise. She touched on her mother's infatuation with the charming Tony Lassiter, their whirlwind romance and the equally fast marriage that followed. Life was beautiful. Or so her mother thought.

Swallowing hard, Jacinta continued.

Halfway through recounting how her mother had stoically faced her new husband's unrelenting intimidation, manipulation and abuse as if it had been a punishment to be endured, Jacinta stopped.

If Daniel hadn't come into her room that night, would her mother ever have found the courage to flee? Had he inadvertently done her a favor? She shook her head, refusing to dwell on the what-ifs.

By the time she had filled Brett in on the period between her and her mother's landing in Melbourne and the sighting of her stepbrother in the café, she felt wrung out. Empty. Numb. Strangely, she also felt lighter, as if in the retelling she had offloaded some of the burden of the past.

Without a word, Brett put his arm around her shoulder, pulling her in close. His skin felt hot against hers.

"I never meant to keep any of this from you." She sniffed, the tears welling in her eyes. "Keeping it locked away just seemed the easiest way of dealing with it."

Brett kissed her lightly on the forehead, and shuffled back on the bed, taking her with him. For a long time they lay still and quiet, snuggled in each other's arms.

Then she remembered her houseguest.

Brett's eyes opened as she started to pull back.

"I'm just going to check on Narelle," she whispered. "I'll be back in a minute."

Yawning, he rolled onto his side. She reached the door and turned. He watched her through half-closed eyes, the corners of his mouth lifting in a playful grin. *Sexy.* She smiled, tickled by the unexpected thought.

However, this light-heartedness proved fleeting. The door to the dining room stood wide open, the empty daybed mocking her. Narelle's suitcase and toilet bag were gone, leaving no evidence that she had ever been there.

Cursing, Jacinta ran from the room. In her panic to check if Narelle might be elsewhere in the house, she almost missed the note propped by the phone.

Narelle's large, round handwriting filled the torn notebook page. Jacinta skimmed over the apology and thank you, her dismay intensifying as she realized that Narelle had returned home to the man who only hours ago she had fled. The same man who, in a drunken rage, had phoned Jacinta, spouting threats.

Narelle's postscript promising to call her the next day did nothing to quell Jacinta's growing fears. Her first reaction was to search for her car keys. But logic told her she was overreacting. Craig hadn't harmed Narelle to date. What made her think he would now?

"Don't get involved. It's not your problem." Brett caught her by the elbow. "It's time you put yourself first."

She shook him off. "That's not what you said last week." His accusation that she always put herself first still smarted.

He dropped his gaze, looking suitably contrite. "Yes, I know. I'm sorry. I said a lot of things I didn't mean."

As pleased as she was to hear that, she didn't have the time to pursue it. "Look, for whatever reason, Narelle came to me for help. What do you want me to do? Turn my back on her?"

"She says here she'll call you tomorrow." He waved the note in her face. "I'm sure she knows what she's doing. After all, she's survived on her own all these years."

So had Kirsty, until that fateful night, she thought.

"If you're that concerned, why don't we get the police to check on her? And if you're worried about getting the run-around, why don't you call Daniel direct?"

Before she could take umbrage, he continued.

"You said yourself you were only kids. Maybe this is a chance for your stepbrother to redeem himself; prove to you that he's not the monster you remember."

"You're not serious?"

"What harm could there be in talking to him?"

Plenty. It would mean acknowledging his existence, and she wasn't ready for that. "Brett, I know you mean well, but can we please just take it one step at a time?"

"Would it help if I phoned him and explained the situation?"

She wasn't sure what situation he was referring to, but shaking her head in an emphatic no anyway, she said, "Besides, the police turning up at the house would undoubtedly only make matters worse."

Brett grinned. "And you turning up wouldn't?"

In a roundabout way, he had forced her to answer her own question.

24

Jacinta had lost count of the number of times she had picked up the phone, listened to the dial tone and hung up again. Brett had left for work early, leaving her alone to prowl the house and wait for Narelle's promised phone call.

Her problem was she had too much time to think. Willing the phone to ring wasn't working. She needed a distraction. Laundry, dishes, dusting, accounts: all needed doing, but none held any appeal.

When the phone did ring, she was elbow-deep in soapy water. Quickly drying her hands with a tea towel, she lunged for the phone, answering with a breathless "hello."

"Where's my wife, you fucking bitch? And don't even think about—"

Jacinta recoiled, the phone slipping from her grip. She caught it, disconnecting the call. What had happened to Narelle? Where was she, if not at home?

The phone rang again. Jacinta's stomach knotted, a bitter, metallic taste filling her mouth. She couldn't not answer it. What if it was Narelle? With her finger poised to end the call, she answered it.

Her voice came out as a squeak. A vaguely familiar woman's voice asked for Jacinta Deller. Covering the mouthpiece, Jacinta cleared her throat.

"Jacinta Deller," she announced in her most confident and business-like voice.

When she heard it was Emily York from Alvico Media, her heart skipped a beat, a bubble of hope welling in her chest. As far as job interviews went, bad news was usually delivered by letter or email.

The phone call lasted less than a minute, but when Jacinta hung up, she couldn't contain her elation, dancing a little jig on the spot. Emily was emailing all the details through, but that was just a formality. She started work Monday at Alvico Media: a regular job with regular hours and regular pay.

Wanting to share her excitement, she called Brett, leaving a message when it diverted to his voicemail. While Brett's reconciliation dinner hadn't gone to plan the previous night, they now had extra cause for celebration. She closed her eyes, already tasting the champagne bubbles.

The ringing telephone broke her reverie, the champagne fizz dissipating on hearing Narelle's subdued voice.

"Thank God! Narelle, where are you?"

"On my way to the doctor. Why?"

"Where did you go last night?"

"Oh, Jacinta, I'm really sorry about running out on you like that. Didn't you get my note?"

"Yes, but where did you go?"

"Home," Narelle replied, her voice tentative, as if she wasn't sure it was the right response. "Why?"

"Craig has just rung here looking for you," Jacinta said, neglecting to mention how het-up he had been. Nor that she had hung up on him without saying a word.

Narelle sighed. "It was probably stupid of me to think he might stay asleep until I got home." She went on to say that when she had arrived home the night before, Craig had been passed out on the couch, a whisky tumbler clutched in his hand. After removing the glass and throwing a blanket over him, she had gone to bed, leaving him to sleep it off. He was still snoring when she left the house that morning.

Narelle didn't volunteer the reason for her doctor's appointment and Jacinta didn't pry, assuming it was to confirm, or otherwise, her suspected pregnancy.

Relieved that Narelle was in no immediate danger, she took a deep breath, relaxing back into her chair. Jacinta's news of her new job with Alvico Media lightened the tone of the conversation considerably. Narelle congratulated her, sounding genuinely delighted, even suggesting a celebratory drink when things settled down.

What things, Jacinta wasn't quite sure. But the mere fact that Narelle had made the suggestion at all had to be a good sign, and the first step in taking back control of her life. After securing a promise from Narelle that she wouldn't think twice about ringing her any time of the day or night, for any reason whatsoever, Jacinta rang off.

She returned to the kitchen sink, the now cold and grey dishwater not enough to dampen her spirits. She had a new job to look forward to. Brett and she were back together. Narelle's problems, while still there, didn't appear quite so dramatic in the clear light of day.

Even the radio station she was listening to was in sync with her mood. She found herself singing along at the top of her voice with the chorus of a long-forgotten dance hit from the late 1980s, 'The Only Way Is Up'. The only way *was* up, and it felt good.

She finished washing up, planning the rest of her day as she wiped down the benches. First stop: *The Acacia Tribune* to thank Anthea for the job reference and, if she could persuade her to leave her desk for long enough, a catch-up over coffee. Then lunch with Brett, if he was free. Broke as she was, any shopping, with the exception of window-shopping, was out of the question. Perhaps then a leisurely stroll through Fitzroy Gardens. She could certainly do with the fresh air and exercise.

In the throes of hanging up the tea towel, the doorbell rang. Still singing along with the radio and without much thought as to who it might be, she went to answer it.

DS Renee White, prim and proper in a dark, tailored trouser-suit, was the last person Jacinta expected to see. But her bewilderment soon turned to dismay as she caught sight of the detective's partner. Instead of the insolent DC Mark Fratta, she was staring straight into the dark eyes of Daniel Lassiter. She gasped, her attempt to slam the door thwarted by a well-placed black boot.

"Ms Deller," said the DS, her foot still implanted between the door and jamb, "can we please have just a few minutes of your time?"

The sergeant's request, while polite enough, didn't touch on the reason for the visit. Surely Daniel wouldn't have had the DS fronting for him if it had been strictly personal. Official police business? Then again, what could they possibly want with her?

With curiosity tempering her instinct to keep the police – and more so, her stepbrother – at a distance, she relented, taking the pressure off the door. Journalist or not, she doubted she would ever lose the innate inquisitiveness that had led her to choose that career in the first place.

"Jacinta…"

She froze, unable to breathe; Daniel's deep liquid voice, his father's voice, piercing the armor she had spent years erecting around herself.

"Jacinta," he repeated, taking a step forward, his hands out in front of him. "You're shocked, and I apologize for that. This wasn't the way I saw us meeting up again after all these years, either." Puzzlement flashed across his face. "Did you get my letter?"

She nodded dumbly, her power of speech deserting her. If she hadn't known better, she would have sworn she'd been transported back in time. Daniel's resemblance to his father was startling: the same espresso-colored eyes; the same strong, square jaw; the same chiseled cheekbones; the same wide mouth. Even his dark, wavy hair, though he had more of it, was identical.

"You two know each other, then?" said DS Renee White, one eyebrow arching as she glanced back and forth between Jacinta and Daniel.

"Yes," replied Daniel, not elaborating any further.

His eyes didn't blink. "Good to see you again, Jacinta. It's been a long time."

She found her breath. "What do you want?"

His mouth opened, but before he could speak, the sergeant cut in. "It would be better if we talked inside."

What choice did she have? Releasing the door, she stepped aside, pressing her back up hard against the wall. Her eyes closed as Daniel brushed past, the warm muskiness of his aftershave unsettling her.

She closed the door, paused, took a couple of deep breaths and turned to face him and the DS.

"Thank you for your time, Ms Deller," said DS White.

"Jacinta, please," blurted Jacinta, countering the disquieting formality. "Come through."

She led them through to the living room, seating them together on one sofa before claiming the far end of the other for herself. She shivered, folding her arms tightly over her chest.

Perched on the sofa edge, Daniel looked as ill at ease as she felt. He cleared his throat. "Jacinta, even though I would like to spend some time catching up with you, unfortunately we're here on official police business. Perhaps we could get together later." She opened her mouth to protest. "Of course, I'll leave that entirely up to you," he added quickly, not giving her any leeway.

Her mouth closed, the clunk of her teeth sending vibrations through her jaw. Would the Daniel of old have been as deferential? She didn't know. Somehow he had her doubting her own memories.

"Here," he said, taking a pen from his shirt pocket and writing on the reverse of one of his business cards, "these are all my contact details, including my home email address. Wendy, my wife, and the boys would love to meet you." He handed her the card, but when she hesitated, laid it on the coffee table.

Jacinta blinked. With everything happening so fast, it all felt surreal. She glanced at the business card, wondering if he had forgotten that he'd enclosed one with his letter. Perhaps the suave Daniel Lassiter wasn't quite as in control as he would have liked her to think.

"DS White happened to mention you were at the Edmonds house when she and DC Fratta called on Narelle Croswell last week."

"So?" replied Jacinta, looking to Renee White for an explanation. Stony-faced, the detective returned her stare.

"I'm sure you're aware that Craig Edmonds was charged with the murder of his first wife, Narelle's sister."

"So?" she repeated, before she could stop herself, her belligerence acting as a defense mechanism. "What could that possibly have to do with me? I wasn't even in the country."

Daniel gave a low sigh. "We're not here to make trouble. Nor are we out on a witch-hunt. Simply put, new information has come forth that may or may not relate to the Edmonds case. I was hoping that you might be able to help us get to the truth, whatever that may be."

"What new information?"

"I'm sorry, we're not in a position to divulge details at the moment. Investigations are still ongoing."

Cop-speak for it's none of your business, thought Jacinta. "I still don't see where I come into the equation."

"How long have you known Craig Edmonds and Narelle Croswell?"

She stiffened. "Not long," she replied, deliberately vague.

"Days? Weeks? Years?"

"Days."

Daniel's right eye twitched. "How did you meet?"

"Does it matter?"

"I know it probably seems irrelevant, but experience tells us that we can't overlook any detail, no matter how insignificant it might appear at the time."

As long as she didn't betray any confidences, she couldn't see any harm in answering his questions. "My boyfriend and Narelle are work colleagues."

Again, his eye twitched. "Can you tell us how you came to meet Craig Edmonds?"

"First," she said, unfolding her arms and planting her hands on her knees, "please tell me what all this is about." If they wanted information from her, they were going to have to barter for it.

"That's not how—" began Renee White.

Daniel took charge, dismissing his sergeant with a reproving glance. She scowled, looking like a petulant child when he dispatched her to the kitchen to make coffee.

"Now," he said, dropping his voice to a conspiratorial whisper, "I'm only telling you this because I trust you to keep it confidential." He held her gaze. "I can trust you, can't I, Jacinta?"

Her journalistic antenna shot up. She nodded, fully aware that it was his way of trying to endear himself to her. And, at the same time, test her. Breaking police protocol wasn't a gamble she imagined he would take lightly; if it backfired, it could cost him his career.

He studied her face, shaking his head as if having second thoughts.

"Jesus, Daniel, don't start playing games with me. Either you have something you can tell me, or you don't. Whatever it is, I assure you it won't make tomorrow's headlines."

He laughed. "Placid as ever, I see."

She glowered at him, already regretting letting him into her house. Didn't he understand what it took for her just to be in the same room with him? Poking fun at her wouldn't help.

He reached out his arm, laying his palm on the coffee table in front of her, his tone suddenly serious. "It's not public knowledge yet, but more remains have been uncovered in the Toolangi State Forest."

"More?"

Before he could elaborate, Renee appeared in the doorway, balancing a black-and-white-patterned mug in each hand.

"Thanks, Renee," he said, as she crossed the room and set the steaming mugs on the coffee table. "My sister and I were just catching up on old times."

The DS's eyes widened, her head jerking from one to the other as if the concept was entirely outside the realms of possibility.

"He means stepsister. For a short time his father was married to my mother," said Jacinta, adding the word *unfortunately* in her mind.

"Jacinta, if you're free later on today, how about we continue our conversation then."

She picked up the cue, realizing she would learn no more about the remains found in the Toolangi State Forest while Renee was in earshot. "Sure, I could meet you somewhere in the city." Meeting in public would be less daunting than being alone with him in private.

Niceties dealt with, at least on the surface, Daniel and Renee pressed on with their queries about her relationship with the

Edmondses. She answered their direct questions, not proffering more than was strictly necessary. When it came down to questions involving her thoughts and opinions, she shrugged and pleaded ignorance.

By the time Daniel and Renee left, they only knew for certain that Brett and Narelle had worked for the same company for three years, that the Edmondses had attended a dinner party hosted by Jacinta and Brett, that Narelle and Jacinta had seen each other a couple of times since, and that the Edmondses had few friends.

What she didn't tell them about was Narelle's admission that the gold and sapphire cross found with the original unidentified skeletal remains could be her sister's. Nor did she tell them about Narelle's fears for her husband's state of mind, or even that she was more than likely pregnant with his child. Jacinta didn't see it as her place.

Of more import was Grace's assertion that she and Kirsty Edmonds had been lovers. True or not, why had she not mentioned that?

25

The garage door closed. Taking a deep breath, Narelle tilted her head back against the headrest and sighed. The air smelled faintly of concrete and detergent.

She stared unseeing at the car's windscreen. Cocooned in the quiet and gloom, she felt oddly disconnected from the world. Her emotions in limbo, she didn't know whether to laugh or cry. Worse still, she didn't know how Craig would react to the news of her pregnancy.

She released her seatbelt, removed the keys from the ignition and gathered up her handbag from the passenger seat. As she went to open the car door, it was wrenched from her hands.

"What the fuck has been going on? Where have you been?" An ugly vein bulged above Craig's right eye, his face beyond red. "And don't lie!"

Narelle shrank back, her arms protecting her head. He advanced, breathing fumes of soured whisky into her face. She tried to close the car door, suddenly scared about what he might do. No contest. He overpowered her easily, grabbing her by the wrist and yanking her from the car.

Treating her like a wayward child, he dragged her into the house and down the hall to the bedroom. She didn't have the strength to resist. His last shove sent her flying. Her body curled into a protective ball as she landed on the unmade bed.

She lashed out with her feet, kicking nothing but air. "Stop!" Bringing her knees up, she rolled on to her back, shielding her abdomen with her hands as she scooted backwards. "What the hell has got into you?"

Craig's chest heaved, his trembling hand suspended in front of his face. "Oh, Christ, I didn't mean it. You know I would never hurt you," he said, dropping to his knees beside the bed.

"Stay away from me!"

He froze, his unshaven face contorted with bewilderment as he registered her fear. Breathing hard, she stared into his bloodshot eyes, looking for the man she loved.

"Narelle, I'm so sorry. I'll make it up to you, I promise." He reached out tentatively, watching for her reaction. "I love you."

She hugged her knees, her body tensing as he touched her bare foot. "I love you, too." Her arms tightened around her knees. "But I'm worried sick about what's happening to you. I—" She paused, correcting herself. "*We* can't go on like this. Bottling it up is doing neither of us any good. Whatever it is, I'm here for you." She forced a smile. "After everything we've been through, we can't give up now, can we?"

His bottom lip quivered. "Please forgive me. I can't help myself. I'm just so scared of losing you. You mean everything to me." His eyes pleaded with her.

She swallowed hard, fighting the ball of emotion welling in her chest. With him exposed and vulnerable like that, she knew she could forgive him almost anything. She loved him with an intensity she couldn't explain.

Unlocking her arms, she slid her left hand down her leg to meet his fingers. "I'm not going anywhere, but things do have to change."

His gaze never left her face as, giving her foot a light squeeze, he moved from kneeling on the floor to sitting on the edge of the bed. "Anything. Just name it."

"We need to put the past behind us, where it belongs. Kirsty is gone and nothing we do will bring her back. We've grieved long enough. Can't you see that living like social pariahs is unhealthy? I want us to be a normal family, living normal lives." Taking a deep breath, she added, "Especially now…"

"Yes, yes. Any—"

She didn't let him finish. "Craig, I'm pregnant," she blurted.

His face seemed made of rubber, his initial look of complete incomprehension morphing to one of excitement and back again. "A baby?"

She nodded, watching his face, not knowing what to expect. Early on in their relationship, they had agreed that children weren't on the agenda. Neither had brought up the subject since.

"A baby?" he repeated.

She nodded again, her lips twitching in a hesitant half-smile.

A broad grin spread over his face as in one fluid movement, he bounded from the bed, taking her with him. Holding her close, he danced around the room. Even though his reaction more than told her he was pleased, she still had to ask.

"Happy?"

Coming to a standstill, he looked straight into her eyes, his own bloodshot ones sparkling. "Mrs Edmonds," he said, the elation in his voice smashing any doubts she might have had, "you have no idea how much."

26

Jacinta took a deep breath and pushed against The Quadrangle Bar's huge, barn-like door. As it swung inwards, she gasped. Flooded with natural light from the vast expanse of skylights high above, the cavernous space looked large enough to house a Jumbo 747. Until Daniel had suggested The Quadrangle as a place to meet, she hadn't known it existed. Certainly, its nondescript street façade belied what lay inside.

Laughter and voices, competing with the music for dominance, bounced off the brick and corrugated iron walls. A young woman wearing bronze dangly earrings that looked more like wind chimes brushed past in a cloud of perfume. The woman's glazed eyes and supercilious grin told Jacinta she had been there for a while.

Then she saw him, his hand raised in a wave as he picked his way around and through the parties of people congregated amongst the maze of couches, chairs, low tables and tall trees.

Her flight instinct kicked in. She wanted out of there. She should never have come in the first place. It was all a mistake.

Instead she froze, her strappy-sandaled feet glued to the bar's polished concrete floor. The closer he came, the faster her heart beat. She glanced over her shoulder at the door, and then back at her advancing stepbrother. He waved again.

Within seconds he was at her side, propelling her along the route he had just come, one hand lightly resting in the small of her back. She gritted her teeth, refusing to let the familiarity and intimacy of his gesture unnerve her. The strained, high-pitched laugh she heard was her own. Laughing on the outside but screaming on the inside.

Eventually they reached a nest of tan leather armchairs, a solid pale-timbered table at its centre. A white tented 'Reserved' sign sat on one corner of the table, along with what looked to be extensive wine and cocktail lists.

Sinking down into one of the plush seats, her thoughts inexplicably turned to Brett. She knew he would have liked the bar, but would he have approved of her meeting with Daniel on her own? More than likely he would have insisted on accompanying her. She didn't want or need him — or anyone else, for that matter — to hold her hand.

Her reasons for meeting Daniel were twofold. First, she needed to confront him; she couldn't keep hiding forever. Second, he had promised her information that could have some bearing on the dormant Edmonds case. Even, perhaps, something that could bring closure for Narelle and the man accused of her older sister's murder. Perhaps.

Daniel sat down in the chair directly opposite and picked up the wine list. "What would you like to drink?" He glanced up, the corner of his mouth lifting in expectancy.

Her lips peeled back in a half-smile, half-grimace, the sick feeling in her stomach intensifying. Reminding herself why she was there, she returned his gaze. "A glass of Chardonnay, please."

She knew that anyone watching could be forgiven for mistaking they were on a first date. Polite small talk. Nervous smiles. Strained body language. Strangers testing the social waters.

The arrival of the waiter provided a brief respite. His departure left them with no distractions.

They both started speaking at once, desperate to fill the awkward void. Whatever it was that Daniel was saying she didn't hear, her own voice drowning out his words. She stopped, waiting for him to continue. He didn't. They tried again, repeating the farce. She might have laughed if the situation hadn't been so damned serious.

Finally, she clamped her lips together and sat back in her chair, resolving to stay mute until after Daniel had his say.

"Jacinta," he sat forward in his seat, "I'm really pleased you decided to come. I wasn't sure you would. For years I wondered what became of you and your mother. I hoped you were somewhere far away, safe and happy."

She frowned, wondering where he was taking it.

"I don't blame you for hating me, but there's something you should know." He cleared his throat, dropping his gaze to the tabletop. "When I came into your room that night, it wasn't to molest you…"

Jacinta couldn't breathe, winded by the invisible punch.

"No," he continued, looking up, "I wanted to talk to you, convince you it would be better for you both to leave. I might have been only a kid, but I wasn't blind. I loved Dad but I had seen it all before. I saw my own mother treated like a possession – her every action, her every thought, controlled by my father. Anyway, when I touched your shoulder to wake you, you sat bolt upright, screaming your lungs out, your arms going in all directions. At that moment, I think I was as terrified as you were. I tried to calm you and perhaps – because I don't remember this – I accidentally touched you somewhere I shouldn't have."

Sucking in ragged gulps of breath through her gaping mouth, she could do nothing except sit and stare at him in disbelief. *Accident?* Over and over, she had replayed every second of that night in her head. From waking with a start, to the touch of his sweaty hands on her skin, to the smell of his cheesy breath in her face. The more she thrashed, the more he fought to pin her down. Her shrieks finally summoned her mother to the rescue, one flick of the light switch turning the scene to stone. A few long seconds later, Daniel had broken away, mumbling something unintelligible under his breath as he hurtled past her mother. A door slammed down the hall. Now he was telling her it had all been some innocent mistake?

"You have to understand, I never meant any malice. It all happened so fast that I didn't have time to explain. And when you and your mother took off, I truly believed that it had all worked out for the best. You were out of harm's way. That's all I ever wanted."

Stunned beyond belief, she suddenly wondered if it was some elaborate ploy to absolve himself of any sense of wrongdoing. Fixing him with an icy stare, she said, "If that was the situation, why didn't you say so at the time? Or even the next day? You had plenty of time to put your case then. Why wait all these years?"

He sighed, averting his eyes for a moment. "I've asked myself that question many times, too. We were just kids. I don't think anyone at that age really thinks through all the possible consequences of their actions. In hindsight, I should at least have tried to explain. But then again, if your mother had known I wasn't trying to molest you, would she have whisked you away like that? I doubt it. She didn't seem to care what happened to her, but when it affected her daughter, that was different. Back then, I thought by staying silent I was doing you both a favor. Now..." his chest heaved. "Now, I realize my actions were probably wrong. Jacinta, I know it's a big ask, but I hope in time you'll find it in you to forgive me."

Her body felt like an overwound spring, ready to snap. Her fingers gripped the chair's arms as if they were all that separated her from life and certain death. Her brain threatened to overheat, the synapses firing in a feverish battle to process Daniel's words.

His body language, the tone of his voice, the pain in those dark eyes all made her want to believe him. But was he sincere or, like his father, a consummate liar?

Part of her wanted to scream at him, unleashing years of pent-up anger. For him it may have happened too fast, but for her it had all been in excruciatingly slow motion.

At fifteen, she hadn't stopped to question his motives for being in her room that night. Why should she have? Good boys didn't creep into a girl's bedroom in the dead of night. Whatever his reasons, her terror had been real. Nor had she imagined his clammy hands on her skin.

Nevertheless, was it possible she had misconstrued the whole situation? Adult logic fought against the petrified teenage girl still deep inside her. The room had been dark. Too dark to see where he put his hands. He hadn't physically hurt her.

In that instant, she hated him even more. His version of events meant the pain and guilt that had wracked her mother for failing her daughter had all been so needless. Up to the day she died, her mother had blamed herself.

He shrank back under her glare. She didn't trust herself to speak.

The waiter arrived, becoming an unwitting mediator as he made a show of first presenting the bottle of wine to Daniel for his inspection and then opening it and pouring two glasses.

Although the diversion gave her the perfect opportunity to flee, she chose to stay, using the brief interval to calm herself. Mentally counting down from one hundred, she focused on steadying her breathing. As much as she wanted to, she knew hurling abuse – or even better, the wine – at him wasn't the answer.

Instead, Jacinta pushed the whole matter back into the dark recesses of her mind to deal with later. She needed time to digest it. Time to come to terms with it. Time to let go.

Like two chess opponents, they sized each other up across the table. Daniel made the first move, sliding one of the two glasses of wine toward her. In a show of bravado, she picked it up, raising it in a quasi toast. Checkmate.

27

Narelle lounged on the bed, her fingers laced over her abdomen as she watched her husband's silhouette through the adjoining en suite's steam-obscured shower glass. In the middle of shampooing his hair, he suddenly burst into song, his deep baritone voice filling the bedroom.

Giggling, she slid off the bed and, taking the phone from the bedside table, left Craig to finish showering.

She dialed as she walked. For some reason the call cut off after only two rings. She tried again, not waiting for a greeting when it connected, her words coming out in a breathless rush. "Great news! It's definite. I'm pregnant."

Nothing.

"Jacinta, are you there?"

"Sorry." Her voice sounded edgy. "I mean, congratulations. I'm so pleased for you. How did hubby take the news?"

"Brilliantly," she said, briefly wondering why she hadn't referred to Craig by name. "Oh, Jacinta, I really couldn't have hoped for more. He's thrilled to bits that he's going to be a daddy." She laughed. "I don't know why I was so concerned. It was obviously meant to be. A new start."

"We'll talk soon."

Narelle frowned, disappointed by her friend's lack of exuberance. Then, in the background, she heard the scramble of muffled voices, music and clatter that could only belong to a bar or restaurant. So completely caught up in her own excitement, she had blocked out all else.

"Oh, shit. I've interrupted something, haven't I?"

"Sorry." Jacinta sounded distracted. "Can I call you later?"

She hung up, turning to see Craig toweling his hair dry as he padded half-naked down the hall toward her. In the space of less than an hour, he had grown in stature, exuding more confidence than she had seen in him in a long time.

"Who were you talking to?"

A simple question asked in a casual tone, yet instantly her guard went up. For a split second, she thought about lying. He had made no secret of his disdain for Jacinta, blaming her for all their current woes. Avoiding the issue wouldn't solve them, though.

"Just Jacinta." She watched his face, trying to gauge his reaction. "I'm so excited I want to tell the whole world our news." She beamed at him, hoping to catch him up in her enthusiasm.

A flicker of something she didn't recognize passed over his features, disappearing almost immediately. With a smile that didn't quite reach his eyes, he traced the outline of her face with his finger, brushing a wayward curl aside.

"My darling Narelle, that probably wasn't the wisest thing you could've done. I wish for your sake you could see through that woman. She isn't to be trusted. How many lies and half-truths has she told you, I wonder? Remember, she's a journalist first and foremost." He paused. "Don't be surprised if you get your wish. Although I doubt the news will be reported in the way you expect."

Inwardly she groaned, hoping her face didn't betray her thoughts. "I'm not as naïve as you seem to think. Yes, Jacinta was a reporter and yes, we were probably just a story to her initially." She hesitated, taking a deep breath. "But think about it: if she hadn't come along when she did, we'd still be hiding like criminals behind closed doors.

She did us a favor. I like Jacinta, and if you would just give her a chance, I'm sure you would, too."

He didn't say anything, but she could see his mind ticking over. At least it wasn't the short-fused, defensive reaction she had come to expect of late. She quickly kissed him, stymieing any further debate. Then, with a cheeky smack on his bum, she sent him to get dressed. An almost naked, towel-clad man with damp, mussed-up hair just didn't gel with deep and meaningful conversation.

A building queasiness in the pit of her stomach interrupted her thoughts and sent her scurrying to the kitchen in search of relief. Now she knew the reason for her nausea, it didn't seem half as bad. But why they called it morning sickness, she'd never know. She'd had bouts morning, noon and night.

By the time the kettle boiled, her nausea was already waning of its own accord. She sweetened the gingery herbal tea with a teaspoon of honey before carrying it down to the living room.

Craig emerged not long after, barefoot but fully clothed in jeans and a black T-shirt. Stepping down into the room, he glanced over at the whisky bottle on the bar. Narelle continued to sip the hot aromatic tea, doing her best to appear nonchalant as she waited to see what he would do. He didn't falter.

"Have the police been in touch?" he asked, flopping down onto the couch next to her.

His question caught her unawares. "What?"

"The police. Any news on when the DNA results will be in?" He gazed at an invisible spot on the floor, stroking his freshly shaven face.

"Not yet. They did say it would be a week to ten days." Setting her cup on the coffee table, she then snuggled up to him. He smelt clean and fresh, the faint scent of soap lingering. "I hope it is Kirsty." She felt him stiffen. "I mean, it's better than not knowing, right? And the insurance company would have no more excuses for not paying up," she added, referring to the $1,000,000 insurance policy on Kirsty's life.

Sighing, he draped his left arm around her shoulders and pulled her in close. "If only it were that simple," he said, his lips brushing her forehead.

"Why can't it be? Think about it…"

"Believe me, I have been. Every moment of every day. Don't you understand? If the remains prove to be Kirsty's, they'll have proof positive she was murdered. I'm going to be back in the frame again. They had no problem charging me with murder when they didn't have a body. What do you think my chances would be *with* a body?" He sighed, his voice dropping as he continued. "You wanted me to be honest with you. Well, the truth is I'm shit-scared. I feel like there's a huge guillotine suspended over my neck and at any moment it could come down…"

His volatile moods and heavy drinking started to make sense. "Oh, Craig, why didn't you tell me sooner?"

"What, and burden you with it? Besides, what could you have done?"

"I'm your wife and I love—" His arms tightened around her. She could barely breathe, let alone speak. She felt a wetness on the side of her face and realized he was crying. His chest heaved in silent sobs.

Pressing her face hard against his chest, smothering her own tears, she silently berated herself for not seeing the obvious. Blinded by her own wants and needs, she hadn't stopped to consider what the real ramifications of unearthing human remains — that might or might not be Kirsty's — would be.

Believing in her husband's innocence would no longer be enough.

28

Jacinta groaned and, unwilling to open her sleep-leaden eyes, groped for the phone.

"Hello."

"I need you out on a job ASAP."

"Anthea?"

"Yes. I wouldn't ask if it wasn't important."

"Ask what?" In Jacinta's half-comatose state, Anthea Sutton, her old boss and the editor of *The Acacia Tribune*, wasn't making any sense.

"I've had a tip-off and I want you to check it out."

Jacinta rubbed her palm over her forehead and eyes. "But that's not my job anymore."

"Please, Jacinta, I don't have anyone else available."

I told you so, thought Jacinta, biting her tongue. Cost-cutting measures had seen *The Acacia Tribune* sack all but one of its salaried staff reporters, using freelancers instead to fill the gap.

"You don't start with Alvico Media until Monday, do you?" Anthea added, in a less than subtle reminder that she was calling in a favor. "Besides, I think it may be in your interest to follow it up. From what I hear, it may have something to do with the old Edmonds murder case."

Jacinta's eyes sprung open. With the phone clamped against her ear, she scrambled to sit up. "What exactly have you heard?"

"Human remains found a week ago in the Toolangi State Forest are thought to be those of Kirsty Edmonds, right? Well, something else must be going on as well, because according to my sources, the area is literally swarming with police. My guess is they've found something or someone else."

So much for confidentiality, thought Jacinta as, still listening to Anthea, she threw back the bedclothes and made a beeline for the walk-in-robe. Against her better judgment, she had stayed on at the bar, not only to prove to herself how tough she could be, but also in the hope of obtaining the information Daniel had baited her with earlier in the day. Speculation or not, it seemed that the snippets Daniel had divulged were far from secret. Anthea knew more than she did. "I'm on my way," she said, taking the top pair of jeans from the shelf. "I'll give you a call as soon as I know anything."

She dressed quickly and then, checking first that she had her mobile phone, Dictaphone, a notepad and pens, she gathered up her satchel and car keys. Closing the front door behind her, she couldn't help but feel a twinge of guilt over how easily Anthea had talked her around. *But this is it*, she told herself. *No more.*

Once in her car, she hauled the UBD street directory from the backseat on to her lap. Although she knew the general direction in which she should be traveling, the last thing she needed was to get lost. However, on checking the map on the inside cover, she realized that was still an option. The UBD would get her to Healesville but not beyond.

She checked the pocket behind her seat and found a slim and much dated book of country road maps, but they didn't prove to be of much assistance either. While the maps named the main roads, the secondary roads and tracks, marked by solid and dotted orange lines respectively, remained unidentified.

With the UBD directory open on the passenger seat, she backed her car out onto the street, deciding her best bet was to get to Healesville first and then take it from there.

Driving against the peak-hour traffic, it took her just over an hour to reach the small township of Healesville, on the outskirts of Melbourne. She cruised down the tree-lined main street and pulled into a parking space outside the historical Grand Hotel.

She removed the keys from the ignition, turning her head to check for traffic before opening the car door. A Channel 7 News van sped past, bringing her plans to buy maps, a drink and a belated breakfast to an abrupt halt. In her panic to follow the TV crew, she dropped her car keys on the floor, losing precious time. Unless some major catastrophe she didn't know about had happened in the area, she was betting that Channel 7 would lead her to where she wanted to go.

Ignoring her parched throat and the gnawing in her stomach, she pulled out onto the roadway. Hunched over the steering wheel, she pushed her little Nissan Pulsar hard, only easing off the accelerator when she was virtually tailgating the other vehicle.

Paddocks replaced housing as they left the township. Jacinta opened her window and breathed deeply, savoring the taste of the clean, green country air lingering like a mouth-freshener. Her stomach grumbled, reminding her of her missed breakfast.

Open farmland eventually gave way to majestic Mountain Ash. She followed the news van deeper and deeper into the dense forest, hoping she would be able to find her way out again. Signposts were few and far between, and with her sense of direction, she could see herself driving around and around in circles.

According to Anthea, she should be looking for an old, overgrown logging road not marked on the map. So far she had passed at least seven dirt tracks fitting that description. She sincerely hoped the TV news crew had been given better directions.

She needn't have worried. Up ahead, police, media and civilian vehicles packed both sides of the road, slowing traffic to a crawl. Flashing neon lights couldn't have been more effective. The Channel 7 van braked suddenly and pulled onto the gravel verge, leaving Jacinta with no option except to continue driving through the tunnel of cars, 4-wheel drives and vans. At the end, she did a U-turn, her passenger side wheels sinking into the road's soft shoulder as she parked behind a black Toyota Prado with tinted windows.

Once out of the car, she walked with long, purposeful strides. Loud-mouthed reporters vying for attention jarred the forest's natural calm. Cameras and microphones jostled for position as young, uniformed constables standing sentry behind blue and white police tape struggled to keep them at bay.

"How many more skeletons have been found?"

"Are they male or female?"

"Is it true that one of the victims is Kirsty Edmonds?"

"What's been done to identify the remains?"

"Are you investigating missing person's files?"

"Who made the gruesome discovery?"

"Who is the officer in charge of the investigation?"

"What can you tell us about how the victims were killed?"

Unfazed, the police officers stood their ground, deftly deflecting the media's endless questions. Jacinta smiled to herself. She had seen the same scene played out countless times before.

Forgetting she had renounced her journalism career and was, in theory, only there as a favor to Anthea Sutton, she squeezed her way to the front. Her skin crawled like a junkie craving a high, the story so close she could taste it.

"Detective Inspector Daniel Lassiter, please," she said, her voice strong and authoritative. Not only did she succeed in attracting the attention of the round-faced constable closest to her, but that of the whole media circus. Reporters thrust microphones in her face, demanding to know who she was, her connection to DI Lassiter, and her purpose for being at the site. She ignored them all, leaning forward to present her business card to the constable.

He dutifully accepted it, stepping away from the tape and turning his back briefly to talk into his radio. He returned, speaking to his colleague before lifting the cordon tape and motioning her under. An indignant clamor rose behind her.

Constable Peter Haggerty, as he had introduced himself, walked her down the rough dirt track leading into the forest. Not as sure-footed as her minder, she had to concentrate hard to avoid stumbling over tree roots and rocks. She struggled to keep pace with him, the dry, earthy air tickling her throat as she gasped for breath.

Once out of sight of the sealed road, Constable Haggerty told her to stay put while he checked on Daniel's whereabouts. Thankful for the respite, she sagged against the nearest tree large enough to take her weight. No longer a moving target, a cloud of bush flies closed in, attracted by the sweat rivulets running down her face. She waved her hand in front of her face, driving them away.

Keeping up the wiper motion, she surveyed the area. Though she couldn't see the police operations, she could hear their jumbled voices floating up from the other side of the rise over which Constable Haggerty had disappeared. Through the trees and some distance away, she caught sight of a couple of intrepid individuals bushwhacking through dense undergrowth in an obvious attempt to circumvent the police cordon. *Brave or stupid?* she wondered. If the snakes and spiders didn't get them, the police undoubtedly would.

This thought sent her scuttling into the middle of the track, away from the bushes and trees. Logic told her that with all the commotion, any snakes would be long gone. Phobia told her it was better to be safe than sorry.

Intent on checking for movement in the scrub off the side of the track, she didn't hear Daniel's footsteps as he came up behind her. In the same instant he spoke her name, he touched her shoulder.

"Shit!" She clapped her hand to her chest. "Give me a heart attack, why don't you?"

"Sorry," he said, not looking the slightest remorseful, "but what the hell are you doing here?"

"On assignment. What's your excuse?"

"Pardon?"

"Kangaroo bones don't warrant this much attention."

Daniel pressed his lips together and dropped his gaze. "Jacinta, I'm sorry," he said, his voice low and soft like he actually meant it this time. "You're right; what I told you last night was more to appease you than anything else. You have to realize I'm not in a position to tell you anything more substantial. Anything you may have heard elsewhere is wild speculation, and nothing more. The investigation is still very much in the early stages, but I promise you, when we have something for the press, I'll let you know. Besides—" his voice rose an octave, "—it cuts both ways. What's your interest in this case? Didn't you tell me you had given up the reporter game? Perhaps there's something more you ought to be telling me…"

Before she could protest, Constable Haggerty turned up to tell Daniel he was required. "Jacinta, we need to talk, but not here and not now. Can I call you later?"

She hesitated and then nodded. Pretending he didn't exist wouldn't make him disappear. And maybe – just maybe – if he could convince her of his sincerity, the monster inside her head she had fed for years would wither and die.

"Peter will take you back to the road."

For a moment or two, she watched Daniel's retreating form before turning to begin the hike back.

"You friends with DI Lassiter, then?" asked Peter, his tone casual as, walking side by side, they retraced their earlier steps.

"He's my brother," she said, surprising not only the young constable but herself. "Stepbrother, actually." Why she had felt compelled to blurt that out, she didn't know.

Peter Haggerty didn't ask any more questions, remaining mute until they reached his colleagues standing guard at the track entrance. All eyes were on her as Peter directed her along the blue and white police tape to a less populated spot.

Ducking under the tape, she knew Anthea would be less than pleased with her lack of results. In her previous life, she would probably have stood her ground: demanding, wheedling, and pleading until she had the information she wanted. But somehow, she knew being obnoxious wouldn't have worked with Daniel, anyway. After all, he hadn't achieved his rank by giving into annoying reporters, stepsister or not.

She straightened up, glancing first at her car, then at the growing pack of reporters and stickybeaks, and then back at her car. She was dehydrated, hungry, tired and sweaty; the air-conditioned sanctuary of her car won out easily over standing around in the building heat, dust and sticky flies.

A blast of superheated air hit her when she opened her car door. She started the car without getting in, leaning across the driver's seat to turn the air-conditioner and fan to maximum. With all the Pulsar's windows open, the hot outside air soon displaced the even hotter interior air, along with a couple of bush flies for good measure.

Leaving the car idling, she dug into her satchel for her mobile phone. Even though she had nothing to report, Anthea would still be waiting for her call. Her phone's signal indicator flickered, steadied and then died. Cursing, she danced around, holding her phone in the air like some demented marionette.

Swinging around, she came face to face with the last person she expected to see.

"Grace!"

Kirsty Edmonds' best friend and self-proclaimed lover, Grace Kevron, gave her a lopsided grin. "Hello, Jacinta," she said, her speech marred by a slight slur. "Fancy meeting you here." She giggled, tilting her head to one side.

Jacinta frowned, wondering from which planet the pale-faced alien with dilated pupils had descended. "Have you been drinking?"

Grace responded with another stupid, lopsided grin, before moving her face in so close that Jacinta feared she was about to be kissed. She instinctively pulled back, but not before Grace had blown a lungful of garlicky breath in her face.

"What are you doing here, Grace?"

"You're not the only one with contacts, you know."

That much was obvious. "What do you think you're going to achieve?"

"Justice."

"I don't see how a pile of animal bones is going to do that," Jacinta said, using the line Daniel had given her the previous night.

That bloody grin again. "You'll see," Grace said over her shoulder, as she turned and walked away.

29

Like a ghost, Grace had faded into the crowd, leaving Jacinta bemused and none the wiser. Who or what had brought Grace into the Toolangi State Forest? Were her cryptic comments about 'justice' and 'you'll see' meant only to taunt, or something deeper? What wasn't she saying?

Using her hand to shield against the glare, Jacinta scanned the surrounding area again, to no avail. She sighed and closed her eyes, immediately wishing she hadn't when the insides of her moisture-less lids sandpapered her eyeballs. Not only her eyes but her whole body craved water.

With dehydration fogging her brain, what hope did she have of corralling her thoughts into anything coherent? She had no choice. She would have to return to Healesville for supplies.

Getting into her car was like going from the oven to the freezer. Before she closed her car door, she flicked a fly comatose with cold from the dashboard. Then, hoping like hell that nothing major happened while she was away, she drove off.

Once in Healesville, she broke the diet commandment, 'thou shalt not shop on an empty stomach', and piled her shopping basket with enough junk food and drink to survive any siege. At the checkout counter, she added *The Acacia Tribune*, *The Age* and *Herald Sun* newspapers, noting that the discovery of the human remains had yet to make the front pages. If nothing else, she would have something to read to while away the time.

Not waiting for the car to cool first, she jumped into the driver's seat, cramming her shopping bags into the passenger-side footwell. With an opened bag of jellybeans on the seat between her legs and a bright blue sports drink in the middle console, she somehow managed to retrace her route to the Toolangi State Forest without getting lost.

In her absence, a couple of new vehicles had arrived and at least one – namely the black Toyota Prado she had been parked behind earlier – had left. Other than that, nothing had changed.

She opened all the car windows, allowing any breeze there might be to flow through, and stretched across the console to retrieve her picnic provisions from the floor. In the middle of this contortionist act, she heard a vehicle slow and stop close by, followed by a mishmash of disjointed voices. Rummaging in the bags in the footwell, her grip tightened on a cold bottle of something in the same instant the voices registered. She froze; her left elbow propped on the passenger seat taking the bulk of her weight.

Snatches of Daniel's deep voice, mixed with Detective Sergeant Renee White's softer tones, drifted through the car window. Not wanting to alert them to her presence, Jacinta kept her head down and held her breath. Her ears strained to pick up every sound, flipping into overdrive when she heard the words 'DNA' and 'Edmonds' in the same sentence.

Stringing together the words she could hear with the ones she couldn't wasn't easy. But if she had the general gist right, it wasn't Kirsty Edmonds' remains out there in the bush. Or at least not the first body. Daniel's last instruction to DS White before she restarted her car was to notify Narelle Croswell and Craig Edmonds of the DNA results in person.

Jacinta waited until she felt sure the coast was clear before she sat up. Able to breathe freely again, she tried to work out where Daniel had gone but, like Grace, he had disappeared from sight.

Renee White, Jacinta presumed, was on her way to the Edmonds house. How would Narelle and Craig react? Would it be good news or bad news? Sincerely hoping that insensitive prat of a sidekick, Detective Constable Mark Fratta, wasn't accompanying her, Jacinta took a swig of her now tepid sports drink.

Narelle wanted closure, but at what expense? She and Craig had more than themselves to consider now. If the remains had been positively identified as those of Kirsty Olive Edmonds, their lives would have been thrown into turmoil. The once dormant and all but forgotten murder case, along with its prime suspect and his new wife, would once again have been thrust into the spotlight. Could either of them have handled the stress again? What would the effect have been on their unborn child?

But if it wasn't Kirsty's body, whose was it? Someone else's daughter, sister or wife had been murdered and left to the elements and wildlife. What else had the police uncovered out there in the undergrowth?

Leaning back into her seat, Jacinta weighed up the little she knew with what she could only surmise. Fact one: skeletal remains of an unidentified female had been unearthed. Fact two: that female wasn't Kirsty Edmonds. Speculation: remains of at least another person – sex unknown – had also been discovered in the same area. If speculation proved to be fact, did that mean this secluded spot in the forest had become a serial killer's dumping ground? How many victims were there? How long had they lain there, waiting to be discovered?

She shook her head. The more she thought about it, the more questions she had. Besides, it wasn't her problem any longer.

Copywriters didn't hang around in the back of nowhere, battling the heat and flies in the slim expectation of a story, wasting a perfectly good day off. And as of Monday, that was what she would be — a salaried copywriter with an air-conditioned office and regular hours. Anthea Sutton could get someone else to do her dirty work for her.

With the media turnout, Jacinta had no doubt any breaking news would be splashed across the television and radio in no time. *What's one less unemployed reporter?* she thought, putting the car in drive and checking the side mirror before easing out onto the road.

All of a sudden, the crush of reporters spread out in front of her, blocking her way. No one looked at her, their focus centered firmly on a white Toyota Land Cruiser leaving the cordoned-off dirt track. She caught a glimpse of its dark-haired driver and immediately wondered if it might be Daniel.

The driver nudged the 4-wheel drive through the milling reporters and cameramen, accelerating quickly once clear. On the other side of the crowd, Jacinta tapped her fingers on the steering wheel, resorting to an impatient toot of her car's horn when they ignored her more subtle engine revving.

She planted her foot, catching up with the Land Cruiser just as it turned left onto Myers Creek Road. Even after catching sight of the driver's profile, she still couldn't be sure it was Daniel. But what did it matter, one way or the other? Shaking her head, Jacinta flicked on the indicator and followed the 4-wheel drive around the corner. Like an itch she couldn't stop scratching, logic didn't come into it.

She hung back, keeping the Toyota in sight but not breaking any speed limits. Until she decided what her next move should be, she didn't want to draw any undue attention her way. Then, in the split second it took to change radio stations, the unmarked police vehicle vanished from sight. With the exception of a small, red car coming toward her on the other side, the road was empty.

While her Nissan Pulsar was no match for his Toyota Land Cruiser, unless he had been called to an emergency, he couldn't have gone far. She pressed her foot to the floor, once again demanding her little car's all. Her frown deepened with each passing kilometer.

She heard him before she saw him, the ear-splitting sound of a siren from out of nowhere startling her. Glancing in the rear-view mirror, she saw flashing lights inside the white 4-wheel drive, the driver signing her to pull over. She cursed, slowed the car and indicated, looking for a safe place to stop. She could ill-afford a speeding ticket.

The police vehicle parked behind her. She held her breath, watching in the side-mirror as the door opened, exhaling in a loud huff as Daniel stepped out.

"Hello again," he said, leaning down into her window. "Do you realize what speed you were doing?"

"Yes... no..." she spluttered, unable to read anything in his deadpan expression. Surely, he wouldn't.

"Let's call it a warning this time." His face softened slightly, moving from cop to real person. "Come on, Jacinta, out with it. Tell me what is so important that you had to tail me."

"I'm entitled to use this road as much as you."

He cocked an eyebrow at her and waited.

"All right, then, I confess." She took a deep breath before continuing. "So far you haven't exactly delivered on your promises. How do you expect me to trust you?"

Both eyebrows rose then. "Jacinta, we're both professionals. You and I both know it's not as simple as that. I might not have told you all you want to know, but I swear I have not knowingly lied to you."

"Surely there must be something you can tell me."

"I can tell you there will be a press conference later today."

"I won't be there."

Daniel narrowed his eyes, holding her gaze in a steely grip. "Come to dinner tomorrow night."

Her jaw dropped, his unexpected request flooring her.

"Bring Brett with you. It'll just be a family dinner – Wendy, the boys and I, Brett and you. Nothing fancy."

Unable to find the right words, her mouth opened and closed like a fish gulping air. She felt torn in two. Half of her wanted to keep her stepbrother at a safe distance; the other half craved what he was offering: to be part of a family again. Hoping she wasn't being taken in by the same magnetic Lassiter charms that had sucked in her mother, she nodded, before adding a quick disclaimer. "I'll have to check with Brett first, though."

With something close to relief in his eyes, he smiled down at her.

"Now about this press conference," she said, before he could say anything else. "Since I won't be there, how about a sneak preview? Off the record, of course," she added.

"First, I have to know what your interest in this case is. If you remember, you told me that you'd given up on journalism as a career."

"Of course I remember," she snapped, annoyed by his oblique insinuation that she might have been making up stories. "I only came out here as a favor to my old editor. And yes, I have a personal interest, too, as you very well know. Narelle Croswell is a friend."

He laughed. "Keep your hair on. I do have something I can share with you. I've just found out about it myself, so don't go thinking I've been keeping it back just to annoy you." He then proceeded to tell her what she had already picked up while eavesdropping.

"What about the bones you found today? Is it possible they could be Kirsty Edmonds'?" Although the skeletal remains found a week ago had proved not to be Narelle's sister, it didn't rule out the possibility that she had been a victim of the same killer.

"Anything's possible, but she's only one of many possibilities. You know as much as I do. And Jacinta…" His face was serious.

"Yes?"

He grinned. "We also found kangaroo bones."

30

When the two little, round faces appeared in the downstairs window of the flat-roofed, brick two-storey house, Jacinta's heart did a flip, the bottle of Pinot Noir almost slipping from her grip. Trying hard to smile, she lifted her hand, waggling her fingers in a timid wave. The two dark-haired boys continued to stare at her until the taller one, poking out his tongue, pulled the other back from the window. She laughed but it came out more like a snort.

"Ready, then?" asked Brett, taking the bottle of wine from her hands.

"As ready as I'll ever be." Reminiscent of her first date, her stomach had been in knots from the minute Daniel had invited her and Brett to dinner. And like that date, she didn't know what to expect. But unlike that date, she had Brett there for moral support. Taking a deep breath, she took a step forward before looking down at her hands. "Oh shit! I've forgotten the flowers."

"You mean these flowers," Brett said, tilting his head at the large bunch of brightly colored gerberas nestling in the crook of his left arm.

She sighed, feeling some of the tension ease from her body. "Thanks, Brett," she whispered as she took the flowers from him. "What would I do without you?"

Giving her an encouraging smile, he opened the low iron gate and waved her through. Before she had a chance to change her mind, the Lassiter family's front door opened. Daniel's broad frame filled the narrow doorway, the two faces from the window now peeking out from behind his jean-clad legs.

Jacinta swallowed hard and took a step and then another. Feeling like she was wearing boots of concrete, she made her way up the short path to the house. As Daniel stepped forward, she thrust the bunch of flowers at him, warding off any physical contact.

Brett frowned and then, with a sidelong glance at Jacinta, extended his hand to Daniel. "Brett Rhodes."

She had forgotten that even though Brett and Daniel knew of each other, they had never actually met. Mortified by her lapse in etiquette, she interjected with a hasty introduction.

Then it was Daniel's turn. "This," he said, planting his free hand on top of the older boy's head, "is Flynn, and this young rascal," he stepped sideways, twisting to reveal the toddler clinging to his leg, "is Liam."

Jacinta guessed Flynn's age at around four or five years old, with Liam twelve to eighteen months younger. Both boys had inherited their father's wide mouth and wavy dark hair, but Flynn's deep brown eyes were in stark contrast to the startling blue of his younger brother's. Daniel's broad grin and the way his face softened when he looked at his sons revealed one proud father.

"Come through. Wendy's in the kitchen, putting the finishing touches to the salad, and then it's over to me."

Jacinta's eyes widened. She hadn't imagined her stepbrother would cook. His father certainly never had.

"I'm no gourmet chef," Daniel said, laughing at her expression, "but I can burn sausages on the barbie with the best of them."

As they followed him through the air-conditioned house, Jacinta unconsciously looked for clues to the sort of man he had become. The sparsely but elegantly furnished formal lounge room at the front of the house had an empty feeling to it, as if merely for show. The real home lay beyond.

Daniel led them toward the back of the house in the direction in which the boys had scampered. Over the light jazz playing in the background, she heard the rat-a-tat-tat of a knife against board. The chopping paused, the soft tones of a woman's voice mingling with little boy laughs and squeals.

An entire wall in the expansive open-plan living area had been devoted to framed family photographs and collages of crayon and paint artworks. Under a window, the artists busied themselves, emptying a massive wooden box crammed with every toy imaginable.

Wendy Lassiter, her glossy auburn hair loosely tied back from her face, joined them just as a tug of war with a miniature red plastic guitar looked to be developing. She stepped in, rescuing the toy from imminent destruction and, with a grin as broad as her husband's, turned to Jacinta. "I'm so pleased you could make it. Isn't it wonderful that you and Daniel have found each other again after all this time?"

Jacinta stretched her mouth into what she hoped was a convincing smile and murmured something about a small world. Even though she had no reason to do so, she felt ill at ease. She looked to Brett for back-up, but he and Daniel were already deep in conversation about football.

Wendy's warm fingers grazed the back of Jacinta's hand. "It's okay, I know how hard this must be for you," she whispered, her voice soft and caressing. "Drinks time, I think."

Accepting a chilled glass of white wine, Jacinta placed another mental tick next to Daniel's name. Not only did he have a family that so obviously adored him, he also didn't keep secrets from his wife. She leaned against the bench, sipping the wine, and watched as Wendy squeezed oranges. Unless she had been told, Jacinta would have never realized Wendy was pregnant, her loose white linen shirt and short denim skirt covering the slight swelling.

Wendy's bump brought Narelle to mind. How was she coping? How had she and Craig taken the news that the human remains weren't Kirsty's? Not wanting to crowd her, Jacinta had left it up to Narelle to contact her. However, with no word in two days, Jacinta decided the time limit on her good intentions was up. Phone call or no phone call, she intended visiting her the next day.

As Wendy poured the freshly squeezed orange juice into one glass and two plastic tumblers, two pairs of small hands appeared out of nowhere from below the kitchen bench, spiriting away the tumblers on offer.

With cold beers in hand and ensconced in two large Aztec-patterned armchairs near the toy box, Brett and Daniel's animated discussion continued unabated. Another tick? Brett certainly seemed to be getting on with Daniel. Leaving them to it, Jacinta followed Wendy outside to the rear brick-paved courtyard.

Under the vine-covered pergola, sipping her wine and soaking in the late summer balminess, Jacinta soon found her guard relaxing. Wendy did most of the talking, her passion for both her job as a legal aid solicitor and her family evident. Making no mention of the past, she asked open-ended questions, allowing Jacinta to reveal as little or as much as she cared to.

Daniel announced his arrival as, balancing a large square earthenware dish piled high with raw meat and sliced onion rings in one hand and a beer in the other, he pushed through the swing door from the kitchen. 'Help Wanted' declared the big, bold, white letters splashed across the front of his long, blue apron. Jacinta couldn't help smiling. If the crew tagging along behind him — consisting of Flynn carrying a pair of tongs, Liam with a plastic spoon, and Brett with a six-pack of beer — was anything to go by, he needed more than help.

The wine, together with the warm evening air, on top of her pent-up stress, soon went to Jacinta's head. By the time dinner was nearly ready, she felt flushed and decidedly tiddly. Excusing herself, she went in search of the bathroom.

Vowing to switch to water, she sat down on the toilet and closed her eyes. She savored the chilled air-conditioned air and took long, slow breaths. She heard footsteps, Daniel's voice and then a door closing. Instinctively, she pressed her ear up against the wall, clearly hearing her stepbrother's side of a phone conversation.

"Are you sure?"

Pause.

"Yes, well, that's not enough. We need to be 110 percent sure on this one. Pull all the old case notes and check his statements again. Look for anything that might link him to these murders, but I don't want him alerted. Not yet."

A longer pause.

"So ballistics are confident that the two bullets recovered could lead to the identity of the weapon used?"

Another pause.

"Okay. Keep me updated."

Jacinta held her breath, waiting until she could no longer hear footsteps before opening the door, and walking straight into Daniel. She averted her gaze, her face flushing as she tried to dodge him.

He caught her by the shoulders, holding her at arm's length. "Once a journalist, always a journalist?"

"It's not like that," she said, shaking her head. "I was already in the bathroom, and the walls are so thin…"

Daniel sighed and dropped his hands from her shoulders. "You're right. I'd forgotten you had come inside when I got the call.

However—" he took a breath, "what you overheard is highly confidential and can't leave these four walls. Do you understand that?"

Jacinta nodded, even though since no names had been mentioned, she wasn't entirely sure who or what the conversation had been about. She still hadn't processed everything Daniel had been saying on the phone.

Bullets.

Old case notes.

Statements.

Murders – plural…

Her heart skipped a beat. "You were talking about Craig Edmonds, weren't you?"

With his hand covering his mouth, he scrutinized her face, as if searching for a way into her mind.

"You've already sworn me to secrecy. Would you rather I speculate?"

Daniel lowered his hand. "Is that something they teach journalists, or does it come naturally?"

"If you don't tell me what's going on, what am I supposed to think? You haven't denied it was Craig you were talking about…" She left the words hanging.

"You don't want to get mixed up in this, Jacinta. Personal feelings can't come into it. Until we've completed our investigations, I strongly suggest you keep your distance from the Edmondses."

She straightened her back, her stance defiant. "Not unless you can give me a damned good reason. I'm certainly not going to abandon my friend just on your say-so."

One eyebrow arched. "I admire your loyalty, but you're just going to have to take my word for it."

"What if I were to tell you that Kirsty Edmonds had a lover?"

"More motive."

"What?"

"Jealousy." Lowering his voice, he caught her by the arm, steering her from the hall into an immaculate book-lined study. "Anyway, who is this lover you're talking about, and where did you get your information?" he said, releasing her and closing the door.

"From the horse's mouth," she said, only answering the second half of his question. Sometimes information had to be bartered.

With a low groan, Daniel plonked down onto the black leather swivel chair behind the polished mahogany desk. "I'm not the enemy, you know. Surely you want to see the killer – or killers – brought to justice as much as I do."

"You're starting to sound like Grace."

"Grace who?"

"Grace Kevron, Kirsty's lover."

He stood up. "Okay, out with it. Tell me everything, and I mean everything, and I'll tell you what I can." He paused and added, "Strictly on the condition it goes no further than this room, though."

"You're on," she said, glancing at the door, "but the others must be wondering where we've got to."

With that, there was a light knock on the door and Wendy entered. "Oh, I'm sorry; I hope I haven't interrupted anything. I thought Daniel must've got caught up in that phone call and lost track of time."

Daniel laughed, wrapping an arm around his wife's shoulders. "You know me too well. We're coming right now." Turning his head to Jacinta, he said, "We'll continue this later. Agreed?"

The three of them returned to the courtyard to find Brett on his hands and knees with Flynn astride his back. Liam had hold of his brother's leg, trying to pull him off. In amidst the arms, legs, giggles and giddy-ups, Brett seemed in his element.

Bracing herself for all the baby hints he would inevitably drop in the next week or so, Jacinta reclaimed her seat at the table. The delicious aroma of char-grilled meat and caramelized onions wafted out from under the sheet of aluminum foil covering the large serving platter at the end of the table. A glass bowl overflowing with crisp green mesclun leaves and cherry tomatoes took centre stage.

While Wendy busied herself cutting sausages into small, manageable pieces for the boys, Daniel served the adults, heaping enough meat onto each plate to make Jacinta think she was at a carnivore's party. After that, with everyone more intent on eating than talking, conversation became rather limited.

Jacinta had a mouthful of steak when Daniel's mobile phone buzzed, breaking the rhythmic clank of metal cutlery against plates. She stopped chewing, looking up as Daniel scraped his chair back, excused himself and went inside.

"You get used to it," Wendy said, with a forced laugh. "Off-duty is not in Daniel's vocabulary. Anyone for a top-up?"

Two phone calls in less than an hour. Jacinta swallowed, absent-mindedly slicing a cherry tomato into tiny eighths as she wondered what the new developments in the Toolangi State Forest case might be. Craig Edmonds had to be involved somehow. Why else had Daniel warned her off? She felt the blood drain from her face as an image of Narelle's trusting face flashed through her mind.

A well-placed kick under the table from Brett to her shin brought her abruptly back to the present. Wendy was talking, but Jacinta caught only the tail end.

"...start Monday?"

Jacinta smiled and nodded, hoping it was the appropriate response to whatever the question had been. Stuffing a forkful of rocket leaves into her mouth circumvented any obligation to elaborate. But she needn't have worried. A frustrated yowl from a restless Liam trying to wriggle out of his chair demanded all of Wendy's attention.

Across the table, Brett lowered and raised his eyebrows, making faces at her.

"What?" she mouthed back, her eyes widening in feigned innocence.

Shaking his head, he rolled his eyes and picked up the opened bottle of Pinot Noir, topping up the wine glasses before meeting her gaze again. She pursed her lips, sending him an air kiss. The corners of his mouth twitched before lifting in a slow grin.

"Sorry about that," announced Daniel, the kitchen door slamming shut behind him. "That should be it for the night," he continued, glancing at his cold, half-eaten meal as he crouched down to see the picture book Flynn wanted to show him.

Wendy intervened, enlisting Brett's aid to read a bedtime story to the two boys as she hustled them away from the table. Jacinta knew it was Wendy's way of making sure stepsister and stepbrother spent personal time together. Right then, though, Jacinta was more interested in Daniel's work than their relationship.

Daniel ate. She talked, telling him everything she knew about Grace Kevron, starting from what she had picked up in the trial transcript, to Grace's over-the-top reaction to Craig and Narelle's marriage, to her demented phone calls, to her unannounced visit when she claimed she and Kirsty had been lovers, and finally to Grace's presence at the crime scene.

When she had finished, she sat back in her chair. Daniel continued forking cold sausage and steak into his mouth, saying nothing for a while. Eventually, he laid his knife and fork down together on the plate and pushed it aside.

He propped his elbows on the table and crossed his arms. "What were you thinking, leaving it until now to tell me?" He didn't wait for an answer. "I don't have to tell you that the police don't look favorably on people who withhold vital information."

He silenced her unvoiced objections with a raised finger.

"What's done is done, but for God's sake, remember we're talking life and death here, Jacinta. It's not a bloody game." He sighed. "And while it may be nothing, it could also mean the difference between a killer being caught and a killer getting away with it." *Again*, his half-closed eyes added silently.

"Look, I understand where you're coming from, but you have to see it from my point of view, too. Initially, I was just following up on an old missing person's story. The trial transcript led me to Grace, but after I met her, I didn't know what to believe. She's not exactly all there. I didn't want to be accused of wasting police time."

Whether Daniel believed her motives or not didn't matter. She had fulfilled her side of the bargain.

31

Jacinta ran her fingers through her hair, tugging at the roots. Daniel, she discovered, had the art of saying a lot without revealing much of anything down pat. "I'm confused. You're telling me that DNA tests showed the remains weren't Kirsty Edmonds; that no firearms are, or have ever been registered, to Craig Edmonds; and that in fact you have nothing linking the Toolangi bodies with him. Yet you're rechecking all the old Edmonds case notes."

"We have to explore every avenue. I'm sure you've heard the old line about everyone being a suspect until they can be ruled out."

Exactly, she thought, *an old line*. "But you haven't told me a damned thing I didn't already know."

"I wish I had more, but," he paused, presenting his palms in an open shrug, "I can't tell you what I don't know."

Fed up with talking in circles, she tried another tack. "Let's say – only hypothetically speaking, mind you – that Craig Edmonds is a serious suspect in these killings. Shouldn't you be doing something to protect his wife? She's pregnant, for God's sake!"

His eyes narrowed into tiny slits, logging the news of Narelle's pregnancy. "Hypothetically speaking, we would probably keep both of them under surveillance. She's survived all these years without incident, so we wouldn't be unduly concerned, unless something was to happen where we thought she," he paused for effect, stressing the next word, "*and* her unborn child might be at risk."

"What could happen?"

He shook his head, pouting his lips. "Nothing or anything."

Jacinta glared at him, fighting the urge to reach out, grab him by the ears and shake his head until something fell out.

The doorbell saved Daniel, giving him a temporary reprieve. Still refusing to admit defeat, she trailed a few paces behind as he opened the door to DS Renee White.

"You weren't answering your phone." Daniel patted his pockets as the DS continued. "Craig Edmonds is threatening to jump from the top of that multi-storey car park in—"

Daniel stepped outside and pulled the door behind him, leaving less than a one-centimeter gap. Despite that and the detectives' hushed tones, by edging closer to the door, Jacinta heard nearly everything they said.

"Somehow the media found out about that credit card we found, put two and two together, and confronted Craig Edmonds at work."

Daniel cursed.

"The news seems to have sent him over the edge. He's that drunk he can barely stand. There's a team there now, trying to talk some sense into him. His wife is being picked up as we speak," said DS White.

Jacinta's breath caught in her throat, her exasperation with Daniel lost in her immediate concern for Narelle. Alternatively gnawing her bottom lip and running her fingernails back and forth across her top teeth, she racked her brain, trying to think what she should do.

"Give me a minute," said Daniel, shoving the door open and only just missing her nose.

She lunged to the side, mirroring his movements as he tried to dodge past her. "Take me with you. Narelle needs someone on her side. I can help."

"I don't have time to argue," he said, his arm sweeping her aside. "The DS will have to babysit you."

Renee White, looking less than impressed and muttering under her breath, turned her back to the door.

Brett responded to the news in much the same way. "God, Jacinta, I hope you know what you're doing," he said, a frown wrinkling his forehead. Then, just as suddenly, the worry lines vanished. "I'll come, too."

Much to his chagrin, she rejected his suggestion outright, giving him a quick peck on the cheek and a promise to see him at home. His bottom lip dropped further when she and Daniel joined the sergeant on the front step. Wendy, on the other hand, appeared relatively unfazed at having her husband called away unexpectedly.

Closing darkness shrouded the houses and cars in the street in hazy shadows. She breathed in the dusk-cooled air and scrambled into the backseat of the unmarked police car parked at the curb behind Brett's Chevy. She buckled herself in, wondering how many murderers and rapists had been there before her, and shuddered.

"If I'm going to be of any help, don't you think I should know what's happening?" Sitting behind Daniel, she saw DS White's sidelong glance at her superior, but not his response.

Met with silence, she added, "At least what's supposedly behind Craig Edmonds wanting to jump off a car park building. I have to be able to tell Narelle something."

Stopped at a red light but with both hands still on the steering wheel, the DS angled her body toward Jacinta. "A Visa card, belonging to a 22-year-old missing woman, was recovered today. Unfortunately, someone leaked this to the media and before we knew it, they had cornered Craig Edmonds. For whatever reason, he flipped."

"You can't be talking about Kirsty – Kirsty was older than that — so what relevance does this woman have to Craig?"

With a nod from Daniel, Renee continued. "At the time this woman went missing," she said, pausing as the lights changed and she pulled into the middle of the intersection, "she worked for the same company our Mr Edmonds did."

Tossing a bucket of iced water over her would have had the same effect. She gasped. Her hypothetical question to Daniel earlier had been intended only to provoke a discussion. Even if she accepted the police viewpoint of Craig Edmonds killing his first wife in a drunken rage, it didn't automatically make him a serial killer. *Did it?* She shook her head, no longer sure of anything anymore.

"But what does that prove?" asked Jacinta, recovering her voice.

Daniel uttered something she didn't catch. Without taking her gaze from the road, Renee nodded, the dashboard's pale glow accentuating her profile. "Nothing at this stage, except he knew her."

Sighing, Jacinta slumped back in her seat, her cheek resting against the cool glass of the side window. Outside, light and dark rushed past in a hypnotic blur. She felt as if she had been caught up in a rip, the swirling currents draining her strength.

She only had herself to blame. In spite of Brett's best efforts, the choices had been all hers. And, even if she had wanted to, she had come too far to back out. Narelle had no one else to turn to.

However, it was more than that. In the short time they had known each other, the two women had formed a strong bond. Jacinta couldn't explain it, but Narelle was like the sister she'd never had. Perhaps part of it was because they were both de facto orphans: Narelle disowned by her parents and she with a dead mother and an unknown and nameless father.

32

Emergency services had blocked off the street. Red and blue flashing lights cast a sterile strobe effect over the scene, highlighting the two uniformed police officers diverting traffic down the side street.

Inside the cordon, all eyes pointed skyward. Daniel leapt from the car the instant it came to a standstill, disappearing into the light-sliced multi-level concrete car park within seconds. Unbuckling her seatbelt, DS White gave Jacinta strict instructions to stay in the car, and then followed her boss in.

Jacinta crooked her neck, looking up, but the angle from her position in the backseat was all wrong. She shuffled across the seat and looked out that window. Nothing much appeared to be happening at street level. Two fire fighters with folded arms stood nearby, talking and occasionally glancing up. A paramedic busied himself in the back of an ambulance. And, on the far side of the street, police officers and civilians, all with their necks craned upward, stood around in clusters.

She tried the car door, relieved to find she hadn't been locked in. Disregarding Renee's orders to stay put, she clambered out, scanning faces and vehicles as she closed the car door behind her. Narelle either hadn't arrived or was already up top with the negotiating team. *Whatever*, thought Jacinta, *I'm no use stuck in the back of a police car.*

She made it as far as the ticket booth before being challenged by a thick-necked constable. "I'm sorry, miss, authorized personnel only."

"I'm with Detective Inspector Lassiter," she said, her hope of bluffing her way past fizzling when he asked for her name. "Please tell him—"

"Jacinta? Is that you?" said a small voice from behind her.

She spun around. Flanked by two burly police officers, Narelle appeared tiny and fragile.

"Thank goodness, you're here."

Narelle's eyebrows drew together. "But what are you doing here?"

The question surprised Jacinta until she remembered that Narelle didn't know about Daniel. She hadn't intentionally kept it from her friend, but with all Narelle's dramas, the right opportunity just hadn't come up. Jacinta extended her hand, suddenly realizing what it must look like.

Narelle shied back, her face contorting in confusion.

"Let me explain. Please. No, wait," Jacinta called out as Narelle's minders guided her toward the lift. "I'm only here as your friend. I only found out recently that my stepbrother, who I haven't seen in years, is a policeman. Brett and I were having dinner with him and his family when he got the call. If you don't believe me, ask..."

The lift doors closed, leaving Jacinta no alternative but to wait and pray. Even if she had been able to convince Narelle of her intentions, the car park's top level had to stay out of bounds. In his unstable state, the last person Craig needed to see was Jacinta, the woman he blamed for his woes.

33

Detective Inspector Daniel Lassiter removed his reading glasses and rubbed his eyes. Dental records had identified the human remains first suspected to be those of Kirsty Edmonds as those of 22-year-old Tamara Whitfield, a securities clerk who had been employed by Siegel Stockbrokers. According to the missing person's report, all employees, past and present, had been questioned at the time of her disappearance. At that stage, there had been no suggestion that Craig Edmonds was anything more than a colleague.

Of course, thought Daniel, leaning back in his chair and clasping his hands behind his head, *it could all be a coincidence*. Sighing, he dropped his hands and returned to scouring the case files on his desk for anything, no matter how insignificant, that might have been overlooked the first time around. He distrusted coincidences.

Expanding the search area in the Toolangi State Forest had yet to yield any new clues or evidence. A dental practice fire in 1995 had destroyed Kirsty Edmonds' dental records, so until DNA testing either proved or disproved that the second body was hers, he had little to go on. In the meantime, DC Mark Fratta had been delegated the unenviable task of searching through the multitude of missing person's reports for other possible matches.

Regardless of the outcome, Daniel felt sure the disappearance of Kirsty Edmonds and the discovery of the human remains in the forest had to be linked. Tamara Whitfield had been reported missing in November 1994, Kirsty Edmonds 14 months later. The gold and sapphire cross recovered matched the description Narelle Croswell had provided of the one her sister always wore, even if she denied it was the same one. Craig Edmonds had worked with one woman and been married to the other. Then there was Grace Kevron, Kirsty's best friend and, if she was to be believed, lover. What had she been doing at the Toolangi site?

Detective Sergeant Renee White appeared in his doorway. Her expression told him she didn't have the answers he was looking for.

"Grace Kevron is proving rather elusive. She hasn't been at work since she called in sick a week ago, and if she's at home, she's not answering the door or her phone. None of her neighbors recall seeing her since last Thursday."

"Stick with it; she has to come up for air sometime." Daniel pushed his chair back from the desk and stood up. "Any news from the hospital about when we can talk to Craig Edmonds?" he asked, placing his hands on the small of his back and arching his spine.

DS White shook her head. "No, they're allowing his wife to see him, but that's all." She gave a small smile. "I guess they're trying to protect him from any undue stress."

Daniel raised his eyebrows. Craig Edmonds' drunken suicide threats had landed him in The Alfred's psychiatry department, and out of the clutches of the detectives. What had driven him to the point of wanting to end it all? What was he running away from? Had guilt finally caught up with him? Had a decade of protesting his innocence come to naught? Had he seen death as a better alternative to a lifetime in jail? All questions that would have to wait.

Renee continued. "Grace Kevron has gone AWOL, we're not allowed access to Craig Edmonds, so for now that only leaves us with Narelle Croswell. What harm can it do to talk to her?"

"No, it's too risky. Whatever we said to Narelle would go straight back to her husband. I don't want him forewarned. Let's focus on what we do have," he said, dropping into one of the black vinyl-upholstered visitor chairs in front of his desk while motioning Renee to the other. "Talk to the forensic anthropologist again. If nothing else, by now she should be able to give us some indication to the age of the skeleton. While you're there, check with ballistics and find out what progress they've made with those two bullets."

"I'll give them a call now." Renee stood and moved toward the door.

"No, go in person. They'll be less likely to fob you off that way."

Daniel stayed seated in the visitor chair, staring blankly at the cream wall behind his desk. He had a difficult decision to make. Jeopardize what was already a fragile relationship with his stepsister, or lose the perfect opportunity provided by a ready-made Trojan horse?

34

Jacinta Deller flicked another page over, looking up as the tram pulled to a stop. Three people got off: a wizened, wispy-haired man with a walking stick; a pink-haired youth in black Doc Marten boots; and a long-limbed, ebony-skinned man in his mid to late twenties. Sighing, she returned to her magazine, reading but not absorbing the words.

From her seat at the weathered picnic table in Fawkner Park, she was able to watch the comings and goings over the road at The Alfred without appearing too conspicuous, but she had already been there three hours. Shuffling on the hard wooden bench, her backside numb from sitting in one place for too long, she hoped she hadn't missed Narelle's arrival.

Narelle had been avoiding her all week, not returning her phone calls and refusing to answer the door. All Jacinta wanted was a chance to explain, but skulking about outside the hospital made her feel like a stalker lying in wait for her victim.

Then she spotted her leaving a footpath at the Punt Road end of the hospital. Jacinta jumped to her feet, shoving her magazine and empty water bottle into her canvas knapsack as she strode toward the pedestrian crossing.

Walking head down, Narelle didn't see Jacinta until she was directly in front of her.

"Leave me alone!" Tears welled in Narelle's eyes. "Stay out of my life!"

"Please, Narelle, give me a chance to explain. I haven't done anything wrong, I swear. You're my friend and I want to help."

"Some friend. Who needs enemies?" Narelle's face crumpled.

Jacinta moved in, wrapping her arm around the forlorn woman's shoulders, and gently drew her toward the edge of the footpath. Narelle buried her face in her cupped hands, fighting the convulsive sobs racking her body, her elbows pulled in tight against her chest.

Using the front of her thigh as support, Jacinta rummaged one-handed through her knapsack, feeling for the soft plastic pack of tissues she kept there. Only when Narelle's tears had weakened to a snivel did she accept the offered clutch of tissues. Keeping her red, puffy eyes downcast, she mopped her tearstained face and palms.

"I don't know what's wrong with me," Narelle said, her voice raspy from crying. "I can't stop bawling."

It didn't take a lot of guesswork to know what was wrong with Narelle. Her husband was in psychiatric care after trying to kill himself. DNA tests had yet to identify or otherwise the second lot of skeletal remains as her sister. She feared the impact the outcome might have on her life, her husband's life and their unborn child's life. Pregnancy hormones ran rampant through her body. She also thought the person she called a friend had betrayed her.

"Well, it's really no wonder, is it?" Jacinta said.

Sniffling, Narelle scanned the area around her, managing to avoid any eye contact with Jacinta.

"What are you looking for?"

Narelle's bottom lip quivered and Jacinta feared she was about to start crying again.

"Let me buy you a cup of coffee. Come on, there's a café just inside the main entrance."

Breathing in ragged gulps, Narelle's flickering eyes scanned the area again, paying particular attention to the line of parked cars across the road. Jacinta's frown deepened. *What or who is she looking for?*

Keen to escape the searing midday sun, she took two paces toward the hospital's concrete steps. "It'll be cooler in there, too." She kept walking, glancing back with each step.

Hugging her abdomen, Narelle kept her head bowed, remaining motionless until Jacinta had reached the top of the first section of steps. Using the handrail, Narelle began to half-pull, half-walk her way up the steps. Jacinta hunted through her knapsack, pretending to look for something, knowing any attempt to help would be rebuffed.

Neither woman spoke as, leaving the glare and heat of outside, they entered the hospital. Jacinta blinked, her eyes adjusting to the artificial lighting. She shivered, the sudden change in temperature raising goosebumps on her arms.

Narelle lagged half a step behind as they crossed the polished floor of the main foyer. The muffled echoes of footsteps, intermingled with low, solemn voices, reminded Jacinta of a church. As Jacinta and Narelle neared the café, the voices became more upbeat, the tone less somber.

Without warning, Narelle darted off to the right, disappearing through a door at the end of a short but narrow corridor. Jacinta saw the sign a moment later and breathed a sigh of relief. Narelle wasn't the only one who needed a toilet.

After washing her hands, Jacinta waited out by the café. When Narelle didn't appear, she began to think that Narelle had either come out before her or had been sucked down the toilet. Following the low partition separating the café from the walkway, Jacinta checked out the people queuing to be served and the others seated at tables. Unable to see Narelle among the hospital visitors, medical staff and even the odd pajama-clad patient, she turned back, her pace quickening when she saw Narelle looking lost outside the entrance to the toilets.

Jacinta joined the queue behind the espresso machine, watching as Narelle made her way through the maze of tables and chairs to a vacant table for two against the far wall. A few minutes later, she joined Narelle, balancing a cup of steaming herbal tea and a cellophane-wrapped muffin in one hand, with a long black and another muffin in the other.

"Phew," she said, setting the hot drinks and muffins on the table. "I made it. I thought for sure one of those hunky young doctors was going to wear this lot." She chuckled, but her attempt at levity failed to raise even a hint of a smile from Narelle.

Jacinta slid her knapsack from her shoulder, dumping it on the floor beside her chair, and sat down. "How's Craig?" she asked, her voice as soft and unthreatening as she could make it.

Narelle looked up. A touch of color had returned to her cheeks, but her brown eyes still lacked luster. "Why are you hounding me, Jacinta? I don't appreciate being followed day and night, and I especially resent you breaking into my house while I'm not there and going through my things."

"What are you talking about? I admit I've left a few phone messages and knocked on your door, but I would never, ever break into your house, let alone rifle through your personal belongings. If you remember, I started a new job this week. And when I wasn't working, I was with Brett. How could I have done what you're accusing me of?"

Confusion flashed across Narelle's face. "How did you know where to find me today if you weren't following me, then?"

"Purely a calculated guess. Craig is in hospital, you're his wife — who else but a wife would be expected to visit every day? If I'd been following you, I certainly wouldn't have sat out in that damned heat for three hours, waiting for you to show up." She paused, taking a breath. "I apologize if my methods seem a little underhand, but I couldn't see any other way. Please just let me explain and then, if you still feel the same way, I promise I won't try to contact you again."

Narelle still looked unconvinced. "If it's not you, who is it? It doesn't make sense."

Mid-shrug, Jacinta froze, her shoulders up around her ears. Did the police have Narelle under surveillance? Daniel had intimated that as much would happen if Craig Edmonds became a serious suspect in the Toolangi murders.

"What is it? What do you know that you're not telling me?"

Jacinta shook her head, her shoulders dropping. "First, was anything taken?"

"Not that I know of. Why?"

"Any idea what they were looking for?"

"No." Narelle's jaw tightened. "Where is this going?"

"I just thought that if we knew what they were after, it might give us a clue to who's following you and why," Jacinta said, determined to keep her suspicions about it being the police to herself until she knew more.

Narelle stared into her untouched tea, her fingers absent-mindedly flicking the crimped edge of her muffin's cellophane wrap. Seconds ticked by.

Jacinta resisted the urge to fill the silence, instead stuffing apple and raisin muffin into her mouth. She swallowed and took another bite, washing it down with coffee. When Narelle eventually spoke, it was just one word.

"Explain."

Jacinta choked on a mouthful of muffin. "Pardon?"

"You wanted to explain, so explain."

Her face deadpan and her eyes downcast, Narelle listened intently as Jacinta did her best to recount, without going into too much detail, how the long-lost stepbrother she had hoped she would never see again had suddenly reappeared in her life.

"I hadn't even told Brett I had a stepbrother. So you can imagine running into him like that came as a hell of a shock. I didn't set out to deceive you. I was going to tell you, but you had more than enough of your own to deal with without having my problems lumped on top. I told Daniel you were pregnant only because I was concerned for your welfare. I swear I haven't discussed anything else you've told me with him."

"What does my welfare have to do with the police?"

Buying time, Jacinta nudged her coffee cup aside and leaned forward. "The less stress you have, the less stress your baby has to tolerate," she said, her fingertips edging across the table. "I'm hoping that now the police are aware of your pregnancy, they won't resort to using shock tactics like they did that time you collapsed at your place. You can't escape what's happened, but if there's anything I can do to make it easier for you, I will."

Tears welled in Narelle's eyes. Fighting a losing battle, she jammed the heels of her palms into her eye sockets. After a few deep breaths, she sat upright, batting her cheeks with the backs of her hands. "God, I must look a fright," she said, running a finger under each eye, smudging her mascara further. "Sorry. I'm not normally like this. Really."

Jacinta retrieved the packet of tissues from her knapsack and passed them to Narelle. "Don't apologize. You're holding up better than I would be in your situation."

"Yeah, right," Narelle said, managing a weak smile.

Jacinta grinned. "Yeah!"

For a fleeting moment Narelle's smile strengthened, her eyes brightening. Then her face dropped. "Oh God, if only I could wake up and find this has all been a bad dream." Pausing, she stared off into the distance. "But it isn't, is..." She didn't finish, her chair toppling sideways as she jumped to her feet. "What the hell is she doing here?"

Jacinta swiveled her head in the direction of Narelle's gaze. None of the faces of the people walking past the café looked familiar. "Who?"

"Grace Kevron, the bitch!"

Jacinta stood up, turned and stepped away from the table, hoping for a better vantage point. At one of the ATMs near the toilets, a tall woman with straight black hair slipped her wallet into her handbag and walked away. From the back, she could easily have been mistaken for Grace. "Are you sure?"

With a weary shake of her head, Narelle bent down to pick up her fallen chair, setting it upright again. "Next I'll be hearing voices," she muttered under her breath. Sitting back down at the table, she swigged her now cold herbal tea as if it were medicine, screwing up her nose in distaste as it went down.

She then opened her muffin, picking the raisins from it and placing them on her saucer but not actually eating anything. Sitting down opposite, Jacinta bided her time, folding the cellophane wrapping from her muffin into tight eighths before releasing it to spring open again.

The show over, the volume of conversation around them soon picked up. Cups clanked. Chair legs scraped against the floor. Although they were no longer the centre of attention, Jacinta would rather have left their audience behind altogether. She glanced at Narelle, but she seemed lost in her own little world, the dissection of her muffin her only concern.

Jacinta gathered up her knapsack, pushed in her chair and stepped over to the other side of the table. "Come on, let's get you home."

Blinking rapidly, Narelle looked up, her mouth forming silent words. She hesitated for a second before standing, but once on her feet, moved decisively toward the exit. However, her sudden burst of energy proved short-lived, lasting not much further than the hospital's main doors.

By the time they reached the car park, Jacinta felt in need of a reviving cold shower. Narelle, too, looked ready to drop as she trudged the last few steps to Jacinta's car.

Whether it was the more comfortable seating, the air-conditioning, the absence of eavesdroppers, or something else altogether, Narelle started opening up within minutes of being in the car.

"Jacinta." She paused. "I'm sorry. I should never have accused you of following me or breaking into my house. I don't know what I was thinking. Of course I should've realized Grace Kevron would be the only one warped enough to do that sort of thing."

"Grace? You really think it could be her?" Daniel's comments had led Jacinta to believe the police were the likely culprits. But then again, she had learned enough about Grace not to put anything past her.

"Who else could it be? She's had it in for Craig and me right from the start. She's crazy."

"Crazy enough to be dangerous? You should be talking to the police about this. They can protect you."

Narelle snorted.

"I'm serious. I think you should stay with me, at least until Craig comes home."

"Thanks for the offer, but I refuse to let that woman drive me away from my own home. Don't worry about me. I've organized for security cameras to be installed right around the house, so if she tries to break in again, she'll be caught in the act," Narelle said, the slight quaver in her voice undermining her brave words. "If all else fails, there's Craig's gun – if I can find it."

Jacinta's heart skipped a beat. "A gun?" According to Daniel, Craig Edmonds had never had any firearms registered under his name.

"Don't panic, I would only use it to scare her off. It's old. It used to belong to his father. I don't even know if there are any bullets for it."

Jacinta's grip tightened on the steering wheel. Loaded or unloaded, old or new, guns were guns. But right then, her deep-seated aversion for anything capable of killing at the touch of a finger wasn't her primary concern. One minute Narelle had been accusing her of betraying her, and the next she was confessing her husband owned a gun. Something didn't add up.

Wanting to gauge Narelle's reaction, Jacinta waited until they were stopped at a traffic light to pose her next question. "You do realize the two women found in the Toolangi State Forest were shot, don't you?"

Narelle's jaw dropped. "What are you saying?"

"I'm not saying anything, I'm just asking."

"Well, if you're implying Craig is somehow involved, you're crazier than Grace Kevron," retorted Narelle, her voice loud and indignant.

"Please, I didn't mean to upset you," said Jacinta, pulling into the Edmonds driveway.

Before she could turn off the ignition, Narelle had jumped from the car. "Thanks for the lift." The car door slammed on her clipped words.

Watching Narelle as she bolted across the lawn toward the front door, Jacinta couldn't shake the uneasy feeling Narelle was testing her allegiance. What was she supposed to do with the information about the gun? Go to the police and betray a confidence? Or pretend the conversation had never happened and do nothing? Did the gun even exist?

35

Narelle Croswell leaned against the door and breathed out, her body sagging as she heard Jacinta's car reverse down the driveway to the street and then accelerate away. The heavy stillness inside the house engulfed her, accentuating her own emptiness. She had never felt so alone.

Nor had she ever felt so exhausted. Every muscle in her body ached. Somehow, she mustered the strength to push herself away from the door and shuffle zombie-like to the bedroom. She flopped down on the unmade bed, kicked off her shoes and fell backwards, sighing as her head hit the soft pillow. She crossed her lower arms over her eyes, too tired to get up again to close the curtains.

Past the point of sleep, she lay there, her mind a jumble of erratic thoughts. Nothing was going according to plan, and feeling sorry for herself wasn't working. She had to stay strong. She needed someone to blame.

Her breathing quickened as anger displaced self-pity. Anger at her family for abandoning her. Anger at Craig for not being there to protect her. Anger at Jacinta for being too nice. Anger at herself for believing in a real future. She knew it had all been too good to be true.

She rolled onto her side, tucking the pillow under her chin, and stared at the wall. Listening to the low hum of the air-conditioner, she concentrated on slowing her breathing, and counted back from one hundred.

...ninety-five...ninety-four...ninety-three...

She froze, her breath catching in her throat. Had she imagined it? Was someone in the house? Her ears straining to pick up every sound, she heard only the hammering of her own heart. Sliding from the bed, she crept toward the doorway into the hall, stopping just shy of the threshold.

Staying close to the wall, she edged forward, all her senses heightened. A faint grumbling sound from the direction of the kitchen sent her pulse skyrocketing. Paralyzed by fear, she stood stock still, one hand touching the wall, the other suspended in mid-air.

Recognition finally kicked in. She sank to the floor, a half-laugh, half-scream erupting from her throat. If the fridge switching on was enough to freak her out, how would she react in the face of real danger? She had to take back control. The fetus growing inside her depended on it.

Forcing herself to take slow, controlled breaths helped. Her heartbeats steadied as the adrenaline dissipated. She felt stronger.

Getting up, she took two steps, stopped and then, before she could give it any more thought, marched straight down the hall. Trying to fool herself into believing she wasn't in the least nervous, she kept her eyes forward, focusing on reaching the kitchen.

Once there, she pulled the blinds. Crouching down in front of the dishwasher, she removed its plastic kickboard. Then, lying on her back on the hard, tiled floor, she reached into the dark cavity. With her shoulder wedged against the square edge of the dishwasher, she strained to feel for the box. Nothing. She grunted in frustration and tried again, almost dislocating her shoulder in the process. Her fingertips grazed tin. Satisfied it was still there, she withdrew her arm.

In the garage she found a pair of long-handled barbecue tongs. Coming back through the door, she glanced across the kitchen bench to the meals area, deciding as an added precaution to draw all the curtains.

Returning in the semi-darkness to the kitchen, she resumed her position on the floor and, using the tongs, reached under the dishwasher to the back corner.

After a couple of attempts, she succeeded in hooking the end of the box and dragging it out onto the tiles. Wiping sweat and grit from her eyes, she sat up, resting her back against the pot drawers. She stretched her legs straight out in front of her and laid the tarnished metal box on her lap. Brushing the dust from its top, she unsnapped the two clasps and raised the lid.

Taking a deep breath, she peeled back the black oilskin to reveal the .38 Special revolver nestled inside. For a few moments, she just stared at it. Then, struggling to control the tremor in her hand, she touched the gun, her fingertips tracing the cold steel barrel and cylinder down to the diamond-hatched grips. She lifted it out, its weight heavy in her hands.

She had fought all her life for what she had wanted, and she wasn't about to give up.

36

"Daniel!" Jacinta's glass thudded against the wooden chair arm, slopping ice-cold lager over her hand. "What are you doing here?" she demanded as, leaning forward, she deposited the glass on the outdoor table and flicked her fingers.

"Nice to see you, too." He flashed her a disarming smile and, without waiting for an invitation, settled down in one of the chairs on the other side of the table. "Any more where they came from?" he asked, nodding at the two empty cans on the table.

Jacinta frowned. "You could at least have rung the doorbell."

"I did. And I knocked."

At least Daniel's request for a beer meant he wasn't on duty. "Be back in a minute," she said, rousing herself from her chair to go inside to raid Brett's supplies yet again.

She returned, plonking a Foster's Lager and an empty glass on the table in front of Daniel. Beads of condensation ran down the beer can, puddling at the base.

"Thanks," he said, pulling the tab and releasing a hiss of carbonation. "I didn't take you for a beer drinker."

"It's too hot for wine. Anyway, to what do I owe this honor?"

"I was passing." He finished pouring his drink and then raised his glass. "Cheers!"

"No ulterior motive?"

Daniel put his beer down and he drew his chair in closer, the shadow from the market umbrella darkening his features. "Jacinta," he said, his demeanor and tone suddenly more serious, "I need your help."

"With babysitting, you mean?" she asked, knowing full well that wasn't the purpose of his visit.

He blinked and shook his head. "No, but," he said, stumbling over his words, "if you're offering…" Clearing his throat, he clasped his hands together on the table in front of him and started again. "The remains of the second body found in the Toolangi State Forest have been identified." He paused, letting the words sink in. "And it's not Kirsty Edmonds."

Jacinta sat upright. "Has Narelle been told yet?"

"No, and this is where – unofficially, of course – you come in. I think she probably knows a lot more than she's telling us, but is too scared of someone or something to say anything." He opened his hands, revealing his palms. "If she thought you were taking her into your confidences and passing on information from the police, she might then trust you enough to do the same."

Jacinta tensed. "You don't seriously expect me to be your mole?"

"That's not the word I would've used," Daniel said, arching one eyebrow.

"What, then? Spy?"

"I know you think of Narelle Croswell as your friend, but how well do you really know her?"

"Better than I know you, obviously."

"What if she's withholding information that could help put a killer behind bars? Information that could put her own life at risk? Wouldn't you want to help then?"

"Daniel, would you quit talking in riddles and tell me what the hell is going on."

Lowering his voice, he said, "Not that you have nosy neighbors, but perhaps we should continue this inside."

If he was trying to pique her interest, he was succeeding. Hoping it wasn't simply another ploy to get to Narelle through her, Jacinta gathered up her glass of beer and the empty cans. Daniel opened the French door, holding it for her, before following her through to the kitchen.

She dumped her load on the stainless steel draining board and turned to see him checking out the front of the fridge.

"When was this taken?" he asked, pointing with his glass at one of the photos Brett had taken the night of the dinner party.

"A few weeks ago. Does it matter?" she said, putting herself between him and the fridge. The photo he seemed most interested in featured Narelle and Craig, Shauna and Patrick, and herself, all crammed together at one end of the outside table, grinning tipsily at the photographer. She gestured in the direction of the living room. "After you."

Daniel started to say something, but the sound of the front door opening interrupted him.

"Honey, I'm home!" Brett sang out, appearing a moment later with his gym bag slung over his shoulder, his hair damp. "Daniel, hi. Didn't realize you were here." He grinned and stuck his hand out. "How are you, mate?"

Jacinta might as well have been invisible for all the notice Brett took. Without even looking at her, he accepted the beer she handed him and ushered Daniel through to the living room. She took the unexpected opportunity to remove all the photos from the fridge, shoving them face down in the utensil drawer. Then she rejoined the men.

When she sat down on the sofa next to Brett, he placed his hand on her knee, acknowledging her presence but not missing a beat in his conversation with Daniel. She listened idly to their banter, her mind more caught up in what Daniel had been about to tell her before Brett arrived home.

The remains of the two women found in the Toolangi State Forest had been identified and neither was Kirsty Edmonds. All Jacinta knew, other than that, was that both victims had been shot and one of them used to work for the same stockbroking firm as Craig Edmonds. Was the second victim also linked to Craig in some way? What had Daniel been alluding to when he mentioned Narelle's life could be at risk?

Daniel's deep voice broke through her thoughts. She jumped, taking a second to realize Brett wasn't beside her any longer and Daniel was looking at her.

"Sorry," she said, shaking her head, "What did you say?" She wondered where Brett had got to and then heard the toilet flush.

Daniel laughed. "I gather the footy is not your thing. Shame, you don't know what you're missing."

"I'll live," she retorted. "Now, what were you about to tell me earlier?"

"Maybe now isn't the best time," he said, glancing at the doorway and then at his watch.

Maybe not, but Jacinta wasn't about to be thwarted. "Answer me one thing: is the second woman you identified in any way linked with Craig Edmonds?"

Daniel's eyes widened. "What makes you ask?"

"Please, Daniel, just tell me. Is she?"

"Okay then, yes. However, it's only a tenuous connection at this stage. She was the architect employed by the Edmonds when they put the extension on the back of the house."

"This is before Kirsty disappeared?"

"Yes, she was reported missing about six months before Kirsty, but the work she did on the house was a year prior to that."

Jacinta stared open-mouthed at Daniel, her brain manically trying to fit the pieces together.

"Now do you understand why I asked for your help?"

Feeling more flummoxed than ever, she started to shake her head, before halfway through changing it to a nod. "But what I don't understand is why, if Craig Edmonds is securely tucked up in a psych ward, you have Narelle under surveillance."

Daniel scratched the side of his face, his eyebrows lowering as he held her gaze. "We don't. Where did you get that idea from?"

Before she could reply, Brett came back, his hands clamped around another three cans of Foster's.

Daniel took it as his cue. "Thanks, but I'd better not, I'm driving," he said, checking his watch again. "I also promised the boys I would take them to the park," he added, getting to his feet. "Jacinta, think seriously about what I said and call me."

37

"I'll tell you about it in the car." Jacinta snatched her keys from the hook. "Hurry up!"

Leaving the front door open for Brett, she raced for her car. He followed seconds later, his unbuttoned shirt flapping about his chest, the fly in his jeans gaping. Jacinta drove hard, taking corners at speed and throwing Brett around as he endeavored to finish dressing.

"Christ, Jacinta! I want to get there in one piece."

Mumbling an apology, she eased off the accelerator a fraction before the thought of Narelle, frightened and alone with a gun, changed her mind again.

The Nissan Pulsar screeched to a stop in front of the Edmonds house. Jacinta left the car idling as she scanned the driveway and the front of the large brick home. Both garage doors were closed and all the curtains were drawn. As far as she could see in the low light, that was the same situation at every house down the sleeping street. Not even the birds were awake.

If it hadn't been for Narelle's hysterical pre-dawn phone call, she and Brett would still have been tucked up in bed, too. A noise out by the swimming pool had convinced Narelle someone was out to get her, and no amount of reasoning was going to sway her otherwise.

Brett yawned, his hand catching only the end of it. Thinking there would be safety in numbers, she had roped a sleep-dazed Brett into coming with her. Now he sat in the passenger seat next to her, his seatbelt still buckled. She glanced at his shirt, stifling a small chuckle when she realized he had miscalculated by at least one buttonhole.

"What's so funny?"

She pointed at his shirt, peering past him to the house while he unbuttoned and rebuttoned his shirt. *Staying home alone in a place that size would be enough to test anyone's nerves*, thought Jacinta. *Without any added stresses.*

Jacinta unbuckled her seatbelt, turned off the ignition and, with the keys clasped in her hand, got out of the car. Brett followed suit, yawning as he waited for her on the footpath.

"Wakey, wakey."

"Wait." He grabbed her arm. "Do you really think this is a good idea? What if Narelle isn't hearing things? Don't you think it's about time we involved the police?"

"No," she said, shaking his hand off her arm, "I promised her I wouldn't. You know how Narelle feels about the cops, and she already thinks I've betrayed her once. Stay here if you want, but I'm going in."

Without giving herself time to change her mind, she strode toward the Edmonds' front door, anxiety heightening all her senses. Brett caught up with her in the same instant she pressed the doorbell. The resulting strident, metallic peal shattered the dawn stillness, making them both jump.

She pressed her ear up against the door, stepping back when she heard footsteps approaching on the other side. A few seconds later, the door opened slightly, Narelle's pasty face appearing in the gap. With a quick check of the area behind Jacinta and Brett, she ushered them inside and hastily relocked the door.

Barefoot and dressed only in pink love-heart boxers and a white singlet, Narelle seemed unable to stand still. Her dark-circled eyes darted from Jacinta to Brett and back again. Wringing, clenching and unclenching her hands, she headed down the hall toward the lighted kitchen and meals area, her agitation growing with every step.

Brett looked at Jacinta, his bemused expression mirroring the expression she was sure must be on her own face as he hurried after Narelle. Jacinta tried to stall him but her fingers clutched thin air. Then she almost collided with him when, rounding the end of the kitchen counter, he came to an abrupt halt. His eyes boggled, his look changing to one of complete incomprehension, as he stared at the revolver lying in the middle of the round glass table.

Seemingly oblivious to the consternation caused by the presence of the gun, Narelle circled the table, her hands constantly moving.

"Shit, Narelle! I didn't think you were serious." Brett glared at Jacinta as if to say: *You knew about this and you didn't think to tell me?* She ignored him, adding, "I sincerely hope it's not…"

Narelle froze, shushing her with a finger to her lip. "Did you hear that?" she whispered.

Jacinta heard nothing. Looking over her shoulder, she took a cautious step forward. Brett met her glance with a shrug, mouthing words she couldn't decipher as he reached out to pull her back. Breaking free of his grasp, she padded across the room toward Narelle.

"There," said Narelle, her voice a low hiss as she sidled to the end of the drape-drawn windows. "You must have heard that."

Jacinta shook her head, but Narelle was too intent on peeking around the edge of the heavy drape to notice. Brett touched the back of her hand, leaning in close to whisper in her ear. "I don't know what the fuck is going on, Jacinta, but this is way past a joke."

Narelle waved her hand in their direction, motioning them to the window. Crowded together and with every nerve on end, they strained to see through the thin slice of half-light to the shadowy courtyard. At that moment, a bird farting would have been enough to send them all into a screaming heap.

Brett was the first to peel away. "If there was anyone lurking out there before, I'm betting they're long gone by now." He sighed, his hands going to his hips. "For Chrissakes, would someone tell me what the hell this is all about?"

Still gripping the edge of the curtain, Narelle responded with nothing more than a cursory glance in his direction before returning to watching out the window. With an exasperated shrug, he looked to Jacinta.

She pulled him aside, whispering, "I only know part of it and it's complicated. But I think it should come from Narelle. Just give her a minute or two."

Pointing at the table, he made no attempt to keep his voice down. "And the gun? I suppose you didn't know a thing about that either."

Before Jacinta could answer, Narelle snatched up the revolver from the table. "The gun is nobody's business but mine," she said, her forceful tone shocking Jacinta. Narelle clamped the gun to her chest, her narrowed eyes challenging them.

"For Chrissakes, woman, you're going to hurt yourself," Brett said, edging forward with his arm outstretched, "or one of us."

Narelle cackled. "Don't be ridiculous, it's not even loaded. See," she said, waving it above her head, her finger tightening on the trigger.

Jacinta dived for the floor as the blast of the gunshot, amplified by the confines of the house, reverberated above her. Instinctively, her arms came up to shield her head, mashing her face against the hard, tiled floor.

The ensuing silence hung like an icy vapor in the air. Gasping for breath, she turned her head to the side. Brett's unblinking eyes stared back at her, fear written all over his face. Twisting around a bit further, she caught sight of the gun abandoned in the middle of the floor, its muzzle pointing under the table.

Breathing slightly easier, she raised her head and peered around. Narelle sat in a clumsy heap on the floor near the wall, her face wet with tears, gaping at the gun.

Crawling commando-style across the floor, Jacinta closed the gap between herself and the stricken woman. Her hand closed over the gun's grip, the sensation so foreign she immediately wanted to throw it as far away as possible. Instead, she slid it gingerly behind her and out of Narelle's reach.

"Oh dear God, what have I done?" Narelle gave a loud hiccup and dissolved into tears.

Jacinta pushed herself up, scooting the remaining distance on her backside. Narelle's sobs turned to howls as Jacinta wrapped her arms around her distraught friend's shoulders. Out of the corner of her eye, she glimpsed Brett retrieving the gun and offered a silent prayer of thanks.

Leaving her ministering to Narelle, he disappeared, returning a few minutes later minus the gun. She had no idea what he had done with it, but right at that moment she didn't care. Out of sight, out of mind.

Lethargic and subdued, Narelle allowed Jacinta to help her to her feet but kept her eyes averted, picking at invisible bits of lint on her singlet. Jacinta's suggestion that she get some sleep met with a vehement shake of the head.

"I don't want to sleep," she said, the deep hollows under her eyes telling a different story.

"When was the last time you slept?"

Narelle shook her head again as she detoured past Jacinta, then Brett, on her way to the kitchen. "I'm fine."

Casting a disapproving glance at Brett as he threw his hands up in the air, Jacinta followed Narelle. "If you're worried about being on your own, don't be. Brett and I aren't going anywhere."

With a sense of déjà vu, she watched as Narelle busied herself filling the kettle, opening cupboards and drawers, setting out cups and other tea- and coffee-making accoutrements.

"Narelle, you know ignoring it won't solve anything. We have to talk about it. You can't keep going on like this." Jacinta leaned across the counter. "For your baby's sake, if not your own."

Narelle flinched, Jacinta's words hitting home. "I'm that tired, I don't know which way is up," she said, contradicting her previous statement, "but I can't sleep. Every time I close my eyes, I'm afraid something terrible is going to happen."

"That's completely understandable. No one could be expected to cope alone with what you've been through, but that's all the more reason you should talk to someone. It doesn't have to be us, but you do need help."

"What are you saying?" retorted Narelle, her face hardening. "You think I'm imagining things?"

"No, of course not. I don't think anything of the kind." Jacinta paused, suppressing a sigh as she wondered how far from the truth she actually was. "Look, let Brett finish that for you," she added, nodding at the cups on the counter, "and come and sit down."

Relief washed over Brett's face. "Yes, yes," he flapped his hands, shooing them away. "Go and sit down and I'll bring it to you." Clearly, the opportunity to do something, even if it was only making hot drinks, was better than doing nothing.

In Jacinta's mind, sitting around a table would be too confrontational and formal, more like a business meeting. So, taking the lead and hoping Narelle would follow, she headed for the large, sunken living room with its comfortable armchairs and couches.

All the blinds were down. Her pulse quickened as she stepped down onto the wooden floor, her hand groping the wall for a light switch. In the gloom, the silhouettes of the furniture looked anything but inviting. Imagining what could be lurking in the dark corners, she told herself not to be so stupid, wondering if Narelle's paranoia was rubbing off on her.

Narelle hung back, not saying anything. When Jacinta turned to make sure she was still there, she saw Narelle had her knuckles jammed in her mouth. Coming up behind her, with a round tray of steaming cups balanced precariously on one hand at shoulder-height, was Brett.

"Okay, ladies," he announced, his smile as forced as his cheery tone, "where would you like it?"

Having visions of spilt drinks and broken cups, Jacinta went to rescue the tray from the theatrical waiter and in the process, almost did what she was trying to avoid. She recovered without mishap.

"Honey…" She never called him that. "I'll look after this if you open the blinds.

Her little endearment earned her a small smile. "No problemo," he said, skipping down the two steps into the darkened room and walking across to the wall of Roman blinds on the far side. He seemed much happier having something practical to occupy him. Emotional women always left him floundering.

Using both hands, Jacinta carefully carried the tray of hot drinks over to the long, narrow coffee table, and set it down. Behind her, she saw Narelle edging her way around the room, keeping her back to the wall and her gaze transfixed on the unveiling windows. Brett had one blind up and was pulling up the next.

Early morning light spilled into the room, banishing any shadowy fears. Outside, the rising sun's rays bathed everything in a crisp light, the polished aluminum table glinting next to the swimming pool.

Except for a barely perceptible ripple across the swimming pool's surface, nothing moved in the tranquil landscape.

Instead of joining Jacinta on the couch, Narelle opted for one of the large leather armchairs, almost disappearing as she curled up in it, her feet tucked under her. She accepted the proffered cup of the sweetly scented tea, cradling it close to her mouth as she took small, rapid sips, her eyes focused inward.

Jacinta stirred Brett's milky coffee while he finished securing the last blind. The familiar, rich aroma of strong black coffee, as she collected the remaining cup from the tray, brought a touch of the normal back to the situation.

For a while, all three sat cocooned in an awkward silence, sipping their drinks. As Jacinta's gaze swept the room, it suddenly occurred to her they were sitting in the extension designed by the architect whose remains had been discovered in the Toolangi State Forest. She shivered, the fine hairs on the back of her neck standing to attention.

"My whole house would fit in here," she said, keeping her tone light and casual. "It's a fabulous room. Was it part of the original house?"

Narelle rested her cup on the arm of the chair. "No, it's an extension," she said, seizing the chance to talk about something she obviously thought was mundane and everyday. "This was Kirsty's favorite room." She paused. "Mine, too."

Jacinta gazed up at the high cathedral ceiling. "Who was the architect, do you know?" she asked, feeling out how well Narelle knew her, if at all.

"I don't recall her name – I only met her on a couple of occasions – but Craig will know." Narelle laughed. "Craig will definitely remember." She clicked her fingers. "Chandra. She was an absolute stunning-looking Anglo-Indian woman, with huge brown eyes and the most gorgeous long, dark, glossy hair." She looked at Jacinta. "I can ask Craig if you like, but she might not still be in business. A lot can happen in," her eyes rolled up, mentally calculating the years, "eleven or twelve years."

Was Narelle playing with her, or did she really not know about the architect's disappearance? *Surely, though,* thought Jacinta, *when Chandra was first reported missing, the Edmondses would've been interviewed by the police, or at the very least heard about it.* Wary of jumping to conclusions, she steered the conversation to furniture and color schemes. She needed more time to think it through.

Brett's eyes glazed over. Talk about contemporary versus traditional, brights versus pastels, floor and window coverings wasn't his scene. Swallowing the last of his coffee, he collected the other empty cups and carried them on the tray back to the kitchen.

With Brett out of earshot, Jacinta hoped Narelle might be a little less reserved. The real issues had been skirted for long enough.

"Narelle." She paused. "What makes you so sure Grace is the one stalking you, the one breaking into your home? What reason would she have to do that?"

Silence. Narelle studied her fingernails, polishing each in turn with her thumb.

"Could it have anything to do with the affair she had with your sister?" Jacinta said, tossing out the words like a lighted firecracker.

38

"Get your fucking hands off me!"

The detective constable recoiled, rubbing the side of his hand as he stumbled backwards. "Ow! The bitch bit me."

He glared at Margaret Kevron as if it was her fault that her daughter had sunk her teeth into his hand. Margaret flinched, powerless to do anything except watch helplessly as the scene unfolded.

Detective Sergeant White scowled at her younger colleague, shoved him aside and dropped to her knee. "Ms Kevron... Grace," she said, her voice softening, "we're not here to hurt you; we only want to talk with you, but we'd rather you came out of there. Your mum and work colleagues have been very concerned about you."

No longer able to bear the sight of her daughter frightened and cowering amongst the shoes and hanging clothes in the wardrobe, Margaret moved sideways. She wanted to help, wanted to comfort her daughter, but experience told her that when Grace came off her medication, a mother's love wasn't enough.

She'd had no choice but to call the police. When Grace didn't return any of her phone calls, she had become increasingly frantic. She'd managed to get a standby flight from Sydney to Melbourne, arriving by taxi outside Grace's home early that morning. But Grace refused to answer the door, even though Margaret was convinced she heard movement inside.

The sergeant was doing her best to coax Grace out but, like a cornered feral cat, Grace hissed at her, steadfastly refusing to budge. The DS stood up, narrowly missing having her leg caught in the wardrobe door, Grace slamming it so hard it vibrated in its tracks.

"You haven't done anything wrong," continued DS White.

Detective Inspector Lassiter entered the small, colorless bedroom, dispatching the wounded DC with a sharp thrust of the thumb in the direction of the door. Margaret suddenly felt claustrophobic, as if the whiteness of the room was closing in on her. She took a deep breath and waited for the feeling to pass.

"Don't listen to them!" shrieked Grace from her bolthole. "Don't believe them!"

"Who, Grace? Don't believe who?"

"Them! They say things!"

Margaret saw the arched eyebrows and sidelong glance DS White gave DI Lassiter. He responded with a weary shake of the head, but motioned for her to keep talking.

"Grace, listen to me. Your mother is here. Wouldn't you like to see her?"

"Make them stop!"

The DS looked at her DI again, just as the DC appeared in the doorway with what looked to be a packet of some kind in his hand. DI Lassiter put one hand up to stop him entering the room while making circular movements with the other, encouraging DS White to keep talking. Then, signaling for Margaret to follow, DI Lassiter crept from the bedroom into the hall.

Margaret recognized the small, pale purple rectangular box with bold dark purple lettering in the DC's hands as Grace's *Zyprexa* medication. "They're Grace's," she blurted as the DC handed them to his DI. "For her schizophrenia," she added.

DI Lassiter's face remained impassive as he opened the box and slid the unopened foil blister sheets of tablets onto his palm. Margaret knew even before the DI checked the prescription label that Grace hadn't been taking her medication.

"If the date on the label is anything to go by, it would seem that your daughter probably stopped taking her medication at least a fortnight ago."

Margaret nodded.

"Has she done this before?"

Another nod. Margaret stared at the floor, a guilty flush enveloping her neck and face. She was Grace's mother. How could she have allowed this to happen again?

"Get on to CAT," Daniel said to the DC. "Ask them to get someone here pronto. Not here, for God's sake," he added as the DC pulled his mobile phone from his pocket and started dialing. "Use your bloody head."

As the DC slunk off down the hall, DI Lassiter turned to Margaret, his voice warm and compassionate. "Mrs Kevron, Grace's mental state has disintegrated to a point where she needs professional medical help. DC Fratta is calling Crisis Assessment and Treatment services now. They should be here shortly."

Margaret nodded again, tears welling in her eyes, grateful that Grace was getting the help she so desperately needed.

From the bedroom behind her, Margaret could hear DS White's low, calming tones empathizing with Grace, not contradicting her in the least but uttering all the right assurances.

"That Deller bitch!" Grace retorted. "She's as bad as the rest of them."

Deller? Margaret frowned. It wasn't a name she had ever heard Grace mention, but it certainly made the DI's ears prick up. He turned, looking as if he were about to march back into the room, but then had second thoughts. He gave Margaret a weak smile.

Her fingers snagged his wrist. "Who's this Deller woman she's talking about, then?" she whispered. "How does Grace know her? Do you know?" she added, her grip tightening.

In the other room, Grace continued her rant. "They're all going to burn in hell!" She erupted into loud, raucous laughter that suddenly stopped short. "Oh God, make them stop!"

39

Narelle's jaw dropped. She stared at Jacinta as though she was from another planet. "Did I hear you right? Did you say Kirsty had an *affair,*" she screwed up her nose, "with Grace?"

"Didn't you know?"

Narelle shook her head slowly from side to side, her eyes wide in disbelief. "You can't be serious. They were girlfriends, but not in the way you're suggesting. Kirsty was as straight as you and I." The pitch of her voice rose as, uncurling her legs, she leaned forward. "And even if it was true, how would you know about it?"

Behind her, Jacinta heard a sharp intake of breath and then the sound of a CD case clattering on the floor. She felt Brett's gaze boring the same question into the back of her head, but didn't turn around.

"To be honest, Narelle, I don't know if it's true or not, but it's what Grace told me. She said Craig knew all about it, and that Kirsty was leaving him for her."

Narelle chortled, her face relaxing. "That woman is more deluded than I thought. The only place she and my sister were having a lesbian relationship was in her head," she said, tapping her temple with a finger. "And, anyway, if Craig knew all about it, as you say, he would've told me. God, if it had been true, nothing would've been standing in our way."

"According to Grace, Craig wanted both you and Kirsty."

Narelle pressed her lips together, her face turning pink before, unable to contain it any longer, she burst into laughter. "What a joke. Was that the punch line?"

"No, there's more," Jacinta said, deciding to press on while Narelle was in her current mood. "She thinks that the night Kirsty disappeared, Craig and she argued about it…" Her voice trailed off, deliberately leaving the words hanging.

Narelle laughed even louder.

Jacinta glanced behind her. Brett sat on his haunches in front of the Edmonds' extensive CD collection, looking like he had been slapped in the face. She turned back to Narelle.

"If it's not that, what makes you think Grace is the one stalking you?"

Narelle's laughter came to an abrupt halt. Jacinta watched as Narelle's gaze fell back to her hands, her mind working overtime to formulate answers.

"In a funny way, knowing Grace had a crush on my sister makes more sense. We always knew, regardless of what the courts said, that she held both Craig and I responsible for Kirsty's death. But continuing to harass us year after year… well, we could never quite fathom the intensity of her vendetta. Losing a friend can't be in the same league as losing your wife or sister." Pausing, she added, "Can it?" looking to Jacinta for confirmation.

In Jacinta's mind, the strength of the bond between two people didn't depend on a blood or marital connection. How could it? Her own father had disowned her even before she was born. Her mother had then married a man who systematically destroyed her, demeaning her at every opportunity. Despite these feelings, she simply shook her head.

"But that still doesn't explain what she…" Jacinta paused before adding, "…or whoever it was who broke in was looking for."

Narelle threw her hands up in the air. "Who knows how that woman's mind works... Oh my God," she exclaimed suddenly, "what if she was looking for the gun? What if Kirsty rejected her advances?" The blood drained from her face, becoming paler with each what-if. "What if she's the one? What if she decided that if she couldn't have Kirsty, no one else could either? Oh my God, what if the gun is," she stumbled over the next words, "the murder weapon?" She was trembling, her eyes large and round as saucers. "Oh my God, where is it? What have you done with it?"

Not admitting that scenario had crossed her mind more than once, Jacinta opted to play devil's advocate. "But if that's the case, what about the two women victims found in the Toolangi State Forest? Grace has no known connection to them, but Craig has."

"What do you mean, he had *links* to both victims? I know Tamara Whitfield worked for the same stockbrokers as Craig, but they hardly knew each other. Have they identified the other body? Who is it?" The pitch of her voice started to rise again. "What connection does she have to Craig? Tell me," she demanded, gulping air.

Before Jacinta could open her mouth, a resounding crash down the side of the house had all three leaping to their feet.

"Shit! What was that?" Like the two women, Brett stood stock-still, his gaze fixed in the direction from which the noise had come.

An involuntary scream escaped Jacinta's lips as a half-naked man, barefoot and dressed only in jeans, appeared at the sliding glass doors. Without his glasses, it took her a moment to recognize him.

Jacinta's gaze flitted between Narelle on the inside and Craig on the outside, her frown deepening. With each savage rattle of the door handle, Narelle shrunk back further, her face frozen in a rictus of shock. She had always been so loving and protective of Craig, so what was it about his sudden appearance now that she found so frightening? What had happened between them to turn her into a quivering mess at the sight of her own husband?

"Shouldn't he still be in hospital?" asked Brett, his voice a harsh whisper. "Do you think we should call the police?"

No one made a move, the tension in the room palpable.

"You have to go now," said Narelle, in a tightly controlled monotone. "I need to talk to my husband alone."

40

Brett's breath escaped in a loud huff, his eyes closing as he tilted his head back over the headrest. The whole situation felt so surreal he'd had to pinch himself to make sure it wasn't some weird dream. If it hadn't been for Jacinta's obstinacy, they would have been on their way home, leaving the Edmondses to sort out their own domestic troubles.

"I'm not going anywhere. If you want to go home, you'll have to walk," Jacinta snapped at him.

He sighed. "If you're so concerned, why don't you call Daniel? He's trained for all this; we aren't. Please, Jacinta," he added, although he knew pleading was pointless.

"Not yet." She glanced down at the mobile phone in her lap. "You heard her. If she doesn't answer the phone when I call in ten minutes, then we call the police."

"A lot can happen in ten minutes."

"At least they can't shoot each other, can they? By the way, what did you do with the gun?"

"I wanted to talk to you about that," he said, wishing he had never laid eyes on it. "For now it's hidden away, but the sooner it's in police hands, the better."

Jacinta visibly baulked, her head jerking back. "Have you even stopped to think it through? We still have no idea if the gun is implicated in any of the deaths or not, but whose fingerprints do you suppose are all over it? Besides yours, of course. Not to mention the matter of it not being registered."

"It's a gun, Jacinta. Guns kill. Don't tell me you've already forgotten hurling yourself at the floor when Narelle fired the so-called unloaded gun at the ceiling. We might not be so lucky next time," he said, cocking his finger at her to emphasize his point.

She batted his hand away. "I know that, but I don't think it's as clean-cut as you seem to think. We need to find out a lot more before we go dobbing people into the police."

"For a start, what's this sudden 'we'? Up to now, you've treated me like a mushroom." *Kept me in the dark and fed me bullshit*, he added silently. "Am I the only one with any fucking common sense here?" he demanded, anger welling in his chest. "Leave the detective work to the professionals, for Chrissakes! Do you want to end up like those women in the forest?"

Her mouth opened, but no sound came out.

"Answer me!"

She swallowed, the corner of her mouth twitching in a small smile. "I didn't know you cared."

"Damn it, Jacinta, I'm being serious!"

She squeezed his hand, her smile fading. "I'm sorry. I didn't mean to sound flippant. I do understand what you're saying, but let's not," her mouth twitched again, "jump the gun, so to speak."

He glowered at her, wrenching his hand from her grip. If she'd thought he would find her gun quip amusing, she'd thought wrong. "If Narelle and Craig are innocent of any wrongdoing, they have nothing to worry about. In fact, it could be the very thing that helps clear their names. And as far as it being an unregistered firearm, I'm sure you could talk Daniel into arranging an amnesty."

"Craig inherited that gun from his father. I still think surrendering it to the police at this stage would be premature, causing a whole lot of what might turn out to be unnecessary grief for Narelle and Craig. Daniel said himself that Narelle had survived all these years without incident. Anyway, you've confiscated it. Surely, that's enough until we know more."

Brett felt his initial resolve faltering. Although his head told him he was right, his heart wasn't listening. *What's another few days after all these years*, he rationalized. Besides, he knew even a bulldozer couldn't stop Jacinta in her tracks once she had decided on a course.

"Okay, I'll leave it for now—" He held up his hand in a stop motion as she leaned toward him. "But only on two conditions. You have to promise me, Jacinta, that if the ballistics tests in *any* way match that gun – caliber, age, brand, whatever — we surrender it to the police and you tell them everything. I don't care how damning it is for Narelle." He waited until she nodded, and then continued. "Second, stay away from Craig Edmonds. You have no idea what he's capable of."

"And you do?"

"No, but that's the whole point. We're dealing with the unknown. Someone murdered his wife and two other women connected to him. And regardless of what you say, until he's ruled out, he has to be the prime suspect."

"But not the only one," she said, glancing back down at her mobile phone.

Sighing, he lifted her chin with two of his fingers, tilting her face toward him. "Do you promise?"

"Yes, yes, I promise," she said distractedly, staring past him to the house. "But," she turned her head, looking him straight in the eye, "where is the gun?"

"I shoved it inside the recycle bin as a temporary measure," he said, pointing at the yellow-lidded blue wheelie bin next to the garage.

"Don't panic," he added quickly. "No one saw me do it. What else was I supposed to do? You had the keys to the car."

He extended his arm through the gap between the two front seats, and groped for something in which he could conceal the gun. "Stay here and make sure no one comes out. I'll go and get it." His fingertips touched something fabric on the floor, almost under Jacinta's seat. Grunting, he strained to hook what turned out to be a lightweight but durable green-printed calico shopping bag.

Once out of the car, he skipped across the dew-laden grass verge to the footpath. He paused, inhaling the cool morning air, and looked around. The street was starting to wake, a magpie choir high in the trees heralding the new day. In the distance, he heard a car start up and drive away, a door slammed somewhere else, but most residents, it seemed, were enjoying a Sunday lie-in.

For once, Jacinta did what she was told and stayed in the car. Trying to appear as nonchalant as possible, he sauntered up the Edmonds' driveway, resisting the urge to keep checking over his shoulder. Although it was only a slight incline, by the time he reached the wheelie bins, he felt he had climbed a mountain, his legs shaking from the exertion.

Standing so his back blocked the view of anyone who happened to pass on the street, he opened the yellow lid and peered in. He skewed the stack of newspapers to one side. He broke out in a cold sweat, his stomach lurching violently. In his mad panic to dig through the carton of plastic soft drink and water bottles underneath, he almost overturned the blue plastic wheelie bin. He even checked the green rubbish bin next to it, on the unlikely chance he had put it in there instead.

He couldn't believe it; the gun was gone.

41

Hoping the fresh air might help revive her, Jacinta wound down the car window, sucking in lungfuls of the slightly damp air as she watched the front of the Edmonds house for signs of movement. Her head buzzed, the culmination of the last few weeks' events threatening to overwhelm her. Perhaps Brett was right. Perhaps she should forget all about it and leave it to the police to deal with. If only it were that simple.

Checking the time on her mobile phone again, she wondered what had possessed her to leave Narelle alone in the house with a psychiatric hospital absconder, even if it was her husband and it was only for ten minutes. Craig had been hospitalized for a reason, and although it was possible medical staff had deemed him well enough to return home, they certainly wouldn't have discharged him in a half-dressed state in Sunday's small hours.

From her angle, she couldn't see much of Brett except his back. He had the lid up on the blue bin and appeared to be rummaging through its contents. What was taking so long? Had he hidden the gun so well he was having trouble finding it? *Thank God he'd had the strength of mind to remove it from the house when he had*, she suddenly thought, imagining what might have happened if Craig had got his hands on it.

A white van drove past without slowing, followed a few seconds later by a carload of teenage girls. Jacinta smiled to herself, remembering the days when she too used to have the stamina to party all night, arriving home as most people were waking. She was still reminiscing when a vehicle she hadn't seen coming stopped behind her. Before she had a chance to look in the rear-view mirror, a police car pulled in front of her into the Edmonds' driveway, cutting Brett off from view.

A car door slammed behind her, and then another. Daniel's broad frame loomed in the side-mirror. From the look on her stepbrother's face, she knew he was less than pleased to see her. As uniformed officers piled out of the police car in the driveway and another parked at the curb, he marched past without stopping, rapping the car roof above her head in brief acknowledgement of her presence. DS Renee White, walking down the footpath on the other side of the car, caught up with him as he and the other officers converged en masse on the Edmonds' front door.

Jacinta's mind reeled, trying to take in what was happening. Why were the police there? Had someone called them? As Brett yanked open the passenger-side door, throwing himself bodily into the car, she realized Craig's disappearance from the hospital wouldn't have gone unnoticed. But why the need for so many officers?

"Thanks a lot, Jacinta." Brett sounded out of breath. "At least you could've waited until I was back in the car."

She shook her head at him. "I didn't call them."

His flushed face paled. "This is no time for games."

"I swear I know nothing about it. Remember, you were the one intent on calling them, not me."

"Well, what the fuck are they doing here, then?" Brett's throat constricted, the last words coming out in a squeak.

"I don't know." Leaning in closer to him, she dropped her voice to a conspiratorial whisper. "Where's the gun now?"

Brett gulped, his eyes downcast like an errant schoolboy called to the headmaster's office. "I don't know."

Her heart skipped a beat. "Say that again," she said, hoping she had misheard but knowing she hadn't.

"The gun's gone. It's not where I left it."

"Could it have become dislodged and fallen to the bottom?"

"What do you think I was doing when the boys in blue rocked up?"

Tapping her forehead with her steepled fingers, she tried to think. If the gun wasn't there, it meant only one thing: Narelle had been right; someone had been staking out the house. But who? With no evidence to back her belief, Narelle had Grace, as Kirsty's rejected lover, squarely in the frame for her murder, convincing herself that Grace had broken into her home to search for the revolver. But how long had Craig been outside the house before making his presence known? After all, the gun belonged to him.

"God, Brett, this changes everything. We have no choice now but to tell the police."

He gave her a sheepish look. "We would've had to sooner or later, anyway."

"Later would have been preferable," she murmured, more to herself than to Brett. All she could think about was Narelle, and to what extent she could protect her from the inevitable fallout of a police investigation. If it helped bring a killer to justice, clearing Narelle's name in the process, it had to be worth the stress and aggravation.

Brett cut through her thoughts. "Something's happening," he said, nodding at the house.

The front door had opened. Escorted by two male, uniformed police officers, Craig Edmonds emerged and made his way across to the police car parked in the driveway. No longer half-naked, he wore a loose-fitting, blue and white striped shirt over his jeans, the cuffs rolled back. A pair of tan leather open sandals shod his feet.

Up until that moment, he had been submissive, putting up no resistance as the officers guided him along the footpath. But as soon as he caught sight of Jacinta and Brett, all that changed. His eyes narrowed, his face becoming pinched as, struggling to escape his captors' hold, he hurled abuse in their direction. Placing a hand on the top of his head, the two officers manhandled him into the backseat, closing the door with a resounding thud.

Jacinta shivered, her arms wrapping tightly around herself. She found it hard to understand what Narelle saw in Craig. There had to be a side to the hostile, hot-tempered man Jacinta hadn't yet seen.

After the police car backed out and drove away, presumedly returning their backseat passenger to the hospital, Jacinta opened her car door and got out. Expecting to see the front door open at any moment, she took a couple of calming breaths, mentally preparing herself to face Daniel before realizing that meant Narelle would be left on her own.

Brett had opened his car door, remaining seated with one foot in the car and the other on the curb. She walked around the front of the car to his side and stood facing him. "Narelle's going to need someone with her. Can you talk to Daniel while I look after her?"

Brett cringed, his face blanching.

"Okay, I'll talk to Daniel while you take care of Narelle, then," she said, knowing that for Brett, a distressed, hormonal woman would be too much to contemplate.

He sighed, his shoulders sagging. "What exactly should I tell him?"

"Just tell him what's happened. Blame me. I'm in that much trouble now, it doesn't matter. What is important is that the gun is found before anyone gets hurt, or worse."

His face brightened a little. "Amen," he replied, the tone of his voice adding: *And about bloody time, too.*

Neither spoke as they returned to watching the Edmonds' front door, waiting for Daniel and his team to leave the house.

After what felt like hours but was undoubtedly only minutes, Brett voiced her own thoughts. "I wonder what the hold-up is?"

Daniel appeared just as Jacinta was asking Brett to pass over her mobile phone. "Okay, guys, this had better be good," he said, striding toward them.

"Excuse me?" replied Jacinta, her hackles rising. "We have every right to be here. Narelle called us."

"And why did she call you?" asked Daniel, closing the gap between them.

"What would you do if you were a pregnant woman all on your own in a large house and you heard noises in your backyard? More to the point, what are your lot still doing here? We saw them take Craig away."

"Not that it's really any of your business, but we're executing a search warrant." He turned to walk away. "Now please excuse me, I have work to do."

Struck dumb, she opened and closed her mouth, willing the words forth. "Wait!" she called, running after him. His step faltered, but he didn't turn around. "Please, Daniel!"

"Jacinta, I don't have time for this now," he said, as she drew level with him.

"Just tell me what you're looking for and I'll stay out of your way."

He groaned, stopped and turned to face her. "If it means you'll leave me to get on with my job, I'll tell you. You'll find out sooner or later, anyway." Gesturing for her to follow, he headed toward the garage, away from the house. Brett cut across the lawn, joining them at the corner of the garage near the wheelie bins.

"We received an anonymous tip-off about firearms on the property. We don't know how genuine it is, but until we can prove otherwise, we have to treat it seriously."

"Was it a man or a woman?"

Daniel shook his head. "We don't know. The voice was computer-generated." He squinted first at Jacinta and then at Brett, his head leaning slightly to one side. "You two wouldn't know anything about that, would you?"

Hooking his thumbs in his jean pockets, Brett studied his feet, leaving it up to Jacinta to answer.

"Well," she stammered, "we don't know anything about any anonymous phone call, but…" She hesitated, fumbling for the right words. "But there is a gun. It was on the table when we arrived." She wasn't about to add she had known of its possible existence the day before.

Daniel closed his eyes, pressing his lips together in a thin line. "And where is this gun now?" he asked, opening his eyes and fixing Jacinta with a steely glare.

"I'll… um… let Brett answer that," she said, taking half a step back.

Somehow Brett found his voice. He rushed his words, as if trying to offload his burden as quickly as possible. Starting from when he had been woken in the early hours by the phone ringing, he told Daniel everything that had happened that morning. When he reached the bit about Narelle accidentally discharging the loaded gun at the ceiling, Daniel cocked an eyebrow but stayed silent, allowing Brett to continue uninterrupted. The corner of Daniel's mouth lifted in amusement at Brett's account of the frightening appearance of a half-naked wild man at the window. Brett's speech became faster, his words running together as they raced for the finishing line.

He stopped, took a deep breath and exhaled slowly. "But I don't understand who could have taken it. I was sure no one saw me."

"So, thanks to your efforts, we have a firearm – possibly a murder weapon – out there somewhere," Daniel waved his hand through the air, "in God knows whose hands. If you had come to me in the first place, we could've avoided all this."

"It's not Brett's fault," Jacinta said. "He thought he was doing the right thing. If you have to blame someone, blame me for getting involved in the first place. We were just trying to help a friend. We had no way of knowing what would happen."

Daniel tugged at his shirt collar with his index finger, scratching his neck. "Haven't we had this conversation before? Jacinta, it's not about blame. It's not even a matter of interfering in a police investigation, which is bad enough. Don't you understand what's at stake? You could've been killed today. Dead's dead, accident or not." He paused. "Not only that, you've put others at risk."

Although his tone hadn't been chastising, nor had he raised his voice, she felt the full force of his words. She accepted the rebuke, knowing it was justified. However, it was his underlying deep concern that really affected her. Her stepbrother cared whether she lived or died, and that meant a lot to her.

Making no promises she couldn't guarantee she could keep, but reminding him he had actually asked her at one stage to act as Narelle's confidante, she apologized. Daniel brushed it aside, more intent on finding out how much more she and Brett knew.

"I want you both to think carefully. Is there anyone you know of, or who you may have heard mentioned, who would know the Edmondses possessed a gun? The person who called it in knew about it long before you removed it from the house."

Folding his arms, Brett shook his head. "The first I knew about it was when I saw it on the table."

As Daniel went to say something, Brett talked over the top of him. "Maybe Narelle made the call herself."

"Don't be ridiculous. Why would she dob herself in?" Jacinta asked.

"Not herself, her husband. What better way to get rid of the gun without Craig realizing his own wife had been responsible. Think about it, Jacinta. She makes an anonymous call to the police; she then phones you knowing you won't hesitate to come. When we arrive, the gun is in plain view on the table. She doesn't make any attempt to conceal it. She wanted the gun to be seen."

"But why would she do that?" Jacinta couldn't believe Narelle could be that scheming.

"Because, after all these years, she's suddenly having doubts about her husband's innocence," Daniel said under his breath. "She wanted to find out one way or the other if the gun had been used as a murder weapon."

"You're both wrong." Even as she said the words, she couldn't help but wonder if there was any element of truth in what they were suggesting. How well did she know Narelle? Regardless, the idea their friendship could have been nothing more than some elaborate ruse didn't sit well with her. *I'm a much better judge of character than that*, she thought. "What about Grace Kevron? She's had it in for Narelle and Craig ever since Kirsty disappeared."

"Sorry to disappoint you, but Grace has a rock-solid alibi for this morning. Although not for the time of the phone call."

"What do you mean? Where is she?"

"I'm not going to go into the ins and outs of it, but suffice to say, she couldn't be in two places at one time."

Daniel refused to be drawn any further on the subject, leaving Jacinta to speculate on how he could be so confident of Grace's whereabouts. If the police were involved, she had to have either committed a crime or been the victim of a crime. But then again, police also attended vehicle accidents. Perhaps Grace had been injured and been rushed to hospital.

"You have Grace under surveillance." It was a statement, not a question. Jacinta didn't know why she hadn't thought of it sooner.

Daniel shook his head. "What's with all the surveillance theories? You thought we were watching Narelle Edmonds, too. We're not a police state. Even if we wanted to, we just don't have the resources to monitor—" He stopped talking as something behind Jacinta distracted his attention.

Turning, she saw DS Renee White heading their way, the top edges of a couple of plastic bags gripped in her latex-gloved hands. Daniel immediately broke away, intercepting his sergeant before she reached the driveway. Scurrying after him, Jacinta managed to catch a quick glimpse of what appeared to be a photograph in one of the bags, before Daniel whipped both bags out of sight.

"Jacinta, this really doesn't concern you," he said, holding the bags behind his back. "Go home."

Not being privy to the police investigation didn't mean she had no reason to be there. "What about Narelle?"

"What about her?"

"Police are crawling all over her home. Isn't she at least entitled to have someone with her? You've already carted her husband off."

A look of exasperation passed between the two detectives. Jacinta waited, confident in the knowledge they couldn't reasonably refuse her request. But before that could happen, a young uniformed officer flew out the front door and down the steps toward them.

"Mrs Edmonds has collapsed." He slowed to a trot, gulping air. "We've called an ambulance," he added, as Daniel strode past him back into the house.

Angry that Narelle had been pushed to the point of collapse, Jacinta tried to go her friend's aid, but DS White barred her way.

"She is being looked after. Please wait outside."

Jacinta wanted to tell her where to shove it, but thought better of it. Although Narelle was ill and alone with a bunch of strangers, the same strangers who had been systematically ransacking her home, causing a scene could only further distress her.

42

It was still dark when Detective Inspector Daniel Lassiter arrived at work on Monday morning. Unable to sleep, he had tossed and turned for the best part of the night, mumbled groans from Wendy's side of the bed finally prompting him to get up. He dressed in the dark, and by the time he leaned over to kiss his wife goodbye, she was snoring gently.

Once under the station's fluorescent lights, he used the mirror in the men's toilets to check his appearance. He ran a hand over his unshaven face, wondering briefly if he could get away with it. Then he glanced at his feet, lifting the legs of his trousers to reveal matching black socks. Relieved he had that right at least, he went to get his toilet bag.

Having finished his ablutions, he spent the next half-hour restlessly roaming the deserted corridors, a mug of double-strength instant coffee clutched in his hands. No phones rang, the low hum of the air-conditioners the only sound. A faint hint of curry — someone's takeaway dinner from the night before, no doubt — lingered in the air.

He walked past the Major Incident room's closed door twice before deciding that was where he should be. Stepping into the windowless room, he flicked the light switch on the wall just inside the door. The resulting burst of light reflecting off the shiny surface of the large mobile whiteboard acted like an exploding flashbulb, temporarily blinding him. He blinked, bringing the room into focus.

An eclectic mix of office chairs lined one side of the long trestle table positioned parallel to the whiteboard. Except for one empty glass and two coffee cups clustered together at one end, the table was empty. Setting his own cup beside the others, he straddled one of the chairs and, with his arms folded across the chair back, studied the whiteboard and adjacent wall.

Enlarged copies of both the photograph and the driver's license seized from the Edmonds' house drew his attention. While not enough to convict Craig Edmonds, their discovery had been a significant breakthrough. The photograph, picturing an obviously inebriated Tamara Whitfield hanging off Craig Edmonds at a staff Christmas party, her arms looped around his neck, clearly showed he had been on more intimate terms with the murdered woman than he had let on. Even supposing the photograph was nothing more than the result of festive frivolity, it didn't explain finding architect Chandra Pinder's driver's license tucked inside the flap of one of Craig's old diaries.

Something bothered him, though. Although he hadn't been involved with the original investigation, he had no doubt the initial search would have been as thorough, if not more so, than the one that had uncovered the photograph and driver's license. One of the items could have been missed, but not both. It all seemed too convenient.

Daniel also wasn't one for coincidences. Acting on anonymous information, he and his team had been granted a warrant to search for firearms at the Edmonds' property. Yet, when they arrived to execute the warrant, the mystery gun had vanished, the only evidence of its existence a bullet in the ceiling. Gut instinct told him they had been meant to find the photograph and driver's license.

The bullet he wasn't too sure about. Could that have been staged, too? Preliminary ballistics results had identified the bullet recovered from the ceiling and those found with the human remains in the Toolangi State Forest as coming from a .38-calibre revolver. Every gun left distinctive marks on a bullet. However, the bullet fired inside the house had hit a steel coach bolt, mangling it and greatly diminishing the odds of matching its striations with those of the others. Without the gun, they had nothing.

His gaze moved to the Toolangi crime scene photos grouped together on the wall. In less than a two-year period, two young women had been murdered, their bodies dumped in bushland, and another had disappeared, assumedly under the same circumstances. Then the killings had stopped. Kirsty Edmonds had been the last known victim, but where was her body? He needed to expand the search area even further. She had to be there somewhere.

But what had been the murderer's motive? Daniel now knew all three women had links to Craig Edmonds, but what reason would he have had to kill them? The discovery of the first two victims' remains, rather than strengthening the case against him, weakened it. When he had been charged with his wife's murder, the prosecution had argued the age-old motives of sex and money. Not only had Kirsty stood in his way of a life with her younger sister, Narelle, but her death meant he also stood to gain $1,000,000 from the life insurance policy he had conveniently taken out less than six months prior. Motive, opportunity, means. He had it all, but without the body, it still hadn't been enough.

Now they had two bodies, but no motive. Maybe the answers lay with the victims themselves. What common characteristics did they share? What sort of lifestyles had each led? What were the relationships in their lives? Who were their friends? Did they have any enemies? Standing up, he selected a green whiteboard marker and added a series of question marks after each of the women's names. By the end of the day, he hoped to know everything there was to know about Tamara Whitfield and Chandra Pinder.

43

Jacinta opened the shower door to find a naked, bleary-eyed Brett holding out the phone. "Daniel for you."

Stepping onto the cotton bath mat, she pulled a towel from the rail. "Tell him I'll call him back in a couple of minutes," she said, bending forward and wrapping the towel around her head. Brett hadn't seriously expected her to talk to anyone – let alone her stepbrother – nude and dripping wet, had he?

Already running late for work, she quickly dried herself off, sprayed her underarms with deodorant, and missing the toner step, smeared moisturizer over her face. Then, with one eye on the clock, she dialed Daniel, dressing one-handedly while she waited for him to answer. She didn't even have time to wonder why he had called.

"Make it quick, Daniel. Being late on my second week on the job is not a good look." Her new copywriter position wasn't as stimulating as journalism, but it paid the bills. She couldn't afford to jeopardize that.

"Are you free for lunch, then?"

"God, I haven't even thought that far ahead," she replied, rummaging through her shoes, looking for the mate of the wedge-heeled sandal on her right foot. "Can I call you when I get to work?"

"Sure, but I thought you ought to know Craig Edmonds is expected to be discharged some time today. I imagine the news would be better coming from you — not that the hospital would let me near your friend, anyway."

Jacinta stopped still. "Are they insane?" she exclaimed, not realizing the irony of her words but provoking a chuckle from Daniel.

"I sincerely hope not." He cleared his throat, serious again. "Call me as soon as you have a few free minutes."

Dumping the phone on the floor beside her, she used both hands in her hunt for the missing shoe. Precious seconds ticked by before she found it. Brushing her teeth took another minute.

Brett, taking full advantage of a late start, had gone back to bed. He lay flat on his back, sounding like a chainsaw. With no time to spare, she grabbed her satchel and, blowing him a kiss, ran out the door.

Hearing the clang of tram bells in the distance, she sprinted for the corner, almost spraining her ankle in the process. Only when she was seated and the tram had moved off did she take stock. Feeling half-dressed, she wouldn't have been surprised to discover she had forgotten to put on her bra — or, worse, her knickers. She ran a finger across her shoulder, feeling for the strap, reassuring herself she wasn't about to turn up at work braless.

With nothing left to do except watch the traffic, her thoughts turned to Daniel's phone call. It was the first time she had heard from him since he stopped her accompanying Narelle in the ambulance. There had only been room for one additional person, and he had wanted that person to be a police officer. For Narelle's own protection, he had said.

Still in hospital under observation, Narelle had yet to speak to the police. Her obstetrician had insisted she was not fit to be interviewed, putting the cause of her collapse down to undue stress. That had restricted Daniel's access to her, but not Jacinta's. The first night she had gone to visit, Narelle had been sleeping. The following evening, she was sitting up in bed, looking the most rested Jacinta had seen her in a while. Narelle didn't mention the police search or the items they had uncovered, and as much as Jacinta wanted to ask, she managed to limit the conversation to small talk.

And now, Daniel had just informed her that Craig was about to be let loose on an unsuspecting public again. Did he know about the search warrant? Did he know his wife had been hospitalized? Did he know his father's gun had disappeared? If he didn't, Jacinta didn't want to be around when he found out.

Sighing, she gathered up her satchel, slid past the petite Asian lady and her wheeled shopping bag in the seat beside her, and waited at the back door for the next stop. The tram trip had been a brief respite, but once her feet hit the footpath, she was off again.

She arrived at Alvico Media's offices gasping for breath, but only ten minutes past her scheduled starting time. Normally ten minutes would be neither here nor there to her, but she had only just started in the job and first impressions counted. Thumping her chest, she took a deep breath, exhaled, and then opened the door. She slunk through the empty reception area, not encountering anyone on the way to her office.

Grateful she hadn't had to use any one of the feeble excuses she had formulated on the way in, she turned on her Apple Mac, using the time it took to power up to phone Daniel. They arranged to meet at midday at Café Face, the same café where she had first thought she was seeing things.

Preparing copy for a new day spa's brochure consumed most of her morning, her cramped muscles hankering to take advantage of its services. She stood up, her intertwined fingers stretching up over her head as she leaned first left and then right. Collecting her satchel from the floor behind her, she made a detour via the toilets, screwing her nose up at the makeup-free face in the mirror. Her sunglasses and a touch of lipgloss didn't remedy the situation, but helped.

By the time she had battled the heat and lunchtime crowds and made it to Café Face, Daniel was already waiting for her. He waved her over. Looking longingly at the chilled drinks cabinet, she weaved her way through the tables to him.

"We can't exactly talk privately here," she noted, taking in the packed tables as she pulled out a chair and sat down. "Anyway, food first, talk second," she said, picking up the acrylic menu holder from the centre of the table. "I'm famished."

Daniel ordered a healthy rare roast beef salad. Jacinta opted for a rocket, goat's cheese and crispy pancetta focaccia, making up for the breakfast she had missed.

Waiting for the meals to arrive, Daniel casually asked after Narelle.

"She's fine, but you have to tell me what it was that got her so stressed out. What did you find?"

Daniel folded his arms, pressing his back against the seat.

"Come on, Daniel, I'm going to find out eventually."

He leaned forward, his arms still firmly crossed over his chest. "As you said before, this isn't the right place to be talking about this."

Jacinta frowned. "So why are we here?"

"Can't a man buy his sister lunch?" he asked, fixing her with a smile.

She caught his omission of 'step' and wondered if it had been intentional, or simply a slip of the tongue. "That's not what it sounded like when you rang this morning."

He dropped his arms, resting his large, square hands on the table, one covering the other. "I'm not good at eating humble pie," he said, his gaze and voice dropping. "Sunday, I told you to stay away from the investigation. Officially, that's still the stance; unofficially, I think you could be in a position to help."

Jacinta hunched forward, keen to hear more.

"There's one proviso, though." He held up a finger. "If, at any stage, I consider you might be at risk, you are to do exactly what I tell you and withdraw. No arguments. I'm putting my job on the line here."

"Anything you say, boss. Why the sudden change of heart?"

Lunch arrived before he could answer. Momentarily forgetting her question, Jacinta descended on her focaccia like a ravenous beast, not realizing until then how hungry she really was. It wasn't until she had swallowed her first mouthful and was on to her next that she looked up.

Daniel had got as far as picking up his knife and fork. "Hungry?" he asked, his eyes crinkling in amusement.

Her mouth full, she simply nodded, continuing to cut off another piece of the focaccia before spearing it with her fork. Swallowing, she reworded her question. "What has happened to make you think I can be of any help now when I was nothing but a hindrance before?" She took another bite, waiting for him to reply.

Daniel held her gaze. He had a way of studying her that made her feel as if he were reaching right into her mind. She stopped chewing, suddenly self-conscious. He glanced down at his salad and then, without a word, started jamming shavings of pink roast beef, mesclun leaves and semi-dried tomatoes onto his fork. "Eat your lunch," he said, nodding at her plate as he lifted his own laden fork to his mouth.

Too hungry to argue, she did as she was told, and ate. Over lunch, they barely exchanged a word, the only conversation coming from neighboring tables.

Daniel wiped his mouth on a paper napkin, tossing it onto his empty plate as he started to rise. "Fancy a walk in Treasury Gardens? We're less likely to be overheard there," he said, reaching into his hip pocket for his wallet.

"I can't," she said, checking her watch and standing up. "Some of us have to work." Arriving late for work was one thing, but a long lunch would really have been pushing it. "I'm sorry, it's going to have to wait." She shoved her chair in. "Narelle is expecting me straight after work, but then I'm all yours."

"What about Brett? I was under the impression he wanted you to stay as far away from this investigation as possible."

Perceptive, as well as a mind reader. "He's flying to Canberra this afternoon for an IT conference. I'm on my own for the rest of the week."

Daniel's eyebrows drew together in concern, the furrow on his forehead deepening. "Maybe this isn't a good idea after all."

She drew herself up to her full height. "Don't you start getting all over-protective on me as well. It might not look like it, but I'm perfectly capable of looking after myself."

He still didn't look convinced.

"I promise I won't do anything stupid."

The cashier dropped the change into Daniel's open hand. "It's not your actions I'm worried about," he said, turning to face her as he tucked the coins into his trouser fob pocket.

They parted company on the footpath, Daniel turning left and she crossing the street to walk back to work.

Kept busy, her afternoon passed quickly. Before she knew it, it was five o'clock. She finished formatting the text she was working on and packed up.

Foraging in her satchel for her tram ticket, she left her office. She found the ticket, almost dropping it again when she caught sight of Daniel sitting in reception, leafing through an album of the company's latest work. She raised her eyebrows questioningly.

He closed the album, replacing it on the low table next to the chair. Standing feet together, he doffed an imaginary cap. "Your car is waiting, ma'am."

"I thought we weren't meeting until later."

"Correct, but since I was in the area, I thought we could kill two birds with one stone, so to speak. You need to get to the hospital, we need to talk and I have a car. I thought we could talk in the car on the way to the hospital. I'll wait for you and then you can either join the Lassiter family for a very informal dinner or, if that doesn't suit, I'll run you home. A win-win situation, don't you think?" He gave her a broad grin.

It certainly sounded more tempting than a bowl of two-minute noodles, with only the television for company. "But Wendy's not going to want a dinner guest landing on her unexpectedly."

He ushered her out the door. "Wendy suggested it."

In the time it took to walk the two blocks to the car park, drive in a spiral down five levels to the exit, nose the car into peak-hour traffic and make it to the CBD outskirts, she could've been at the hospital. Except for when some mindless driver decided to cross the tram tracks before checking it was clear on the other side, trams on St Kilda Road didn't have to contend with vehicular traffic.

With outbound traffic at a crawl, Daniel had no excuse for avoiding her questions. "You still haven't told me what changed your mind."

Having had all afternoon to come up with what he wanted to say, he didn't hesitate. "To be honest, Jacinta, I'm at a bit of an impasse." Somewhere behind them, a couple of impatient motorists were having a tooting contest. "So far I have three people on my list to talk to." He didn't need to name names for her to know to whom he was referring. "But it's proving rather difficult," he said, tapping his finger against the underside of the steering wheel. "Besides the fact that we've been refused access to all three on medical grounds…"

"What's happened to Grace Kevron? She is the third person, right?"

"Grace is fine. She's responding well to treatment, but I can't give you any details."

"Can't or won't?"

He glanced sideways at her, the tensing of his jaw almost imperceptible.

"Look, Daniel, I'll do everything I can to help, but you have to be straight with me. No bullshit."

As the lights at the corner of St Kilda and Commercial Road changed to green, he mumbled something under his breath that sounded like, "Ditto." Turning left into Commercial Road, he said, "Do you have any idea how far I've already put my neck out, telling you what I have?"

"Of course I do! But if this is going to work, we have to pool our resources. What the hell do you think I'm going to do with the information? Sell it to the highest bidder? Now there's a thought," she added sarcastically. Seeing the hospital up on the right, she started to unbuckle her seatbelt.

As the car passed under The Alfred's helipad, the mobile phone in the dashboard cradle rang, its display screen lighting up. After three rings, it answered automatically, leaving Daniel no option but to respond.

"DI Lassiter," he announced, glancing down at the screen.

"Daniel, it's Renee. Craig Edmonds has been shot. The bullet penetrated his shoulder, causing massive bleeding. He's alive but critical."

Jacinta's mouth opened in a silent gasp, her gaze flitting from the mobile phone to the expansive multi-storied hospital complex across the road.

"Where did it happen?" Daniel pulled into a no parking zone, leaving the engine idling.

"Outside his house. His wife is beside herself. She can't give us any information. I don't think she knows what day it is. A couple of neighbors heard what they thought was a car backfiring, but so far we haven't found any eye witnesses."

He glanced at Jacinta. "Where's his wife?"

"Inside the house. A paramedic is with her."

"Where's the gun now?"

"There's no sign of it, but we're still looking. Crime scene are here now, doing their bit. Let's hope they come up with something soon."

Jacinta found it all too hard to take in at once. When had Narelle been discharged? Why hadn't she let Jacinta know? Had she been with Craig when he was shot? Had he been the intended victim, or had he been shielding his wife? Had either of them seen his attacker? Was the weapon used the missing revolver? Question after question raced through her head, the answers nowhere in sight.

44

Jacinta sat unnoticed in the middle of a row of vinyl-covered seats, that bowl of two-minute noodles in front of the television looking more inviting by the minute. Around her, the bustle of hospital activity continued unabated. A steady stream of medical staff, only distinguishable from the visitors by their identification tags and a general air of belonging or the stethoscope around their neck, passed by without a second glance in her direction.

A disposable coffee cup rested on the seat beside her, its contents gnawing a hole in her stomach. She stifled a yawn, collected the empty cup and, grateful for the excuse to stretch her legs, went in search of a rubbish bin.

She gave the stocky police officer on duty outside Craig Edmonds' room a small smile, but he didn't even acknowledge her presence, the corners of his mouth remaining down-turned. With Craig not long out of surgery, his visitors had been restricted to immediate family. She had hoped for a chance to talk with Narelle before the detectives did, but Narelle had yet to leave her husband's side, and there was no way Constable Gloomy was going to let Jacinta past.

Down at the nurses' station, she spotted Daniel deep in conversation with a tall, officious-looking woman. She nodded as he spoke, jotting something on the front of the file sitting on the counter. Tossing her empty cup into the nearest bin, Jacinta walked toward them, hoping to catch what was being said. Unfortunately, like a schoolteacher she'd once had, Daniel had eyes in the back of his head.

"If there's any change," he said, half-turning as Jacinta came up behind him, "please call me on my mobile." Giving Jacinta a dismissive glance, the woman dropped the business card Daniel had handed her into her pocket and walked away, the file clutched to her chest.

"I just need a minute with Constable Grant, and then we'll be away," Daniel said, striding off in the direction from which she had just come.

Waiting for his return, Jacinta loitered around the nurses' station, peeping over the countertop on the off-chance that information pertaining to the gunshot victim might have been left lying around. Over the years, she had become adept at reading upside down, but in this case, nothing viewable interested her.

Daniel was soon back, an edginess about him that told her he was keen to get home. Trotting alongside him, she wondered how Wendy coped with the unpredictable nature of her husband's job, the long hours and call-outs seemingly so at odds with a stable family life.

Outside the hospital, streetlights and car headlights punched hazy patterns in the settling dusk. A light wind, carrying the last of the sun's heat, tickled Jacinta's skin. She breathed deeply, displacing the chilled antiseptic air of the hospital in her lungs.

They walked quickly, detouring around other pedestrians and sidestepping the occasional jogger or dog-walker coming their way, not speaking. Once at the car park, she followed him up the concrete ramp, the echoes of his heavy footsteps dominating her lighter clip-clop. Low light and looming shadows laced the car park, generating a flutter of irrational fear in her chest. She quickened her pace, intent on staying as close to her stepbrother as possible. Sixteen years earlier, it would have been the other way around, yet now here she was, looking to him as a protector, an irony not lost on her.

Rounding the corner, Daniel pressed the remote on his key ring, the resulting beep piercingly loud in the stillness. "We'll call Wendy on the way," he said, crossing to the car. "She wasn't going to start dinner," he glanced at his watch, "supper, until she heard from us. I can promise you it won't be anything fancy," he added, before Jacinta could protest. He laughed. "Don't be surprised if it's only baked beans on toast. Wendy gave up trying to cook meals for me a long time ago. If I'm there when she's feeding the boys, all well and good, but if not, I usually fend for myself."

Anything had to be better than eating on her own. Reassured that Wendy wouldn't be going to any extra trouble on her account, Jacinta opened the car door and got in.

"Do you ever turn that thing off?" she asked as Daniel clipped his mobile phone into the cradle.

"Unfortunately, it's part of the job. Fingers crossed it doesn't ring again tonight."

Jacinta waited until they had exited the car park and were heading down Commercial Road before she pounced. "Now, where were we? That's right; you wanted my help and you were about to fill me in on the details of the investigation."

For a few drawn-out seconds, Daniel said nothing. Then, clearing his throat, he began to speak. "Craig Edmonds, his wife, Narelle, and Grace Kevron are all people of interest to us. That's not to say they're all suspects, but we do need to eliminate them from our inquiry." He took a breath. "That's where you come in. The police can ask as many questions and use as many techniques as they like, but these people have all had years to bury their secrets. Your friendship with Narelle means you're already a lot closer than we could ever expect to be. If you believe in her innocence, getting to the truth sooner rather than later can only be in her best interests."

"Daniel, I understand that, but you haven't told me anything I don't already know. How am I supposed to know what to look for if you don't tell me everything? I can't work with only part of the information."

Eventually he capitulated, addressing her as she imagined he would brief his colleagues. Starting with a background summary to the original Edmonds' case, where Craig Edmonds had been charged with his wife's murder – most of which she had already surmised from the trial transcript – he led her through the investigation up to Craig's shooting.

If everything he said was true, the case was far from simple. And, whether he'd had time to rethink his position or he had decided he could trust his stepsister after all, he had probably just broken every police procedure in the book.

Her mind reeling, she leaned back in her seat. If she had known all the facts earlier, would she have been so keen to be involved? Up to the point when he told her the bullets recovered in the Toolangi State Forest and the one Craig Edmonds had been shot with more than likely came from the same weapon, she had been prepared, until it was proved otherwise, to write off everything else as a series of bizarre coincidences.

How she had possibly entertained that idea, she didn't know. What were the odds on three women connected in some way to Craig Edmonds being murdered; a gold and sapphire cross owned by the last victim found in the vicinity of the remains of the other two?

After talking with their families, Daniel didn't believe the women had been randomly targeted. Tamara Whitfield and Chandra Pinder had both been shot at close range. And, while both women had been extroverts, they had also been extremely security-conscious and would have been wary of any stranger. He felt certain they had known their killer.

"That may be so, but where's the motive?" For Narelle's sake, Jacinta prayed Daniel's suspicions about Craig Edmonds were wrong. If Daniel was right, the cold-blooded murder of the two women cast the murder of Craig's first wife in a completely different light. Had Craig, as argued by the prosecution, killed Kirsty in a drunken rage then, realizing what he had done, disposed of the body? Or was it more sinister than that? Had it been premeditated?

"Sex. Lust."

"What do you mean?"

"According to her sister, the first victim, Tamara Whitfield, had been besotted with some man. That's all she could tell us, but because Tamara had refused to name names, her sister assumed he had to be a married man. At this stage, the rest is circumstantial, but I'll leave you to draw your own conclusions. First, we know Craig Edmonds, a married man employed by the same firm, has shown he's not averse to a bit of adultery. Second, he lied about how well he knew her. The Christmas party photo refutes his claim they were barely acquainted. Third, she wasn't the only victim linked to him."

"And I thought only journalists speculated," Jacinta said, trying to follow Daniel's chain of thought.

"As I said, it's purely circumstantial, and only one scenario. It doesn't fit neatly into all the boxes, but nothing ever does. As police, we're trained to look at everything, no matter how obscure or improbable, from every angle. From there, it's a process of elimination."

"What about the architect? How does she fit into this particular scenario? Another of Craig's flings?"

"We don't think so. Chandra Pinder was engaged to be married. I know that doesn't preclude her from having an affair, but her mother and her fiancé both said she had been jittery in the months leading up to her disappearance. She thought someone was stalking her. Friends and family said she was flirty by nature, but perhaps that someone misread her signals. Is it possible Craig Edmonds became infatuated with his architect? Who knows?"

Closing her eyes, Jacinta kneaded her temples. "If that's the case, who shot Craig?" She paused, dropping her hands. "Is it possible he shot himself to deflect suspicion away from himself?"

"Not unless he's a contortionist with very long limbs. He was shot from the back, and the evidence is pointing to it being a drive-by shooting."

"Grace Kevron has a car," Jacinta said.

Daniel chuckled. "So do you. Don't worry, we've already checked out that possibility. Grace is still tucked up safely in hospital, where she can't hurt herself or anyone else. So unless she can be in two places at once, that rules her out. Any other suggestions?"

Jacinta clammed up, the lilt in Daniel's voice making her think he might be winding her up. For now, she would keep her thoughts to herself.

45

The taxi had left. Daniel and Wendy were probably already curled up together in bed, their sons sleeping soundly in the next room. Brett was hundreds of kilometers away in Canberra. She didn't own a cat. Jacinta had nothing but her thoughts for company. And they weren't much fun.

Light conversation over a delightfully simple but tasty supper of grilled open sandwiches of mozzarella, tomato and fresh basil had provided a welcome but brief respite from thinking about murder and guilt. Now, home alone with little to distract her, her earlier conversation with Daniel kept running around in her head, playing like an audiotape on loop. If only she could find the stop button.

Double-checking the front door lock, she headed to the kitchen for a glass of water. She drank half of it standing at the sink, refilling the glass before carrying it with her through to the bathroom. A few minutes later, she emerged fresh-faced and clean-teethed.

Intent on not being late two mornings in a row, she set the alarm clock for fifteen minutes earlier, telling herself the snooze button was out of bounds. Then, turning out the light, she scrambled under the covers, sighing as her weary head hit the pillow. She closed her eyes, expecting to fall asleep almost instantly. Instead she found herself staring at the insides of her eyelids, a black nothingness. She squeezed her eyes harder, hoping to convince her brain it was time to switch off. When that didn't work, she tried counting imaginary white, fluffy, cartoon sheep. But as tired as she was, sleep evaded her.

With a resigned groan, she rolled onto her side and felt for the bedside lamp switch. Blinking against the light's sudden glare, she retrieved her spiral-bound notebook and a ballpoint pen from the bedside table's single shallow drawer and sat up. She knew the only way she was going to get any sleep was to clear her head. In the past, writing down her thoughts had helped.

For the next half-hour, she wrote furiously, dumping her thoughts on paper. When she read the jumble of words back, they made even less sense, but at least she had something to work with. She tore out the filled pages, laying the loose sheets on the bed in a semicircle around her, gazing at them as if expecting the answers to materialize.

In the middle of a fresh page, she wrote CRAIG EDMONDS in bold capitals and circled it. Then, in mind-map fashion, she added a series of boxes, connecting each to the circle with a solid line. She stared at the diagram for a while, and then began to add labels. She wrote 'Kirsty Edmonds' in the top box, inserting her sister's name, 'Narelle Croswell', in the one at the bottom of the page. With the two wives taken care of, she then allocated a box to each of the first two murder victims, Tamara Whitfield and Chandra Pinder. Opposite them, on the right-hand side of the page, she added Grace Kevron's name, leaving the box below hers blank. All these people were connected, but to what extent?

Using dotted lines and starting from the top, she added in the known links. Kirsty had been married to Craig, Narelle was her sister, Grace was supposedly her best friend, and she had been architect Chandra Pinder's client. Because Jacinta wasn't sure if Kirsty had known, or known of, securities clerk Tamara Whitfield, she inserted a question mark between the two names.

In fact, Tamara Whitfield's only definite link to the group was she had worked for the same stockbroking firm Craig Edmonds had. Unless he had indeed been having some illicit affair with her, then it was highly unlikely Grace would even have known she existed, and the likelihood Chandra Pinder had known her would be even less. Narelle had told her that Tamara worked for the same stockbrokers as Craig, but claimed they hardly knew each other. Is that what Craig had told her? How long ago?

A possibility she hadn't wanted to contemplate leapt out at her. She closed her eyes, thinking back to what Narelle had told her about the start of her affair with Craig. If she remembered correctly, the original affair between Craig and Narelle had lasted for about five or six months, breaking off about a year before Kirsty disappeared. That meant that for Daniel's scenario to be right, Craig had to have been having an extramarital affair with not one woman, but two. Love square? Her mind boggled.

However, that didn't explain how the next victim, Chandra Pinder, fitted in. True or not, affairs were consensual; stalking wasn't. Narelle's throwaway comment about Craig definitely remembering the architect because of her stunning looks needled Jacinta. Was it possible Craig had made a play for Chandra, not accepting no for an answer when she rebuffed him? Had he been such a philanderer that a wife *and* a mistress weren't enough to satisfy him?

The diagram began to look like a warped spider web as, adding yet another dotted line, she joined Chandra's and Narelle's boxes. Like her husband and sister, Narelle had been acquainted with everyone on the page, with perhaps the exception of Tamara Whitfield.

Skipping the blank box, Jacinta moved on to the final one. With her pen poised, she studied the lines radiating from the box labeled Grace Kevron, connecting her to Kirsty, Craig and Narelle. Question marks hung over the remaining two. Because Chandra Pinder had been contracted by the Edmondses, it was possible but not certain that Grace, as Kirsty's best friend, had met the architect. She made a mental note to ask Narelle.

That left Tamara Whitfield. Even if Craig had been involved with the securities clerk and Kirsty had found out, would she have told Grace about it? Jacinta had her doubts. As it was, Grace's hurt at only finding out about the affair between Kirsty's sister and husband at the murder trial, and not from her so-called best friend, was still evident years later.

Absent-mindedly clicking and unclicking her ballpoint pen, Jacinta stared unseeing at the end of the bed. Grace might have had it in for Craig and Narelle for what she perceived they had done to Kirsty, but what possible reason would she have had to want Tamara and Chandra dead? None that Jacinta could immediately see.

However, who was the mystery contact Grace kept alluding to? A journalist or someone with insider knowledge? News of Narelle and Craig's marriage had only been published after Grace had found out about it. Moreover, how had Grace come to be at the Toolangi State Forest crime scene? Someone must have tipped her off.

Jacinta's imagination ran rampant, conjuring up an endless list of possible, if not improbable, plots and motives. In her mind she could make anything fit, even briefly entertaining Grace's notion that Narelle and Craig had been in it together, before dismissing the idea as ludicrous. Sisters didn't kill each other. Besides, divorce would have been the simple option if the pair had wanted Kirsty out of the way.

More confused than ever, she gathered up the loose pages and jammed them together with the notebook and pen back into the drawer. Writing her thoughts down had had quite the opposite effect to the one she intended. Instead of clearing her mind, all she had done was shuffle everything around, making room for more sleep-robbing notions.

She glanced at the empty bed beside her, wishing Brett were there. Apart from missing him, sex never failed to put her to sleep. Hoping a warm cup of milky cocoa would go at least some of the way to having the same soporific effect, she padded down to the kitchen. Opening the fridge door, she half-expected to find Brett had drunk all the milk that morning, as he was inclined to do, but to her amazement, she found a new, unopened carton wedged in beside the one she had bought on the weekend and that was already virtually empty.

In the night stillness, the purr of the microwave as it warmed a mug of milk seemed magnified, the end ping ear-splitting. Even the clank of the teaspoon against the inside of the cup as she stirred in the cocoa sounded like she was bashing a toy xylophone. Tossing the dirty spoon into the sink, she lifted the mug to her mouth, inhaling the rich cocoa aroma.

She froze, a sense that something wasn't quite right engulfing her. Then she heard what sounded like soft footsteps outside the kitchen window. Jacinta's chest constricted. Her breathing tightened further. In slow motion, she set the warm mug on the kitchen bench and flicked the range hood's light switch, plunging the room into darkness. For a few moments, she stood clutching the edge of the bench, the pounding of her own heart the only sound she could hear.

Mustering the courage to move, she lifted the corner of the blind and looked out. Her stomach lurched, her mouth opening in a silent gasp. She jumped back, dropping the blind as she ducked below the bench. Huddled against the kitchen cupboards, she tried to stem her panic. It was pitch-black out there, yet she was convinced she had sensed, if not seen, movement.

Scrambling on all fours in the dark, she managed to locate the cordless phone, breathing a little easier when she heard the dial tone. But who to call? Brett was too far away to be of any real help. Daniel and Wendy certainly wouldn't appreciate being woken in the small hours for something that might turn out to be nothing more than her overactive imagination.

Was she being neurotic, or was someone prowling around outside her home? The tables had turned. Now she knew how Narelle must have felt. She hugged the phone to her chest, her whole body so hypersensitive to her surroundings that she felt sure she would have sensed the vibrations of a spider's eight legs crawling up the wall.

For what seemed hours, she sat motionless, too petrified to move, until finally she plucked up the nerve to phone Brett. She needed to hear his voice, needed him to tell her nothing bad was going to happen, and needed to reassure herself he was in bed alone. She had forgiven him his indiscretion at a similar conference in Sydney, but she hadn't forgotten. She almost laughed. If scaring herself witless hadn't been enough, she had to torment herself with what Brett might or might not be up to.

You have to trust him, she thought, running her fingers over the phone's raised buttons. She located the menu key, knowing Brett's mobile was the first number listed. Before she could stop herself, she had pressed the talk button.

46

Brett Rhodes woke with a start, the unfamiliar texture and scent of the heavy cotton sheets disorientating him. It took him a while to work out where the ringing sound was coming from. At the same time he realized it was his mobile phone, he remembered where he was, his pounding head adding to the picture building in his mind. Whose bright idea had it been to pub-crawl their way across Canberra?

Unwilling to open his eyes, he groped blindly for the phone, answering with a pained grunt.

"It's me," a woman's voice whispered.

Groggy with sleep and the aftermath of countless beers, he grunted again, his parched mouth struggling to form words.

"Did I wake you?"

"Jacinta?" With a mammoth effort, he managed to open one eye and look at the alarm clock. Pain darted through the retina to his brain. Covering both eyes with his clammy palm, he groaned. "Do you know what time it is?" Still half-asleep, it hadn't yet registered that Jacinta wouldn't be calling him before dawn for no reason.

"No," she said, her voice a harsh whisper. "Brett, I don't know what to do. I heard noises and I saw movement by the kitchen window. I think someone's out there."

"What noises?" She had his attention now.

"Like shuffling footsteps."

"Could it have been a possum?" he asked, hoping that was all it was. Stress could wreak havoc on the mind and the amount of stress Jacinta had been under in the last few weeks, he wouldn't have been surprised if she had seen Martians. Perhaps he should have cancelled the Canberra trip after all.

"Bloody big possum," she hissed.

"Just asking." Opening his eyes slightly, he pushed himself up into a sitting position. "Have you called the police?"

Silence.

"Jacinta, are you still there?"

"Yes."

"For God's sake, have you called the police? Yes or no?" His anxiety levels rising, he clamped the phone to his ear, his hangover all but forgotten. Narelle's prowler had turned out to be her husband, but a bullet to the shoulder meant it couldn't be Craig skulking around outside Jacinta's house. However, his shooter was still on the loose.

"Not yet... Shush, I heard something."

"Jacinta, don't do anything stupid!" He jumped out of bed, feeling no pain as his thigh connected with the sharp corner of the narrow, wall-mounted ledge-cum-desk. "For God's sake, call the police!"

So far away, he felt powerless. Useless. He paced back and forth between the tiny en suite and the bed, feeling like a caged dingo, the compact motel room providing everything except room to move.

He could hear her creeping around, her light tread hesitant, a sharp intake of breath before another step. "Call Daniel!" he yelled down the phone.

He held his breath, listening. Ragged breathing, a muffled jangle in the background, then Jacinta's scream, a loud clunk the last thing he heard before the phone went dead.

47

The doorbell rang again, its shrill peal jolting her body like an electric shock. Abandoning the phone where it had landed in two pieces on the hard floor, Jacinta crept toward the front door, her pulse surging with each shaky step.

Steeling herself, she took a deep breath and looked through the peephole. She squinted, trying but failing to make out her visitor's face in the shadowy dawn light. Although something about the silhouette was familiar, it wasn't until the person turned that she recognized the profile. Jacinta fumbled with the door lock, wondering what had happened for Narelle to turn up on her doorstep so early. Still wary, she opened the door barely enough to talk to her unexpected caller.

Narelle's tired eyes stared through the door crack at her. "I hope I didn't wake you," she said, wringing her hands and moving in so close that Jacinta could taste her sour breath. "I would've phoned but the damn thing's flat. I haven't had a chance to recharge it." She shifted her weight from foot to foot, her narrowed eyes imploring Jacinta to understand.

Visions of her prowler danced through Jacinta's mind. "How long have you been here?"

Narelle stopped moving, her eyebrows drawing together. "I've just arrived. I was on my way home from the hospital to have a shower and pick up some things for Craig. I saw you hanging around last night but I couldn't face you or anyone else then." She paused. "I'm sorry if I've disturbed you," she added, backing away.

"Narelle, stop!"

Narelle faltered, half-turning.

"You haven't disturbed me. I just wasn't expecting you, that's all," Jacinta said, opening the door wider.

The slam of car doors and muffled voices diverted both women's attention toward the street.

Narelle's already ashen face blanched further. "You called the cops on me?" she stammered, her eyes wide in disbelief.

Slowly shaking her head, Jacinta watched as two male, uniformed officers, one much taller and stockier than the other, opened the front gate and walked up the short path toward them. What were they doing there? Then she remembered her phone call to Brett.

She stepped forward to greet them. "I'm sorry, officers, I think you've been called out unnecessarily."

"Jacinta Deller?" asked the short, wiry one, surprising her with the deepness of his voice.

She nodded, opening her mouth to tell them it had all been a false alarm, when she spotted Daniel pulling up at the curb. What next? The fire brigade?

Narelle started edging away from the house, her gaze flitting between the police officers and the street, as if looking for an escape route. Jacinta caught her by the elbow, gently drawing her back.

"I'm sorry," she said, positioning herself between Narelle and the men, "to have wasted your time, but as you can see, I'm perfectly all right."

The police officers exchanged glances, but said nothing. Wrapping her arms around herself, Jacinta shivered, suddenly conscious of her half-dressed state. Daniel came to her rescue, sending the two uniformed men on their way.

"After you," he said, extending an arm in the direction of the door.

"I should be going," Narelle said, backing away again.

Daniel blocked her way. "A couple of extra minutes won't hurt. You look like you could do with a sit-down and a good strong cup of tea. Herbal, of course," he said, as he corralled the two women into the house.

"I should call Brett," Jacinta said, scooping up the two pieces of the phone from the floor and slotting them back together. "I dropped it," she added in response to Daniel's raised eyebrows, before making a beeline for her bedroom. "Make yourselves at home. I'll be back in a minute." Long enough to call Brett and put some clothes on.

Closing the bedroom door behind her, she let out a loud huff, taking a few moments to get her thoughts in order. As much as she wanted to suppress them, little doubts were starting to niggle at her. Had she been blinkered into thinking what Narelle wanted her to think? Or was she letting other people's perceptions – and that was all they were – sway her beliefs? Although they had nothing to back it up, Grace Kevron, Daniel and even Brett had all intimated that there was more to Narelle than Jacinta was seeing.

Narelle claimed she had just come from the hospital, but was it possible she had been outside the house for a lot longer? What conceivable reason could Narelle – pregnant, her husband lying seriously injured in hospital – have to want to spend a chilly night stalking the only person trying to help her? *No*, decided Jacinta, pulling on a denim skirt, *something isn't right, but it's not Narelle.*

Talking to Brett, reassuring him she was still in one piece and that cutting short his trip wouldn't achieve anything, took longer than expected. "Love you, too. Please don't worry about me. I'll call you tonight." Hanging up, she heard cupboard doors banging in the kitchen. Hoping Daniel wasn't searching for the non-existent herbal tea he had offered Narelle, she went to join them.

Daniel was alone in the kitchen, systematically opening and closing cupboards and drawers. On the bench top, he had amassed three mugs, the large coffee plunger, the tin of ground Arabica coffee, the sugar bag from the pantry and the crystallized remains of a jar of honey. "Where do you hide the tea?" asked Daniel, checking the cupboard under the sink.

"Ordinary tea, I have," she said, presenting him with a green, hinged-lid tin that used to house mint chocolates. "Herbal, I don't. Where's Narelle?"

"Other room."

Jacinta rolled her eyes. *Ask a stupid question,* she thought, heading for the living room. But Narelle wasn't there. Nor was there any sign of her in the dining room, bedroom, laundry, bathroom or toilet. Some minder Daniel made. Although, to give him some credit, it wasn't the first time Narelle had slipped away unnoticed.

"She's gone."

Daniel stopped pouring, the kettle suspended mid-air. "What do you mean she's gone?"

"Not here, AWOL, absent, missing, gone!" she said, her pitch escalating with each word.

Shrugging, he finished filling the coffee plunger. "She won't have gone far. Not with her husband in hospital."

"Why do I seem to be the only one concerned about her? Have you forgotten that the man — " Daniel cocked an eyebrow at her " — or woman who shot her husband is still at large? Not to mention she's pregnant and probably not thinking straight."

"Hormonal, you reckon?" He chuckled. "You might be able to get away with saying that, but if I even hinted at it, I'd be ducking for cover. Ask Wendy."

"No, that's not what I mean." She sighed, shaking her head. "Forget I said anything." Stress, fatigue, illness, or hormones: whatever the cause, the result was the same. Jacinta felt close to the edge herself. "Black, thanks," she said, counting on the coffee to revive her enough to get her act together. Her job required her to be a functioning human being.

As Daniel concentrated on pressing the plunger down and filling two of the mugs, she studied his face, the tightness of his lips and the deep V above the bridge of his nose evidence of his stress levels.

"Any news on Craig's shooter or the missing gun yet?"

Daniel continued stirring his coffee, not looking up. "No."

"I'm not trying to tell you how to do your job, and I know you told me Grace Kevron couldn't have done it, but have you considered she could have an accomplice?"

"You really have it in for Grace, don't you?"

"She's hiding something, I'm sure of it. And you have to admit, she's made no secret about her feelings for Craig and Narelle."

Daniel nodded. "Sure, she blames them, but if you were in her position you might have, too. It's a natural reaction to seek out a scapegoat when there are no definitive answers. Grace might be a bit screwed up, but that doesn't automatically label her a psychopathic killer. In fact, the psych report suggests she's more likely to harm herself than anyone else."

Jacinta still wasn't convinced. He hadn't been on the receiving end of her outbursts. "But you haven't completely ruled out her involvement, right?"

The corners of his eyes creased, his mouth twitching in barely suppressed amusement. "Have you thought about changing career? Doggedness is one of the prerequisites to being a good cop."

"Ha, ha, very funny." But it wasn't. She knew her strength lay in her tenacity. Without it, she couldn't have survived. "You're such a comedian. Have *you* thought about changing jobs?"

"Frequently." The smile faded from his face. "But in answer to your question, until we have evidence to prove otherwise, we won't be eliminating anyone from our enquiries. Shuffled down the list perhaps, but not ruled out." He poured himself another cup of coffee. "Don't worry; we'll be talking with Grace in the next day or two. She was released into her mother's care late yesterday, but even though she's responded well to treatment and is considered stable, I'm told she's still a little on the fragile side. Don't, whatever you do, go bothering her. You'll just make my job twice as hard.

"Now," he said, glancing at his watch, "I have to be somewhere else. Are you going to be all right on your own? I could always have someone come and sit with you."

"Thank you for caring," she replied, his concern tempering her indignation, "but I don't need babysitting." She forced a smile. "Besides, having a police officer tagging along with me to work wouldn't be a good look."

After Daniel left, she hurried from room to room, opening blinds and curtains, the early morning light diluting the emptiness and heavy silence.

In the bathroom, she turned the shower taps to full, undressing while she waited for the water to warm up. She tested the temperature and was about to step in, when a flash of movement through the bathroom's frosted glass window caught her eye. She froze, her breath catching in her throat. She hadn't imagined it that time. Over the noise of the shower, she heard a scraping sound, like one of the wooden outdoor chairs being dragged across the brick paving. Then nothing.

Leaving the shower running, she wrapped a towel around herself and tiptoed into the bedroom. She was careful to avoid the windows. The phone lay less than a meter away on the bedside table. It rang. She jumped, letting out an involuntary squawk.

She snatched up the ringing phone, wanting it to be Daniel. "Hello?" she whispered, her hand cupped around the phone's mouthpiece.

"Jacinta?"

"Shit, Narelle, why did…" She stopped, convinced she had heard voices. "Can't talk now. Someone's creeping around outside."

"It's—"

"Call Daniel." Jacinta paused, listening. "Call the police. Call anyone—"

"Jacinta, listen to me. It's me. I'm outside your house. I'm at the door now."

Struck dumb, Jacinta stared at the phone. If Narelle was at the front door, why was she phoning?

"Jacinta?"

"Jesus, Narelle," she hissed, her voice no longer a whisper. "What the hell are you playing at? Do you realize you scared me half to death?" She took a breath. "But hang on, when I answered the door earlier, you told me you had just arrived."

"I had."

"But that means…"

"This is silly. How about letting me in so we can talk face to face?"

For a split second, Jacinta considered leaving Narelle out there and calling Daniel. But if she couldn't trust her own instincts, whose could she trust?

With the phone still in her hand, she went to let Narelle in, checking she was on her own before opening the door.

Narelle's sunken eyes widened slightly. "Oh God, I've done it again, interrupted you."

Following Narelle's gaze, Jacinta looked down; the navy-blue towel barely covered her torso. "Not this month's fashion, then?" she said, hoping to inject a touch of levity into the situation. For her own sake, if not Narelle's.

Narelle didn't smile.

"Please don't worry about it. Come in," Jacinta said, ushering her inside. "I can have a shower any time." That wasn't quite true. If she didn't have a shower within the next half hour, she would be late for work. Again. "Just give me a minute to put something a bit more respectable on." *And don't disappear this time*, she added silently.

She entered her bedroom, cursing as she saw steam billowing from the bathroom and heard the sound of water running. She'd be lucky if there was enough hot water left to have a shower. Managing to turn off the taps without getting too wet, she dumped her towel on the floor, replacing it with the white cotton waffle robe from behind the door.

She found Narelle on the daybed, her back against the wall with her knees drawn up, staring blankly out the window. Jacinta joined her, sitting on the opposite end. Seconds ticked by.

"How's Craig?"

Narelle's gaze didn't flicker. "Off the critical list."

"That's good news."

Silence.

"Narelle, I know you're scared." Of what or whom, Jacinta wasn't sure. "I'm here for you, but I sense you're not telling me something. Whatever it is, I can help you deal with it." *Anything except a confession to murder*, added a small voice in her head. Shoving that thought to the back of her mind, she said, "But if we're not honest with each other, it can't work."

"Why are you doing this? What do you get out of it?"

"What are friends for?"

"You're telling the story."

Jacinta flinched, taken aback by Narelle's abrasive tone. "Why did you come here, then?"

Narelle shrugged, looked at Jacinta and promptly burst into tears. Sitting on her hands, Jacinta refrained from reaching out to her. The next move had to come from Narelle.

"I'm sorry," Narelle blubbered. "I shouldn't be taking my moods out on you."

Jacinta said nothing.

"I'm not making excuses, but with everything that's been happening, I'm all over the place." Shifting to the edge of the daybed, she dropped her feet to the floor and stood up. "I'm sorry, I shouldn't have come."

"You have to stop running sometime."

"I'm not running."

"No? What are you doing now, then? What was your little disappearing act earlier all about? What have you been doing for the last ten years?"

"You don't understand."

"Obviously not."

Tears streamed down Narelle's face. "I want to be normal. I want to live a normal life with my husband and," she paused, her hand straying to her abdomen, "our child. I want to put the past behind us. I wish it was that easy…" Her voice trailed off.

Feeling her façade cracking, Jacinta swallowed hard, resisting the urge to reach out and comfort the teary woman. For things to change, Narelle couldn't be allowed to retreat back inside her shell. To date, compassion hadn't worked; perhaps confrontation would. "Forget being honest with me, you have to be honest with yourself."

"What do you mean?"

Jacinta took a punt. "You know what I mean," she said, her tone all-knowing, although she had no idea what she meant herself.

Narelle dropped her gaze, her bottom lip quivering as she slumped back down onto the daybed. "But that's it; I don't know what's real and what isn't any more. My sister and two other women are dead, shot through the head. That's real. That Craig's father's gun, the murder weapon and the one used to shoot him could be one and the same? How could that possibly be?" She paused, her long fingernails clawing the backs of her hands. "Craig didn't tell me about the gun," she said, her voice soft and sad. "I found it by accident when I was cleaning up some broken glass and took off the dishwasher kickboard to check if any had slid underneath."

Jacinta opened her mouth, thought better of it, and closed it again.

"Do I wonder why he didn't tell me about the gun?" Narelle continued. "Yes. Do I want to believe the man I love is capable of murder? No." She stopped scratching her hands and glanced at Jacinta. "But him being shot proves it couldn't have been him, doesn't it?"

She had a point, but Jacinta's what-if brain had already kicked into gear. What if, in a misguided attempt to divert suspicion from Craig, Narelle had shot him? Could love, or whatever it was, really be that blind? What if he was innocent after all? What if the gun had been planted? Who hated him enough to want to destroy his life? "It certainly helps his case," she said, not quite giving Narelle the answer she was looking for, "but there are still too many unanswered questions. Who," she said, knowing before Narelle opened her mouth what the answer would be, "do you think would want to kill, or at least maim Craig?"

Straightening her back, Narelle met Jacinta's gaze. "Grace Kevron."

"I know that's what you think, but unfortunately she has a rock-solid alibi for the time of the shooting."

Narelle's lip curled. "She probably hired someone to do it. I wouldn't put anything past that bitch."

That was one possibility Jacinta hadn't contemplated. An accomplice, perhaps, but not a hit man. "You of all people know what it feels like to be unjustly accused. Do you have anything, besides a feeling, to support that suggestion?"

Narelle sighed, her sagging shoulders answering the question.

"When Craig was shot, where were you?"

"Just what are you implying?"

Oversensitive or a guilty conscience? "Nothing. What I meant was, were you in a position to see the car? Did you see anything? Did you hear the shot? That's all."

Looking sideways at Jacinta, Narelle said, "I'm surprised your policeman stepbrother hasn't told you everything. Aren't you two like," she raised a hand, crossing two fingers, "that?"

Jacinta closed her eyes, inwardly screaming as she took a deep breath. "Do you want my help or not?" she snapped, Narelle's mood swings more than testing her patience.

48

Fortunately for DI Lassiter, the same charge nurse was on duty. "How's our patient today?"

"Resting comfortably and doing remarkably well. We're watching him carefully, but except for a slight fever, his obs are all within the normal range. He's one lucky man. If that bullet had been any lower, we wouldn't be having this conversation."

"Any chance I could talk to him for a few minutes?"

She frowned, her mouth pursing.

"Nothing heavy, I promise," he said, holding up his hands. "I just want to see what he does and doesn't remember. The longer we leave it, the less he's going to recall." He held her gaze, using his eyes to draw her in. "Five minutes; ten at the most. You can supervise, if you like," he added, his last comment swinging it for him.

Escorted by the charge nurse, Daniel entered the small hospital room. Propped on a mound of white pillows, the head of the bed raised slightly, lay Craig Edmonds, one shoulder bare, the other heavily bandaged. The tubes, catheters and wires connecting him to monitors and other equipment reinforced the seriousness of his injury.

The patient's eyelids fluttered, then opened, his dark eyes accentuating the paleness of his face. Whether it was a side effect of the drugs or not, he struggled to focus on his visitors, his pupils remaining dilated, his face impassive. Recognition dawned slowly, his bottom lip drooping as the DI advanced.

Daniel pulled the plastic, padded visitor chair in close to the bed and sat down. The less intimidated Craig felt in his presence, the better.

Craig's voice crackled as he tried to speak, his chapped lips stretching thin over his teeth. He motioned toward a disposable cup on the bedside unit next to him. The nurse nodded as Daniel, glancing her way, picked up the cup of half-melted ice cubes, holding it still while Craig hooked one of the slippery fragments with his fingers. Sucking greedily on it, he dipped his fingers back in the cup and smeared icy water around his mouth and stubbly chin.

"Mr Edmonds," Daniel said, replacing the cup and sitting back in the chair, "we need to find whoever did this to you, and fast." Craig turned his head away, looking to the nurse. "Don't you care," continued Daniel, "that while you're safe here under police guard, your pregnant wife is out there, fending for herself? Think about it. Someone out there is desperate enough to want you or her or both of you dead."

His face contorting, Craig made a valiant attempt to sit up. "You have to protect her," he said, his voice a husky whisper.

"But that's it, Craig," Daniel said, switching to Craig's first name in an attempt to convince him he was on his side. "She refused our help point-blank. Your wife is one headstrong woman, but the longer your assailant is at large," he paused, adding emphasis to his next words, "the longer her life is in peril. We need your help."

Craig's voice filled with despair as he gazed down at his inert body. "But what can I do?"

"Lead me through everything that happened that day. Start from when you were discharged from the hospital."

Craig's mouth twisted. "I don't remember much. It's all so patchy. Please," he said, tears welling, "whatever it takes, you have to protect Narelle."

The nurse stepped in, stretching a protective arm across her patient. "That's enough."

Craig moved his head from side to side. "No, not yet." He gave a low sigh, sinking back against the pillows, his eyes closing as if the effort of shaking his head had been too much. "What do you want to know?"

"What time did you leave the hospital?"

"I'm not sure. Sometime around four, I think. The taxi driver will have a better idea."

"Why didn't Narelle collect you from the hospital?"

"I wanted to surprise her."

"You bought flowers," prompted Daniel, recalling the bouquet of six pink roses found in the gutter.

Craig opened his eyes, nodding. "That's right, I did."

"Okay, you're in the back of the taxi, holding a bunch of flowers and looking forward to surprising your wife. The taxi turns into your street and pulls up where? In the driveway? At the curb?"

"At the curb."

"How did you pay the driver?" An inconsequential detail, but Daniel hoped it would help stimulate his memory.

"Credit card. I had no cash."

"You get out of the taxi and look up and down the street. What do you see?"

Craig closed his eyes again. "Only what you would expect to see. Cars parked on the street and in driveways. A kid on a bike. A pregnant woman pushing a pram..." He screwed up his eyes. "A white courier van with orange writing. Not a company I recognized. I only noticed it because it slowed, like the driver was looking for an address or something, but I really didn't think that much of it. It drove past."

"The driver, was it a man or a woman?" Daniel leaned forward, keen to catch every word. For a moment, he thought Craig had drifted off.

"I think it was a woman, but I can't be sure." Craig paused. "Or it could have been a small man with long black hair. The driver was wearing sunglasses..." His voice trailed off mid-sentence and then started again. "...and I only saw her or him for an instant. Sorry..."

Ignoring the daggered look the nurse threw his way, Daniel leaned in even closer to Craig. "You're doing great. We're nearly there..."

Narelle burst into the room, the pitch of her voice escalating as she stormed Daniel. "I don't believe you people. This is police harassment. Get out! Get out now!"

Daniel jumped up, grappling with her flailing arms as she came at him, her cheeks blazing like beacons.

"Can't you see he's ill? He doesn't know what he's saying. Leave him alone." Her nails gouged the skin on his wrist, drawing a beaded line of blood.

"Calm down. You have it all wrong." His hand pushed down hard on her shoulder. "Sit!" And like an obedient dog, she did.

Breathing hard, she gulped air, tears streaming down her face. "It's not fair," she sobbed, plucking handfuls of tissues from the box the nurse held out. "Craig's the victim here."

"Narelle." Craig waggled his fingers in his wife's direction, his voice rasping as he tried to attract her attention. "Darling."

"Oh, Craig, I'm here now," Narelle whispered, standing up and wiping her eyes. Squeezing his fingers, she brushed her lips over his closed eyelids. "Rest now. I'll still be here when you wake up." The tension ebbed from her husband's face, his eyelids twitching but not opening.

Leaving Narelle fussing over her husband, Daniel went to check who had been on duty the previous night. Jacinta had been adamant that someone or something had been outside her house. He had a possum or a cat tagged as the prime suspect, but still needed to confirm that Narelle had been at the hospital all night, as she claimed. At least Jacinta would know then he had taken her concerns seriously.

Waiting at the nurses' station for someone to turn up, he wondered how much more Craig knew but didn't realize he knew. If only there had been more time. His wife's dramatic entrance had put a stop to that. She obviously didn't want her husband talking to the police, but what had she meant when she said Craig didn't know what he was saying? What had she thought he had been saying? Or about to say?

Daniel strode back to the room and peered through the small, rectangular window in the closed door. Craig appeared to be sleeping, the rise and fall of his chest almost imperceptible. Narelle perched on the front edge of the chair, her forearms and head resting on the white-sheeted bed next to Craig's thighs, her face obscured by a mass of brunette curls.

"Aaron," he said, turning to the bored-looking police officer stationed outside the room, "there's been a change of plans. I need you inside the room. Under no circumstances is the patient to be left alone with anyone except a police officer or a doctor. Make sure you verify everyone's identity. I'll arrange for someone to relieve you shortly. Do you understand?"

Nodding, Constable Aaron Grant picked up his chair and shouldered the door.

"And Aaron, I want to know every word that is spoken by or to Craig Edmonds." Daniel hoped the constable's presence in the room would be enough to deter the Edmondses from concocting some story to suit themselves. Distrustful of the police and dependent on one another, Daniel knew they would do whatever it took to shield each other. But why couldn't they see they were sabotaging themselves? Hiding from the truth wouldn't make it any less real.

49

Margaret Kevron fought to keep the quaver from her voice. "Grace?" She stood in the lounge doorway and waited for her daughter to look up from the magazine in her lap.

Grace scrambled to her feet, the blood draining from her face. "Oh my God, Mum, what are you doing with that?"

"I thought you could tell me." Margaret held the revolver away from her body, her arms trembling so hard the gun jiggled in her palms. "Oh, Gracie," she said, resorting to her daughter's childhood name, "don't you know how dangerous guns are?"

"Of course I bloody do. Put it down, Mum."

As Grace advanced toward her, Margaret angled her body away. "I don't understand. After what happened to your father, I thought you hated guns."

Pain flared in Grace's eyes, the rawness of her father's suicide still evident. "I do! What are you on about?" Then she gasped. "Oh, no, I hope you don't think it's mine."

"It was with your things."

"What things?" demanded Grace, her voice escalating to a screech. "What are you talking about? Where did you find it?"

"Please, Gracie, let's try and discuss this calmly."

"It's not mine."

Margaret wasn't about to contradict her daughter. "I believe you."

"Do you?" Grace gave her a baleful glare. "You never have in the past, why start now?"

Margaret's stomach churned. Had Grace come off her schizophrenia medication again? She had only her daughter's word that she had been taking the prescribed dose. On the two occasions Margaret had managed to check the Zyprexa pack without Grace seeing, the right number of tablets had been missing. But why hadn't Margaret been more forceful and insisted on watching her swallow them? "Of course I believe you. Who it belongs to isn't important."

Grace's gaze fixed on the gun in her mother's hands. "It's not mine," she repeated, her voice surprisingly calm, "and I don't know anything about it. Where did you find it?"

Biting her lip, Margaret racked her brain for the best way to tell her daughter she had been poking through some of her personal belongings. "I know how much you like everything to be neat, and when I was in the garage, I saw the corner of a newspaper sticking out of that old wooden trunk of your father's. I wasn't prying, Gracie, honest."

Grace scowled, holding her hand out, palm up. "Whatever." Skepticism ran in the family. "Give it to me."

As heavy as the gun felt in her hands, Margaret wasn't about to relinquish it to Grace. Losing a husband to suicide had been devastating enough; allowing it to happen again would destroy her. Whatever Grace's problems, they could work through them together. "It's not the answer."

"The answer to what...?" Grace stared at her, bursting into laughter as she read Margaret's face. "Oh, Mum, you didn't really think I would use a gun to top myself, did you?" She laughed again.

"I guess not," murmured Margaret, looking around the all-white room. "Too messy."

Grace howled, her hysterical laughter loud but unconvincing. "Sometimes you're too much, Mum."

Margaret didn't think she was too much. What mother wouldn't be concerned to find a gun hidden amongst her child's things? Even more so when her child's father had selfishly ended his own life with a firearm, no matter that it had been a rifle and not a revolver? And Grace had been diagnosed with schizophrenia, the same mental illness suffered by her father. No, she wasn't too much.

Grace's laughter died. "Sorry, Mum. I know you worry, but there's no need to. I'm in no hurry to join Dad. That," she pointed at the gun, "isn't mine, and I had..." she corrected herself, "have no intention of using it. You can think what you like, but I swear I don't know how it got inside the trunk."

"In that case, you'll have no objection to me surrendering it to the police."

Grace baulked, her fingers splaying to cover her gaping mouth.

"It's the only sensible thing to do," continued Margaret.

"Forget sensible," Grace said, recovering her composure. "Have you stopped to think of the trouble you could get me into?"

"What trouble? I don't understand." Margaret understood her daughter less and less with each passing minute.

Exhaling loudly, Grace clapped her hands together on top of her head, as if her mother was beyond comprehending. "Let's start by you showing me exactly where you found the gun in the first place. And for God's sake, put the bloody thing down somewhere. I've already promised you I'm not going to take it."

A tug of war started in Margaret's head. If she put down the gun, Grace could take it. If she didn't, her daughter would know she didn't trust her. She had no choice. Carefully, as though it were made of fine crystal, she laid the gun on the white shelf to her right, nudging it behind one of the stereo's speakers.

Her hands felt dirty and clammy. Although desperate to wash them with soap under running water, she trailed Grace out to the garage, wiping her hands against each other as she went. Squeezing past the wing mirror on Grace's white Hyundai hatchback, she then followed her down the side of the single car garage to a suitcase and two cardboard cartons stacked atop the old wooden trunk.

Grace frowned. "You say you found it in this trunk?"

Margaret nodded.

"Tell me if I have this right. You moved the suitcase and the boxes, opened the trunk, saw the gun, took it out, closed the trunk again, and then lifted the suitcase and boxes back onto it?"

Margaret nodded again.

"Why?"

"I wanted to leave it as I found it," Margaret said, not mentioning that at the time she hadn't known what she was going to do with the revolver.

Grace sighed. "Except for the newspaper sticking out," she said, lifting the uppermost box and setting it on the concrete between the car and the trunk. She then sat the next box on top of it, before balancing the empty suitcase on that. "You sure went to a lot of trouble for a scrap of paper, Mum."

Margaret made no comment, continuing to watch as Grace wrestled with the trunk's ancient latches. With one last grunt, Grace hefted the solid wooden lid upright.

"What the…" Grace gasped and, reaching in, pulled out a glossy black wig, dangling it in front of her mother. "What's this doing in here?"

"Why are you asking me?"

"Well, it's not mine."

"Are you sure, Gracie?" Margaret didn't recall amnesia being a schizophrenia symptom.

Grace snorted. "Of course I'm bloody sure. What would I want with a black wig?" She tossed the hairy clump at Margaret before turning her attention back to the contents of the trunk. "And what the hell is all this crap? Citrus Couriers?" She held up two white, limp circles the size of large dinner plates, with bold orange borders and print. "Ever heard of them? I haven't."

The 'Citrus' part of the name meant nothing to Margaret, but something about a courier and the orange color nagged at the back of her mind. Something she had seen. Something she had heard.

Then she remembered. She had been watching the news on television while Grace soaked in the bath. A man had been shot outside his home and police were appealing for information about a white courier van with orange signage that had been seen in the vicinity. The driver was thought to have long, dark hair.

Margaret shook her head, her fingers twisting the long synthetic hairs in her hands. Refusing to think the worst, she studied her daughter's face for answers. If Grace's lowered brow and clamped lips were an act for the benefit of her mother, she deserved an Oscar. But if the gun, wig and signage didn't belong to Grace, how had they come to be inside a trunk in her garage? What person would go to the trouble of breaking into a stranger's garage to hide something? Why?

The other alternative was far bleaker. During a psychotic episode, could her daughter have lost touch with reality and done something terrible? Would she have remembered if she had?

"Mum, are you all right? You look like you've seen a ghost."

Margaret managed a small smile. "I don't believe in ghosts."

"Thank God for that. I thought you were going to tell me Dad was standing behind me." Grace slapped the two magnetic signs together, putting them aside as she delved back into the trunk. "It's been ages since I went through all this stuff. Hey," she said, emerging from the trunk, holding a green and red rubber monster mask to her face, "maybe that gun you found isn't even real. Now wouldn't that be a laugh?" Grace's high, pealed cackle bounced from wall to wall.

Call it gut instinct, call it woman's intuition, call it whatever, Margaret knew with a certainty that she hadn't been holding a replica or toy gun. As much as she wished otherwise, it was no laughing matter. "Listen to me, Grace."

"I'm listening," Grace said, dropping the rubber mask back into the trunk and picking up a scruffy teddy bear.

"No, really listen. I don't know all the details, but..." Margaret paused, undecided about what she should and shouldn't say. "...A man's been shot."

Straightening up, Grace clutched the teddy bear to her chest, her eyebrows arching as if to say: *So what? It happens all the time.*

"The police want to speak to the driver of a white courier van with orange signage."

With each word her mother said, Grace's head tilted further to the side.

"The description of the driver is vague," continued Margaret, looking down at the wig gripped in her hands, "but the person is believed to have long, black hair."

"What are you on about now? What man? When? Where?" Grace's clenched fists dug holes in the hapless teddy bear's back.

"It was on the news. I only caught the tail end..."

Taking a deep breath, Grace bowed her head. When she looked up again, her face was an expressionless mask. "Mum, I think you've been watching too many of those crime shows." She tried to laugh, but it fell flat, sounding contrived. "I remember now," she said, gathering up the black wig from Margaret's hands. "I bought this ages ago, for a fancy dress party."

Bewildered, Margaret didn't protest as Grace, not giving her mother a chance to respond, ushered her out of the garage and into the kitchen.

One minute Grace claimed she had never seen the items in the trunk before, the next her memory was miraculously restored. Margaret knew her daughter well enough to know when she was hiding something. She also knew her well enough to know when to back off.

After a light lunch of tomato on rye sandwiches, Grace excused herself, saying she needed to sleep. "You look tired, Mum. A lie-down would do you good, too."

Sleep was the last thing on Margaret's mind. The discovery of the gun and her daughter's erratic behavior had made sure of that. Until she found out what was happening, she doubted she would ever sleep again. Despite that, she stretched out on the couch, waking with a jolt when she heard a loud clank outside. Half-dazed, she clambered off the couch and went to investigate.

She crept past Grace's closed bedroom door. Another clank. Louder. She froze. Taking a moment to orientate herself, she realized it was coming from the backyard. She entered the kitchen, her nose wrinkling at the toxic stench of burning nylon and plastic wafting through the open window.

Careful to stay out of sight, she edged along the bench and peeked out. Grace stood with her back to the house, shrouded in a haze of dirty smoke. Squinting, Margaret drew her face closer to the window. The lid of the kettle barbecue sat on the concrete near Grace's feet. She appeared to be poking at something black and smoldering in the barbecue's base. A flash of orange.

Margaret gasped, jerking back from the window. Why would Grace be burning the wig and courier signs if she wasn't trying to hide something? But then again, and she had thought long and hard about this, if a dark-haired woman wanted to disguise herself, wouldn't she wear a blonde or a red wig? Anything but a black one.

Clutching at the table to steady herself, Margaret sat down. She could no longer ignore the growing dread that her daughter was indirectly, if not directly, involved in something bad. Who was she covering for? Who was she protecting?

50

Darkness signaled the end of another day, the end of another week. Looking forward to a weekend of nothing, Jacinta kicked off her shoes, curling up on the sofa with a glass of wine and the television remote control, content in the knowledge Brett would be home the next day. Maybe then she would stop jumping at her own shadow.

Perhaps Daniel had been right. Perhaps possums did wear big boots. Certainly, she'd had no more late night or early morning visitors, invited or otherwise. His confirmation that Narelle had been at the hospital with her husband all night also helped quash any lingering doubts she may have had about her friend, but left her feeling doubly bad that she had suspected her in the first place.

The police were no closer to tracking down Craig Edmonds' assailant, but nor had there been any more attempts on his or his wife's life. Jacinta was convinced the attack on Craig, his wife's murder and the Toolangi murders were all related. But how to prove it? Leads were scarce, evidence virtually non-existent. The gun had to be the lynchpin. If only she hadn't let it out of her hands.

Swirling her glass of wine, she glanced at the television. Her mind elsewhere, she absently watched the actors playing out their parts, heard their rehearsed lines. People living in a world of make-believe.

Narelle's world wasn't much different. Despite her friend's protestations about wanting a normal life, Jacinta knew it would remain out of reach until the killer or killers were brought to justice.

Until then, Narelle would have to continue living with uncertainty, doubts and suspicions. A life spent looking over her shoulder.

Skolling the rest of her wine, she dumped the empty glass on the side table, pressed the off button on the remote control and put her shoes back on. The only person who could help Narelle was Narelle. Intent on making her see that, Jacinta collected her car keys and headed out into the night.

She turned into Narelle's street, pulling up in front of the large, brick house. She let the engine idle, not convinced she was doing the right thing, wondering if interfering could cause more harm than good. She switched off the ignition and sat watching the house. Except for a glow from the pool area, the house was in complete darkness, the streetlights casting eerie shapes over the front lawn. She hadn't stopped to think Narelle might not be at home. But then, movement in one of the darkened front windows caught her eye.

Gathering up her shoulder bag, she unbuckled the seatbelt and got out of the car. She stretched her neck and rolled her shoulders, uncrimping the tight muscles. Determined not to leave until she had the answers she was looking for, she marched up the path, her resolve almost shattering when she triggered the security light sensors. White light flooded the area, making her feel like a rabbit caught in a hunter's spotlight.

The front door loomed. She took a deep breath, steadying her pulse, and kept going. Had Narelle seen the lights come on? Reaching the doorstep, she hesitated, half-expecting the door to open. When it didn't, she pressed the doorbell and, stepping back off the mat, waited. Nothing. She pressed it again, adding a knock for good measure.

Still nothing.

Then a thump, a stifled scream, another thump.

Then nothing.

Jacinta's heart raced, the saliva in her mouth drying as she backed away from the door. Something wasn't right. Adrenaline-pumped and with no time to call for help, she ran around the side the house, ripping her jeans as she hoisted herself over the locked iron gate. In the unlit corridor, she had difficulty seeing where she was going, stumbling on the uneven cobblestones.

She rounded the corner of the house by the swimming pool. Immediately she ducked back. Silhouetted in the light by the pool, two figures tussled on the ground. Crouching down and shielded in the shadows, Jacinta crept forward. She heard Narelle's plaintive voice and another, more strident female's, but couldn't make out what they were saying.

Pressing her back up hard against the wall of the house, she felt in her bag for her mobile phone, panicking when she realized she had left it on the kitchen bench. She glanced back at the two women, unable to staunch her cry as she caught the glint of metal, the split-second interruption enough for Narelle to escape the clutches of the other woman.

Narelle scuttled backward, yelling at Jacinta to run, as she made a dash for the house. Narelle wasn't quick enough, the other woman pouncing and snagging her ankle, bringing her prey down with a thud.

Letting out a blood-curdling shriek, Jacinta hurtled across the paving. She threw herself on the woman's back and gouged at her eyes. Howling with rage, the woman bucked, tossing Jacinta aside like a rag doll. She heard the crack in her arm before she felt the pain.

The woman advanced, laughing and brandishing a long-bladed knife. "You should have kept your reporter nose out of it, bitch."

All of a sudden, Grace's voice rang out. "Kirsty!"

The scene froze, an instant snapshot. Jacinta's mind spun, the moment too surreal to grasp. *Kirsty? Narelle's sister? Craig's wife? The murdered woman? That Kirsty?*

"It's over, Kirsty. No more."

Baring her teeth, the woman laughed. "Grace, darling, how right you are," she said, her eyes narrowing at the gun pointed at her. "So you found it."

"You used me. After everything I did for you, how could you? I thought you loved me." Tears streamed down Grace's cheeks as, using both hands to hold the gun, she moved forward.

"Grace, give me the gun."

Grace continued to advance.

"Darling, you know I love you." Kirsty lunged for the gun, grabbing first the barrel and then Grace's arm. Both women fell to the ground, wrestling for control of the weapon.

A gunshot shattered the night.

Grace toppled back, a look of disbelief on her face.

Kirsty clutched her abdomen, blood blooming under her shirt, pooling on the pavers under her body.

EPILOGUE

Jacinta adjusted the sling, the cast on her fractured left wrist weighing heavy on her neck, the afternoon's heat only adding to her discomfort. Seated at the end of the outdoor table, Narelle and Wendy chatted non-stop about babies and pregnancy matters. Pain and gory bits not exempt. If they wanted to put Jacinta off ever having children, they were succeeding.

She glanced across to the men congregated around the barbecue. Brett and Craig supervised while Daniel cooked, talking men's business, no doubt. Craig caught her eye and smiled, raising his beer in a toast. She raised her glass in return. Who would ever have thought they could've been in the same space together without tearing each other apart, let alone be on friendly terms? All those years of being unfairly persecuted would have hardened the most placid of people.

Kirsty Edmonds' funeral had been a small, private affair, restricted to direct family. That hadn't stopped the media jostling for position outside the church, waiting for the mourners to emerge. Bids for the Edmonds' story had come thick and fast, but Narelle and Craig hadn't been swayed by promises of riches and celebrity, preferring to keep a low profile. Instead, they'd handed the scoop to Jacinta, trusting her to be their spokesperson.

Pulling the pieces together had been the hardest part. With salvaged memories and Grace's help, the picture became clearer.

Kirsty had always been a jealous person, but marrying Craig had only aggravated it, not alleviated it. Unless she knew where he was and what he was doing every minute of every day, she wasn't happy. Suspecting Craig was cheating on her fuelled her insecurities. She became obsessed with finding the other woman. She stalked him incessantly, watched his every move, eavesdropped on his conversations, checked his pockets, smelt his clothes, scrutinized his mobile phone bill, read his SMS messages, rifled through his briefcase. The thought it could be her own sister obviously didn't cross her mind at that stage.

Irrational with jealousy, Kirsty saw relationships where none existed. A friendly smile, a look, a touch perhaps, but that was all. Tamara Whitfield and Chandra Pinder were hapless, innocent victims, their only sin that they had been acquainted with Craig Edmonds. But as far as Kirsty was concerned, these two women were vying with her for her husband's affections, and they had to be stopped. Permanently.

It must have cut deeply when she eventually found out her husband's lover was her own sister. The two people she loved most had betrayed her. She wanted them to suffer. In her mind, death would've been too kind. She went one step better, framing them for her own murder.

Filled with hatred, she must have spent months plotting her revenge. The insurance policies, a new identity, seducing Grace, fabricating evidence, an escape route – all meticulously planned. All the while, Craig and Narelle carried on their illicit affair.

Biding her time, she waited for the right moment, slipping Rohypnol or a similar stupefying drug into his whisky before provoking him into an argument. Mixed with the alcohol, the drugs would have taken effect quickly, ensuring he wouldn't remember anything that happened next.

Time to stage the scene. As a nurse, she had no problem drawing her own blood. Smearing it around the house, she used it to full effect, creating the bloodbath illusion. Planting the hairs in the boot of her car was even easier.

Then, under the cover of darkness, with her husband passed out on the bed, she made her escape, flying out of the country that night under an assumed identity, using a false passport and looking a far cry from the photo splashed across the media in the ensuing days and weeks.

She no doubt followed all the news reports, reveling in the havoc her untimely disappearance had caused. The coup de grâce had to have been seeing her husband charged not once, but twice for her murder.

And she would have pulled it off without a hitch, if she had been able to stay away. After years of relying on the media to keep her informed, Kirsty wanted to see for herself the impact her actions had had on the lives of her betrayers. Jacinta could only imagine her fury when she discovered her unfaithful husband and traitorous sister were married, with a baby on the way. She was prepared to go to any lengths to ensure the couple didn't live happily ever after.

Using Grace's infatuation for her for her own ends, Kirsty convinced Grace to be her eyes and ears. She then set about systematically incriminating Craig and Narelle again. Dropping the gold and sapphire cross in the forest near the victims' bodies, planting the gun inside the house, tipping off the police: it all went according to plan. What Kirsty hadn't counted on was Grace developing a conscience and coming off her schizophrenia medication. Hiding the gun at Grace's place after she retrieved it from the recycle bin was probably Kirsty's worst move. Grace thought Kirsty was setting her up in the same way she had set up Narelle and Craig.

Accident or not, Grace had saved the lives of two women and an unborn child that night, and perhaps her own. With Kirsty no longer manipulating her, Grace was free to live her own life. A week after the funeral, Grace had packed up her house, moving to Sydney to be closer to her mother and to start life afresh.

A couple of days later, the For Sale sign had gone up in front of the Edmonds house. Finally, Narelle and Craig were laying the past to rest.

Brett tossed a wine cork at Jacinta, breaking through her reverie. She looked up, smiling. Through it all, he had been the one constant. She owed him a lot, and even more so since he had convinced her life was too short not to do what she wanted. Monday morning, she would quit her job.

ABOUT THE AUTHOR

Based in rural Victoria, Australia, Vicki writes fast-paced mystery and suspense novels in contemporary Australian settings.

Born and raised in New Zealand, she moved to Western Australia with a single suitcase when she was nineteen years old. She has travelled extensively, spending a year touring the world before terrorism was an influencing factor. She has lived in the central business districts of large cities, suburbia, idyllic seaside locations, rural areas, bushland, and remote desert mining camps.

In the lead up to her writing career, Vicki worked in a multitude of different industries including banking, stockbroking, importing and wholesaling, human resources, mining, hospitality, civil engineering, and toys, in predominantly accounting, IT and management roles.

All these life experiences are brought to bear in her writing.

Outside of writing and reading, her main interests are design and photography. She likes to laugh, drink coffee, spend time alone, spend time in company, and get close to nature. She dislikes crowds, hospitals and offal.